Titles by Jessica Clare

THE GIRL'S GUIDE TO (MAN)HUNTING
THE CARE AND FEEDING OF AN ALPHA MALE
THE EXPERT'S GUIDE TO DRIVING A MAN WILD
THE VIRGIN'S GUIDE TO MISBEHAVING

Billionaire Boys Club

STRANDED WITH A BILLIONAIRE
BEAUTY AND THE BILLIONAIRE
THE WRONG BILLIONAIRE'S BED
ONCE UPON A BILLIONAIRE

Praise for the Billionaire Boys Club novels

STRANDED WITH A BILLIONAIRE

"A cute, sweet romance . . . A fast, sexy read that transports you to the land of the rich and famous." —*Fiction Vixen*

"[Clare's] writing is fun and sexy and flirty . . . *Stranded with a Billionaire* has reignited my love of the billionaire hero."
—*The Book Pushers*

"Clare's latest contemporary is gratifying for its likable but flawed hero and heroine, sexy love scenes, and philosophical quotes Brontë perfectly articulates at the right moments."
—*Library Journal*

BEAUTY AND THE BILLIONAIRE

"Clare really knocked it out of the park again . . . This series has been a pure and utter delight." —*The Book Pushers*

"I am in love with this series." —*Love to Read for Fun*

Praise for the Bluebonnet Novels

THE CARE AND FEEDING OF AN ALPHA MALE

"Sizzling! Jessica Clare gets everything right in this erotic and sexy romance . . . You need to read this book!"
—*Romance Junkies*

"What a treat to find a book that does it all and does it so well. Clare has crafted a fiery, heartfelt love story that keeps on surprising . . . matching wit and warmth with plenty of spice . . . This is a book, and a series, not to be missed."
—*RT Book Reviews* (4½ stars)

continued . . .

"Very cute and oh so sexy."   —*Smexy Books*

"[Clare] did a fabulous job of creating a very erotic story while still letting the relationship unfold very believably."
—*Fiction Vixen*

"A wonderful good-girl/bad-boy erotic romance . . . If you enjoy super-spicy small town romances, *The Care and Feeding of an Alpha Male* is one that I definitely recommend!"
—*The Romance Dish*

THE GIRL'S GUIDE
TO (MAN)HUNTING

"Sexy and funny."   —*USA Today*

"A novel that will appeal to both erotic-romance fans and outdoor enthusiasts. Set in the small town of Bluebonnet, Texas, this rollicking story of a wilderness survival school and a couple of high-school sweethearts is full of fun and hot, steamy romance."   —*Debbie's Book Bag*

"Clare's sizzling encounters in the great outdoors have definite forest-fire potential from the heat generated."
—*RT Book Reviews*

"A fun, cute, and sexy read . . . Miranda's character is genuine and easy to relate to, and Dane was oh-so-sexy! Great chemistry between these two that makes for a *hot* and steamy read, but also it is filled with humor and a great supporting cast."
—*Nocturne Romance Reads*

"If you like small-town settings with characters that are easy to fall in love with, this is the book for you."
—*Under the Covers Book Blog*

STRANDED
with a
BILLIONAIRE

JESSICA CLARE

BERKLEY SENSATION, NEW YORK

THE BERKLEY PUBLISHING GROUP
Published by the Penguin Group
Penguin Group (USA) LLC
375 Hudson Street, New York, New York 10014

USA • Canada • UK • Ireland • Australia • New Zealand • India • South Africa • China

penguin.com

A Penguin Random House Company

STRANDED WITH A BILLIONAIRE

A Berkley Sensation Book / published by arrangement with the author

Berkley Sensation Books are published by The Berkley Publishing Group.
BERKLEY SENSATION® is a registered trademark of Penguin Group (USA) LLC.
The "B" design is a trademark of Penguin Group (USA) LLC.

For information, address: The Berkley Publishing Group,
a division of Penguin Group (USA) LLC,
375 Hudson Street, New York, New York 10014.

ISBN: 978-0-425-26907-7

PUBLISHING HISTORY
InterMix eBook edition / April 2013
Berkley Sensation mass-market edition / July 2014

PRINTED IN THE UNITED STATES OF AMERICA

10 9 8 7 6 5 4 3 2 1

Cover photo "diamond ring" © Masterfile.
Cover design by Sarah Oberrender.
Interior text design by Laura K. Corless.

For my sister
Who has always supported me in my writing
and been one of my biggest fans, and who said
this was her favorite book in the entire world
. . . until she read the second one.

ONE

∽

Even though the bar was thumping with loud music and the crowd was shoulder to shoulder, no one approached Logan Hawkings. He stood alone, an island of calm in a roiling sea of bodies. It might have been the "fuck off" expression on his face, or the crisp cut of his expensive tailored clothing that told people he didn't belong in this neighborhood. It could have been because he walked with an arrogant swagger that made men get out of the way and women nudge their girlfriends with interest.

None of that mattered. He wasn't here to socialize.

He moved past the bar, down a narrow hall to a back room. A man—tall, head shaven—stood in front of the door there. The guard wore sunglasses despite being indoors, a suit, and an earpiece with a black cord that wound behind his ear and around the back of his neck. His posture becoming alert, the bodyguard watched Logan as he approached.

With a practiced ease, Logan swept the second and third fingers of his right hand over his shoulder and then rested them on his biceps in the exact spot where his tattoo lay under his clothing.

The man nodded and stepped aside.

Logan pushed the door open and strode down the stairs into the basement. Already there was a thick haze of cigar smoke above the large green octagon table set up in the center of the room. A buffet had been set up off to one side and was being ignored. Beer bottles and poker chips littered the table. Ah, Brotherhood night. His favorite night of the week. Logan gave the room a quick once-over. Everyone was here already; he was the last one to arrive. No surprise there.

The men seated at the table were roughly the same age. All were clean-cut, fit and wore clothes that spoke of money. They all carried themselves with the confidence that success brought, though in some, the confidence was more swagger than anything.

Beside the empty chair held for him sat Hunter Buchanan, the scarred, silent real-estate tycoon, and Logan's most trusted friend. Next to him sat Reese Durham, a young, brash man on the cusp of hitting his billion-dollar fortune. Beside him sat Griffin Verdi, English aristocracy and the 'professor' of their small group. Then was Jonathan Lyons, owner of Lyon Automotives and notorious adventurer and thrill seeker. At his side was Cade Archer, the philanthropist of their group.

The five men barely glanced up from their cards as he entered.

"You're late," Reese Durham told him, a cigar hanging from his mouth. He examined his cards, face impassive.

Logan slipped his jacket off and tossed it into a corner, then moved to the only empty seat at the table. Cade raised a hand in greeting. Logan grasped it and then turned to clap Hunter Buchanan on the back. The man's scars looked hideous in the dim light of the room.

"About time you got here," Cade said in a pleasant voice. "Reese was just asking about Gloria."

Logan frowned, shaking his head as he sat down between the two men. "Gloria who?"

Reese grinned at him across the table. "You know. Stacked Gloria with the big blond hair. I guess you're not seeing her anymore? You brought her to the Stewart fundraiser a few months ago."

Had he? Logan couldn't recall. He hadn't had a second date with anyone since . . . well, since Danica. Hadn't been interested enough and hadn't made the time. "I don't recall a Gloria."

"So you wouldn't care if I dated her? I met her at a party the other night and wouldn't mind seeing her again."

"Care?" Logan snorted. "I can't even recall her face. She's all yours."

"Did you know she's a friend of Danica's?" Reese asked.

"Then you're more than welcome to her," Logan said, his voice cool. "If she's a friend of Danica's, she can burn in hell for all I care."

"Thought you'd say that," Reese said cheerfully.

"Just do me a favor and don't bring up Danica again," Logan said, his tone friendly but with a touch of warning.

The last thing he wanted to do was discuss a money-grubbing gold digger. She was in his past, and he had no intention of dwelling on her. His father had mocked him for falling for Danica. He'd said that Logan was being a stupid fool. Turned out the old buzzard had been right all along.

And that grated more than anything.

"So what took you so long?" Hunter pulled out a stack of chips, glancing over at Logan.

A smooth, effortless change of subject. Logan turned to Hunter and gave the scarred man a check for his share that evening. Hunter added it to the bank and shoved the pile of chips in his direction.

"I have a new driver," Logan said. "He got lost." His tone implied that it wouldn't happen again.

Reese snorted and shook his head. "Excuses, excuses." He gestured at the pile of chips in the center of the table. "Everyone in?"

The six men consulted cards as they were dealt. As cards were laid face up, Cade immediately tossed a bid into the pile. Four of the men folded. "The paladin there's got three of a kind showing," Jonathan said with a disgusted glance at Cade. "You know he can't lie to save his ass."

Reese sighed and put his cards down as well, the last in besides Cade. "Hell, you're right. I fold, too."

Cade grinned and raked the money toward him. "I might have been bluffing."

"You weren't," Jonathan said, and took another swig of his beer, then leaned back to the catering table and snagged one for Logan. "You don't know how."

"All right," Logan said, taking the bottle and twisting off the cap. He took a quick drink. "Now that we're all here . . . This month's meeting of the brotherhood is called to order."

The men raised their drinks, clinking bottles together. "*Fratres in prosperitatem*," they all said in unison, as they did every month. It was the motto of their clandestine society—"Brothers in Success."

"First order of business is the round table," Logan said. "We'll start with Jonathan."

"Lyons Automobiles continues to sell strongly in all quarters. We're looking at adding a line of high-end convertibles that will have an electric engine but with enough horsepower to compete at Daytona." He grinned. "I'm thinking about driving one myself. I'll spare you the technical details."

"Please do," said Griffin in his cultured, bored voice.

Jonathan was undeterred. He picked up his cards, beginning to deal the next hand. "Prototype won't be ready until next quarter at the earliest, but when we roll them out for mass production, you'll each get one, compliments of the brotherhood."

He discussed his car business a bit longer as the hand went on and then turned to Griffin. "You're up."

Griffin shrugged, examining his hand. "It's money. It accumulates on its own."

"Says a man that grew up with wealth," Reese pointed out. "Not all of us were so lucky."

"It's not my fault I was born rich. Besides, I invested in Cade's medical research facility," Griffin pointed out, waving an idle hand. "I'm doing something with my money, at least."

"Reese?" Logan asked.

"My newest acquisition, the Vegas Flush, seems poised to take the Stanley Cup this year. You're all welcome to tickets, of course. Just contact my secretary. I'm also looking at acquiring a football team." He grinned. "Maybe soccer. It's a sport that can grow here in the States. Might be a solid investment worth looking at if I can get a superstar player to get people into the stands. Still debating."

They discussed sports teams for a bit and then went on to Cade Archer, who talked about medical breakthroughs at his research facility and some upcoming charity events. Cade was their white knight. He made money, but he insisted on it having some sort of higher purpose or focus on the good of mankind.

The rest of them? They just liked to make money.

Reese, Logan, and Griffin all took their turns, sharing any news of the week, and then the conversation moved on. Hunter was last, and he kept things brief, as he always did. The real estate tycoon man was never one for talking much. He just sat back and enjoyed the company of his brothers most meetings. Tonight, though, he had something to share, and his dark gaze moved to Logan as he spoke. "Got wind of an investment property if you're interested. There's a large resort on an island in the Bahamas that's in need of a cash influx. Exuma District. I have a friend that's willing to sell to an interested investor, and I think it could be a solid deal."

Logan nodded, only half paying attention to his cards. It did sound like something up his alley. Hawkings Conglomerate was all about buying failing businesses on the cheap, turning them into profitable organizations, and then reaping the benefits from that. "Prime location?"

"So I've been told. Worth taking a look. There's a French billionaire interested, but I thought I'd bring it to the brotherhood first."

Logan grunted, considering. For Hunter to have brought it up, it must have been an excellent deal. Normally Hunter was silent. He contributed funds if one of the others needed cash flow to ensure that his business did well, but other than that he kept to himself. Logan admired that. The man was an island. Logan suspected that he didn't have many— if any—friends outside of the brotherhood.

"I'm busy right now, but I'll see if I can work it into my schedule," Logan said with a nod.

"Maybe you should check it out and take a vacation at the same time," Reese told him. "Get away from the office for a few days. Forget your troubles."

Logan scowled at Reese, throwing his ante for that hand onto the table. "My troubles are long gone." After all, he'd shaken off Danica before they'd ever made it to the altar— a bullet dodged. And his bastard of a father had passed away at about the same time. That was two millstones no longer around his neck.

Reese looked amused at Logan's response, as if he didn't believe him. "Oh, really? Because that's not what—"

"Stay out of it," Logan said in a warning tone.

Reese simply grinned and shrugged, turned his attention back to his cards. "Suit yourself."

Logan did keep thinking about Reese's words, though, and was distracted enough that he stayed in despite having a garbage hand. He ended up losing two grand to Jonathan without even realizing it.

Reese thought he should take a "vacation."

He wanted to laugh at the thought. Successful men didn't get vacations. They just got more opportunities. Still, it sounded like an interesting investment, and he liked to keep Hawkings Conglomerate diverse. An island resort was definitely diverse.

He noticed Hunter watching him out of the corner of his eye. Had the real estate mogul decided that he'd toss the gem Logan's way because he thought Logan could do an admirable job of flipping it? Or did he, too, think Logan needed a distraction?

That thought made his mood sour. First Reese was needling him, and now Hunter was in on it? He wouldn't have thought that of Hunter. He was the quietest of their small, successful group, but sometimes he saw straight into the heart of the matter.

His father would have sneered at the thought of a vacation. To stay strong and on top of business, you kept a close eye on things and one hand on the rudder at all times. Vacation made you weak. Soft. And Hawkings men weren't soft. They had poor taste in women, though. His father had married his mother, and that had been a mistake for all parties. And Logan had almost been fooled enough by Danica's sweet face to go to the altar with her.

Logan stared at his cards, frowning, and tried to conjure up the face of someone named Gloria. Nothing. His memory was full of business meetings and contracts. No women.

Maybe a vacation/business trip was just what he needed at the moment.

"I'll take a look at it," he told Hunter.

Two Months Later

"Hate to say it, girl," Sharon told Brontë and flopped down on her queen-sized bed. "But this is the shittiest resort I've ever stayed in."

"It was free," Brontë replied, trying to keep the irritation out of her voice. "You can't really complain about free. Epicurus said, 'Not what we have, but what we enjoy, constitutes our abundance.'"

"Uh-huh," Sharon said in a tone of voice that told Brontë that she wasn't listening. Instead, she'd picked up the remote and, pointing it at the TV, began to hammer on the buttons. "They water down the drinks at the pool. Did you notice that?"

For the ninth time in two days, Brontë regretted bringing Sharon. When she'd won the trip through her local radio station, 99.9 Pop Fever, she'd been just thrilled to go. Her friends in Kansas City hadn't been able to come, though—none of them could get off work. Her old roomies from college had "real" jobs with responsibility, and they couldn't get away from work for a last-minute getaway vacation, no matter how free it was.

Seeing as how Brontë was a waitress at a diner, she had no problem getting the time off. She'd simply asked for someone else to cover her shifts. Sharon had overheard Brontë's conversation, though, and just happened to have a passport and enough vacation time to be able to make the trip. She'd broken up with her boyfriend, and she could really use a few days away, and wouldn't Brontë want company on the trip?

Sharon wasn't Brontë's favorite coworker, but they got

along well enough. And Sharon had given her sad eyes and mentioned the trip so often that Brontë had felt guilty about letting a second ticket go to waste. So she'd relented and brought Sharon along.

Big mistake.

After a rocky flight, during which Sharon had whined the whole time, a horrible ferry ride out to the island (Sharon had whined all the way through that, too), and now sharing the world's smallest hotel room? Brontë was starting to think that next time she'd just go alone. Forty-eight hours with Sharon was about forty-seven too many.

Even though Brontë was determined to enjoy the vacation, Sharon was making it difficult. She was a slob. Her clothing and shoes were strewn all over the small room. She hogged the bathroom and used all the hot water and took all the towels. She'd stayed out all night the previous night partying *without* Brontë. And she'd nearly cleaned out the minibar already, despite the fact that Brontë had pointed out that it would be charged to Brontë's credit card since the room was in her name.

"This place is a total roach motel," Sharon said, tossing her suitcase onto the bed and throwing clothing onto the floor until she uncovered her pink bikini. "You should have asked them to upgrade you to the penthouse."

"The radio station gave me the vacation. I couldn't exactly demand anything."

"I would have demanded a room larger than a closet!" Sharon stripped off her sundress and began to change.

Brontë went back to her guidebook, ignoring Sharon's incessant complaining. So the resort was a little on the . . . rundown side. Seaturtle Cay in the Bahamas was still a win in Brontë's eyes. It was free, for starters. She hadn't spent a dime on travel or the hotel, thanks to the radio station. Which was a good thing, seeing as how she didn't have two nickels to rub together. Mostly, it was just nice to get away from work. The beaches were gorgeous, and she'd seen a few advertisements for fun excursions like parasailing and snorkeling.

It just had to stop raining.

Brontë glanced out the window at the gray, gloomy skies and pouring rain. She sighed and flipped to the back of the guidebook, wondering if it included a list of rainy weather events.

Sharon finished adjusting her bikini and then glared out the window. "We're not going to get one day of sunshine, are we?"

"I don't know. I'm not a weatherman," Brontë said without looking up, her voice as cheerful as possible. "Maybe you should go to the bar and see if anyone there has a weather report."

"Now that sounds like a great idea." Sharon put on a pair of enormous hoop earrings, slid into her sandals, and waved at Brontë. "I'll be back soon. You want anything?"

Some peace and quiet? "I'm good."

As soon as she was gone, Brontë exhaled in relief and stretched out on the bed. She grabbed a pair of earbuds and turned her music up to blot out the sound of her neighbors having sex—again. Brontë picked up her guidebook and flipped back to the beginning. A vacation was a vacation was a vacation, and she was going to enjoy this one, damn it. She turned a page. Swimming with stingrays. Huh. Maybe she'd try that. She glanced at the angry, cloudy sky again.

Just as soon as it was sunny.

———

A hand roughly jarred her awake from her nap. "Brontë! Ohmigod. Brontë! Wake up!"

She jerked up, tugging out the earbuds, only to see Sharon looming over her bed.

The other woman looked frazzled. "Did you not hear the loudspeakers?"

"Mmm? Loudspeakers?" Sure enough, there was a low tone echoing over and over. As she cocked her head to try to distinguish the sound, Brontë heard a voice chime in over the loudspeaker.

"*Please make your way to the bus loading area*," it said, calm and smooth. "*All guests will be transported to the evacuation site as soon as possible. Please remain calm and do not panic. There is plenty of time to evacuate the area prior to the hurricane. Refunds will not be issued. Guests will be given a voucher for a future visit.*"

"Hurricane?" Brontë repeated slowly, as if trying to make the word register in her mind. "Are you serious?"

"Hurricane Latonya," Sharon said, moving to her bed and throwing her suitcase onto the mattress. "Category three currently and heading toward category four or five. They're evacuating this entire stupid island."

A hurricane? It seemed ridiculous. Brontë had seen something about it on the news. Something like "not heading anywhere near the Bahamas." The news was apparently a big fat liar.

She sat up in bed, alert. "Where do we go?"

"We're all going to be shuttled over to a nearby cruise ship and taken back to the mainland." Looking stressed, Sharon pulled a pair of jean shorts on over her bikini. "This whole vacation has been doomed."

Brontë believed in making lemonade out of lemons as much as the next person, but she was starting to agree with Sharon. "I can't believe the hurricane's heading this way."

"Yeah. It's supposed to be a big one, too. Pack your stuff. We have to *go*."

They packed quickly, Brontë far more than Sharon, who had crammed her suitcase full of clothing and shoes and now found it wouldn't all fit back in since she'd purchased some things in the gift shop. Sharon spent a good twenty minutes deciding which outfits to take with her and which to leave behind, and wailing about all of it. Just when

Brontë was about to leap over the bed and take over, Sharon said she was ready. Suitcases in hand, they made their way out of the room.

A sea of people wandered the hallways, tourists with suitcases and small children. People were crying and arguing, and everyone was shoving to get ahead. The line for the elevator stretched down the hall and the bland, too-calm evacuation message played over the loudspeaker over and over again.

"Stairs?" Brontë asked Sharon.

"In heels? Down twenty floors? Are you kidding me? We can wait for the elevator."

Brontë bit back her retort. "Fine. We'll wait for the elevator."

They did, and had to wait nearly half an hour just to get on the stupid thing. They made it down to the lobby only to find that it was packed shoulder to shoulder with guests. It was a complete and utter mess, and Brontë's stomach sank at the sight of it.

Sharon pushed her way forward, and Brontë followed her. There was a line of buses in the parking lot, barely visible through the relentless rain and the crowd of bodies waiting to get out of the hotel. One harried looking man with a clipboard was trying to keep order—and failing miserably.

As they stood waiting, a man with a Red Cross symbol on his rain slicker headed inside. "All right," he yelled, and the room quieted. "We're going to need you to form an orderly line. Have your identification and your passport out and available. We'll be taking you all to a nearby cruise ship that has agreed to sail back to the mainland and out of the storm's way. Again, please have your passport and identification ready."

The crowd murmured, digging into pockets and pulling out wallets. Brontë pulled out her small purse and removed her passport and license.

Sharon got a panicked look on her face and started digging through her purse.

"Sharon?" Brontë said nervously. "What is it?"

"I can't find my passport," Sharon said, moving aside as the line of people surged forward to get onto the bus.

Brontë pushed her way to Sharon's side, trying not to be annoyed. "Is it in your suitcase?"

"I don't know! It should be in my purse." Sharon opened her purse and began to dig out a random assortment of makeup and brushes. She dropped a lipstick, and it rolled away under a sea of feet. Sharon stared after it, her gaze full of longing. "Shit. I loved that color."

"You can buy a new one," Brontë told her, her patience nearly gone. "Find your passport."

Sharon's eyes widened. "Do you think it's at the bar?"

"Either the bar or the room." Seeing as how those were the only two places Sharon had been since they'd gotten to the resort.

"Bus number two is loading," the man called. "Please form an orderly line for the evacuation!"

They ignored him. Sharon clutched a double handful of makeup and was still digging in her purse. "It's not in here. Can you go back to the room and check?"

Brontë stared at Sharon. "Seriously?"

"Yes!" Sharon snapped, no longer bothering to be friendly. She stuffed the makeup back in and sat down on the floor, unzipping her luggage and ignoring the mob glaring at her. "I'll check my suitcase here and then go to the bar and see if it's there. We can save some time if you go double-check the room for me."

"Line up for bus number three!" the man yelled.

"How many buses do they have?" Brontë asked nervously. "I don't want to be left behind."

"I'll call your cell if I find it," Sharon said. "Leave your suitcase here, and I'll watch it for you."

Brontë hesitated. She really didn't want to go hunting for

the missing passport. Sharon had been awful to room with, and it had only been two days. Two very, very long days. She was almost at the point where she didn't care if Sharon stayed or not. And now there was a freaking hurricane on the way, which just made things go from bad to worse. "There's a hurricane, Sharon. I'm sure they're not going to bother to check everyone's passports. They'll let you on without it."

"Please, Brontë," Sharon said, and her voice sounded tearful even as she began to rip her suitcases open and frantically dig into messy piles of clothing. "Help me, Brontë. It won't take five minutes! I promise I won't let them leave without you. Look at all these people standing here. It's going to take them an hour to evacuate everyone."

There were a lot of people, Brontë had to admit. And there had been a line at the elevator upstairs. It would take a while for the resort to clear out. She thought of the upset wobble in Sharon's voice. Damn it. With a sigh, she pulled out her cellphone and waved it in front of Sharon's face. "Call me the moment you find it," she said in a firm voice.

"Hurry," Sharon told her.

No "Thank you." No "I appreciate it." No "You're the best." Just a "Hurry." Figured. Parking her suitcase next to Sharon, she turned and ran for the elevator.

She was definitely going on the next trip alone.

———

The passport wasn't in the room. At least, Brontë was pretty sure it wasn't. It was hard to tell with the mess Sharon had made of things. But Brontë had dutifully upended the garbage can, searched through the assortment of half-used bottles in the small bathroom, shaken out every towel, and even looked between the mattresses.

And then, because she hadn't gotten a call from Sharon and because she felt like she couldn't go back without

Sharon's passport, she checked one more time. Anxiety made her stomach feel as if it were tied in knots. Were the buses still downstairs? They wouldn't leave anyone behind, would they?

Brontë moved to the window and peered out, but it was raining even harder, the skies gray and dark. It was impossible to see anything out there except more rain.

She checked under the bed one last time and then couldn't stand it any longer. She was just going to have to admit defeat. With a final glance at the empty room, Brontë closed the door behind her.

The hall was empty this time, but that annoying tone was still going off over the loudspeakers. Crossing her arms over her chest, she headed to the elevator and hit the button. She drummed her fingers as she waited, every second seeming like a million years. She checked the screen of her phone for a message from Sharon. Nothing.

The elevator door chimed. It opened slowly, revealing a lone occupant. A man in a double-breasted gray suit stood at the back of the elevator. There was a white name badge over one breast of his jacket, indicating that he worked at the hotel. He frowned at the sight of Brontë, looking as if he was incredibly annoyed that the elevator had bothered to stop on her floor.

Yeah, well, she was annoyed, too. Brontë stepped inside and smacked the lobby button, even though it was already lit up. She punched it a few more times for good measure. Great. She was probably in the elevator with the manager or something. She supposed it was lucky that she'd gone back to the room and not Sharon. If Sharon had seen the manager, she'd have filled his ears with complaints about how horrible the hotel was. The *free* hotel.

She stared at the buttons, watching them light up as the elevator moved down. Twenty floors, and she'd been on the nineteenth. The man on the elevator must have been in the floor above her. The penthouse. If she had to guess,

Brontë would have assumed those guests had been evacuated first. Maybe the manager had gone up to count the bathrobes or something.

They were evacuating the entire island. Good lord. So much for her fun, relaxing vacation. She'd been trying so hard to make this vacation enjoyable, and it had fought her at every turn, as if determined to suck, and hard. So much for "fun" or even "relaxing." Brontë'd never felt so stressed out in her entire life.

A freaking hurricane. The perfect way to cap off the world's most horrible vacation.

The elevator panel lit up on two. Brontë drummed her fingers on her arm, waiting for it to roll over to one. And waited . . .

And waited . . .

The elevator shuddered just as the power went out. The elevator car was plunged into darkness, and Brontë lost her breath, terror gripping her.

"Great," the manager said behind her. "Just fucking great."

A hysterical giggle rose in Brontë's throat. Nope. *That* was the perfect way to cap off the world's most horrible vacation.

TWO

⟨⁓⟩

Brontë's wild laughter echoed in the small elevator, the only sound breaking the silence. She couldn't seem to stop. It was just so ridiculous. She'd been stuck in what was supposed to be paradise with a horrible roomie and a hurricane. Now? Now she was trapped in an elevator with a stranger. Truly, she must have racked up some sort of hellish karma to have this happen to her.

"I'm glad you find this funny," the man behind her said in a cold, biting tone. "I assure you that I do not."

"It's funny because it's so awful," Brontë said between giggles. "This is the worst day ever."

"I don't laugh when I'm in a life-threatening situation."

"I do," she said, and burst into more giggles. They were part hysteria, of course, and part anxiety. Not exactly endearing her to the manager she was currently stuck with. "Sorry," she apologized, but it came out wobbly, as if she were suppressing more laughter. "I'm what you would call a nervous laugher. I'll try to stop."

"Good."

She giggled again and then clapped a hand over her mouth.

He said nothing. She wished they had the lights at least, so she could look over at him and judge his expression. Probably just as well that she couldn't. He was probably glaring hatefully at her. She couldn't really blame him for that. She was kind of being an ass. A hysterical ass.

Silence fell, almost oppressive in the darkness. Neither said anything, and Brontë found herself silently wishing that the blaring monotone of the loudspeaker with the hurricane warning chimes could be heard. Just to break up the silence. Something. Anything.

Her phone. Of course. She felt stupid for forgetting about it. She could call Sharon and tell her that she was stuck in the elevator. Fishing around in her purse, Brontë located it with her fingertips and pulled it out, clicking it on. Bluish light flooded her end of the elevator, nearly blinding her with its brilliance. One bar left—that was what she got for reading books on her phone, she supposed. Not that it mattered. The screen was lit up with a message—"Area out of service." Shit.

Across the elevator, another light flared to life, and she glanced over at the man in the suit, his features illuminated by the phone's light. Good-looking. A few years older than her, with a strong jaw and nose. He immediately clicked his phone off again. "No service." He sounded disgusted.

Thrown back into darkness again, Brontë blinked at the red spots in her vision. She reached out into the darkness, trying to recall exactly how big the elevator was. Fifteen feet across? Less? More? She hadn't paid attention. Brontë suspected that if she took a step forward, her outstretched arm would smack into the stranger, though.

Cozy. A little too cozy, considering they were trapped.

Exactly how long could they be trapped here before someone would notice? What if the ferry had already left the island for the mainland? Brontë tried not to think about that, or the hurricane heading their way. Someone would be coming to get them. She waited for the inevitable sound of voices, of rescuers.

And waited . . .

And waited . . . The darkness was stifling, the only sounds in the elevator that of her accelerated breathing. Hers and the manager's.

When the power didn't appear to be coming back on, she slid down to the floor of the elevator. It felt cool against her legs, a welcome change considering that the air in the elevator was becoming a little stuffy. How long had they been sitting here in the darkness? Ten minutes? Twenty? How long did they have before the hurricane hit? She clutched her purse close.

Air brushed past her as if he was moving forward, and she clung to the wall. "What are you doing?"

Buttons clicked. He seemed to be ignoring her.

"What are you doing?" she asked again.

A buzzer rang out, startling her so much that her heart jumped into her throat and she jolted in her seat.

"Emergency buzzer," he said in a low voice. "Someone should hear it and come looking for us."

"If they're still here," she pointed out.

"Well, aren't you Miss Suzy Sunshine?" he said. "At least I'm doing something instead of sitting around and giggling."

" 'Human behavior flows from three main sources: desire, emotion, and knowledge,' " she quoted.

"What?"

"Plato," Brontë told him, lifting her chin in the darkness.

There was a long pause. Then: "I don't think Plato had 'giggling' in mind when he wrote that."

"Hey," she said, her nostrils flaring with anger. "It's called nervous laughter, you jackass. I laugh when I'm uncomfortable. So sue me. And here's a thought: Since we're stuck in here together, how about you try not being such a jerk for five minutes?"

He said nothing, just continued to hammer on the buzzer.

After about twenty minutes of his endless pushing on the buzzer, she wanted to cover her ears and tell him to knock it off. But that would be stupid, of course. If someone heard the buzzer, they could get out of here. And yet . . . no one was coming. The power was still off. She clicked on her phone, looking at the time and trying to ignore the fact that her battery was almost dead.

They'd been in here an hour. The buses would still be outside, surely. With all that rain, it would take a while to pull off any kind of evacuation. The elevator was becoming stuffy, too. Either that or she was just in the early stages of hyperventilation. She put a hand to her damp forehead and willed herself to breathe slowly. This would be a lot easier if she wasn't trapped with the unpleasant manager. No wonder the hotel was such a dump if he was in charge.

"Shouldn't someone come looking for you soon?" she asked. Surely they'd need the manager to help coordinate the evacuation.

"You would think so."

No sarcasm that time. Well, goody. They were making progress. Brontë dug through her purse and pulled out a piece of gum, popping it into her mouth and nervously chewing it. Every action in the oppressive darkness seemed of monumental importance. She picked through the contents of her purse with her hand, looking for anything useful. A pen. Her checkbook. Passport. Wallet. Loose change. Birth control. When her hand touched upon that, she smothered another hysterical laugh.

She heard him sigh at her laughter. He sounded frustrated. Too bad for him—she was at her wit's end herself. But she needed to talk, so she asked, "Think the buses are still outside?"

"I don't know, and I don't care."

Jeez. Could he be any ruder? "Aren't you supposed to be good with customer service or something? You seem to be failing on that front."

He seemed amused. "Am I?"

"Yeah, as a manager, you might want to work on your people skills. I'm just saying."

"I'll keep that in mind," the dry voice said.

She yawned. Now that the initial terror had worn off, she was busy being annoyed at him and not frightened. Combine that with the rising humidity, and she was getting sleepy. "I think we're stuck here."

"Theoretically."

"I assume the buses left by now."

"You also assume I was going to leave by bus."

"Oh? I guess you have special transportation to take you away before the hurricane gets here?"

Silence for a moment. Then: "A helicopter."

Well, wasn't he high-class management? "Okay, let's try this again. Do you think your helicopter is still there?"

A long pause. Then he grudgingly admitted, "Not if the weather is getting worse."

"You might have to ride the bus with us plebes, then." She lay down on the floor, using her purse as a pillow. " 'As the builders say, the larger stones do not lie well without the lesser.' "

"More philosophy?"

"Just a little something to think about," she said tartly.

"Indeed," he said slowly, and she noticed he had let off on the infernal buzzer. Maybe he was giving up. She sure was. After a moment, he asked, "Will anyone be looking for you?"

Her sigh in response seemed overloud in the darkness. "I don't know. I came here with a friend, but she's a bit . . . flighty. I don't know if she'll realize I'm missing or just assume I got on another bus." Brontë hated to think about it, but if it came down to Sharon staying behind to make sure Brontë was safe or Sharon getting out of Dodge? She knew which one Sharon would pick. "I like to think that someone will come and check that the building's been completely evacuated before they all run off to the mainland."

"Mmm." His tone was noncommittal. As if he wasn't sure that was the case at all but wanted to humor her.

Yeah, she wasn't sure about that either. But it sounded good, so she adjusted her purse and rested her cheek on it, waiting for rescue.

———

Brontë woke up some time later, her mouth dry, her body aching. The silence was deafening, the blackness almost overwhelming in its depth.

Still no power. Still in the elevator. She rubbed at her eyes and sat up, wincing. "Hello?"

"Still here." The man trapped with her sounded more weary than annoyed. "You haven't missed anything."

"I must have slept. How . . . how long have I been out?"

"About six hours."

Six hours? Dear God. Panic made her heart flutter in her chest. "They're not coming for us?"

"My guess is no."

She sucked in a deep breath, willing herself not to panic. Stuck in an elevator on an evacuated island. *Stuck.* It felt oppressively hot in the elevator now, as the power had been out for several hours and the tropical humidity was taking its toll. "How could they leave us behind?"

"Again, just a guess, but I would say that in the chaos of the evacuation, someone dropped the ball." His tone was analytical. Bored.

Was he still pissed at her, or pissed at their situation? It didn't matter, she supposed. Neither of them was going anywhere anytime soon.

She sat up, wincing at how stiff her body felt, and how sticky with sweat. Ugh. She was thirsty as hell, too, and there was no relief from the heat. The jeans and T-shirt she'd put on for the evacuation felt stifling. She kicked off her sandals and then glanced over to his corner of the elevator, not that she could see anything. If she undressed, would he notice? Would he mind? Was it dangerous? He didn't seem like the type to leap over here and rape her, and she was miserable in the heat.

After a moment more of hesitation, she began to slowly shimmy out of her jeans, frowning at the loud noise her zipper made.

"What are you doing?"

Naturally he'd caught that small sound. Figured.

"I'm getting undressed. It's hot in here. Just stay over on your side of the elevator, and I won't bother you."

She heard the rustle of clothing from his side of the elevator as well. "Good idea."

"Was that a compliment? My. Am I forgiven for my insane giggling?" she teased.

"Not yet." His terseness threatened to shut down the conversation.

"'Forgive many things in others; nothing in yourself.'"

"Are you going to sit here and quote Plato all afternoon?" He sounded almost amused.

"That was Ausonius, actually. And yes. My philosophy degree has to be of some use." Stripping off her shirt, she sighed with pleasure when the air hit her flushed skin. Clad in nothing but her bra and panties, she immediately felt cooler, much to her relief, and she folded her discarded clothes and tucked them against her purse.

"You can get down to your boxers, you know," she told him. "I can't see you, and it feels much better."

"I don't think so."

"Briefs, then?" she couldn't resist asking. "You struck me as a boxer man."

Actually, he hadn't struck her as much of anything. She'd only had a quick glimpse of him before the power had gone out. But she liked teasing him. It somehow made this hellish ordeal slightly less suffocating.

"Why are you asking about my clothing?" His tone was stiff, unpleasant.

She sighed. "It's called making conversation. You should learn how to do it." Curling up with her phone in her hand—though she didn't dare open it and run the battery down—she thought for a minute and then offered, "My name's Brontë."

"Brontë? After Charlotte or Emily?"

Her esteem of him grudgingly went up a notch. Normally people cracked jokes about dinosaurs rather than realizing where her name was from. "Either. Both, I suppose. My mother had a fascination for classic literature, not that it got her anywhere."

"I see we share a commonality in mothers, then."

"Do we? Was yours a total dreamer, too?"

"Mine was a showgirl," he said flatly. "I am told she was highly impractical and extremely irresponsible."

"Oh. Um." That hadn't been quite what Brontë had meant. Her mother had been a sweet, caring woman, even if she didn't have a practical bone in her body. She'd also stubbornly refused to see anything but the best in people, which was why Brontë's childhood had been so idyllic . . . and so very false. She shoved away the bad memories. "I didn't mean to sound negative about my mother. She just didn't have a sensible side. That's all. She was a good woman. Anyhow, she liked books—especially classics."

"And you have inherited her love, I take it. You seem to have an obsession with ancient philosophers."

"Everyone has a hobby," she said cheerfully. "What about you?"

"I do not."

"You don't have a hobby? At all?"

"I work. It takes up all my hours. Though I suppose I could spend my time memorizing pithy quotes to zing back at unsuspecting men in elevators."

Well, now she felt stupid. "I . . . wow. Sorry. I just—"

"I was teasing you," he said, his voice that same crisp, abrupt sound that she'd mistaken for rudeness. Perhaps that was just his manner and she hadn't realized it because she couldn't see his face.

"Oh." Now she felt silly. "I didn't realize." There was a long pause between them, and she rushed to change the subject. "So, what's your name?"

He hesitated, as if he were weighing the benefits of telling her. "Logan Hawkings."

"That's a nice name."

"Indeed." There was a hint of amusement in his voice now, definitely.

"What's so funny?"

"Nothing at all."

It sure sounded like he was amused by something, but what it was, she didn't know. A smidge annoyed, Brontë lay back down on the floor, resting her cheek on her folded clothing. "So how long do you think we'll be here?"

"I suppose it depends on how direct of a hit the hurricane makes on Seaturtle Cay. Then it depends on the organization of rescue efforts."

She yawned, feeling sleepy again due to the heat. "So far I'm not impressed with them."

He snorted. "That makes two of us."

There was another lull in the conversation, and she figured she'd best fill it again before he decided he was fine being silent once more. "Do you have a family, Logan?"

"No." That syllable was definitely clipped and short. Not a conversation he wanted to have, then.

"Me either. Since I'm supposed to be on vacation, work

won't be missing me for a week at least." A distressing thought crossed her mind. "God, I hope we're not stuck in here for a week."

"I doubt that will happen."

"Why is that?"

"Because we'll die from dehydration long before that."

She felt the sudden urge to fling one of her sandals at him. "Don't say stuff like that."

"All right then, we'll die thanks to the hurricane."

"The glass is definitely half empty for you, isn't it? Don't think of things that way. Maybe one of the hotel employees stayed behind and will come looking for you. Did you assign anyone to check the floors?"

"Assign anyone? Why on earth would I do that?"

She frowned into the darkness. "You're wearing a badge. Aren't you the manager here?"

"Ah . . . yes. And no, I didn't assign anyone to check the floors."

Lovely. Not only was the man kind of abrasive, but it didn't seem like he was good at handling an emergency. She yawned into her hand again. This heat was making her so sleepy. She hadn't gotten much rest the night before, thanks to the people in the next room and their acrobatics. Which reminded her . . . "Since you're the manager, can I make a suggestion?"

"I can't stop you."

"Thicker walls."

"Pardon?"

"You definitely want thicker walls. You can hear everything through some of them. I'm just saying."

"I'll keep that in mind." He sounded amused again.

The wind whistled, and she heard a crack in the distance. She bolted upright. "What was that?"

She heard him get to his feet. "Hurricane must be arriving," he said.

"Oh, shit." Panic began to surge through her again. "We have to get out of here, Logan."

"I know."

Brontë chewed on her fingernails, her mouth dry as she strained to hear more noise from the hurricane. What was happening out there? Had Sharon even noticed that she'd never come back? Doubtful. She'd probably found her passport at the bar and then had started flirting with the nearest guy. Some friend.

Definitely taking the next vacation by herself.

There was an odd scraping sound, and a crack of light appeared then grew larger. She watched in surprise as Logan forced the doors of the elevator apart. They were stuck between floors. She could make out a bit of brick, and then more light flooded in as he pushed the second set of doors open. His body was lit up, and she could see he was down to his slacks, his chest bare and gleaming with sweat.

As soon as he let go of the first set of doors, though, they began to slide shut, so he grabbed them and braced them again, glancing back at her. "I think we can jump down."

She grabbed her clothes and her purse, then moved forward, peeking over the edge. They had about a foot and a half of clearance, and it looked like a six foot drop to the floor, at the very least. "Is it safe?"

"Safer than staying here."

He had a point. "So how do we do this?"

Logan continued to hold the doors open, thinking. His face looked angular in the low light. "If you can hold the doors, I'll slide through and then look for something to brace them apart."

That sounded . . . nerve-racking. She'd have to trust him to come back for her. "What if I go first?"

"I'm stronger. If I can't find something to brace the doors, I'll have to hold them open for you while you climb down. I'm not sure you'll be able to do the same for me."

He had a point. Brontë bit her lip, then nodded slowly. "Okay. I'll hold them."

They traded places, and Brontë held the doors while he grabbed his clothes and put them back on quickly. She tried not to think about the fact that she probably should have gotten dressed, too, and was standing in an elevator wearing nothing but a leopard bra and bright pink boy shorts. It could have been worse, she supposed. "Ready?"

He squatted on the floor and examined the space, then glanced at her. "Would it bother you if I went between your legs?"

"Oh, no," she said. "Be my guest. My legs welcome your invading presence."

This time he chuckled, and she blushed. "I just don't want you losing your grip on the door," he told her. "That's all. I promise I won't look up."

"Just get us out of here," she said, wincing and spreading her legs wide so he could slide out from between them. This was not a story she was going to repeat if she got home.

When I get home, she told herself. *When.*

As Logan shimmied out of the elevator, Brontë focused on the weather. She could hear the pounding rain occasionally and wind gusts that sounded dangerous. They'd been isolated from the worst of it inside the elevator, but with the door open, it was all too obvious that the hurricane was upon them and they were trapped.

Suddenly Logan's body was gone, and then she heard him smack the tile floor below. She was startled and almost let go of the doors. "Are you okay?"

"I'm fine. Just off balance. Stay there, and I'll look for something to brace the door open so you can crawl out."

"Okay," she said, licking her dry lips. She tried to peek down and get a good look at his face, but the angle at which she was holding the doors made it impossible. She heard him walk away, and panic surged through her. He was gone. What if he wasn't coming back? "Hurry!" she squeaked out, hoping he'd heard that last entreaty.

The elevator was feeling a bit oppressive now, and her arms were beginning to ache from holding the doors open. It wasn't that they were hard to hold apart, but she was exhausted, thirsty, and starving. And a little terrified.

Okay, a lot terrified.

Time creeped past, every minute ticking by in slow motion. It seemed like forever before Logan returned, and she nearly sobbed in relief when she caught sight of him below. He set up a short ladder, then grasped the doors at the bottom, keeping them apart.

"You're going to have to slide down between my arms," he told her. "Get on your stomach and lower your legs first."

She nodded. "Gotcha. Can I let go now?"

"Let go."

She did, holding her breath for a moment as she released the doors. Then she hesitated. If she shimmied down, she was going to more or less shove her ass in his face. "Maybe I should get dressed first—"

"Just come on!"

"Well, then close your eyes!"

"I'm not going to close my eyes, Brontë. Just come on already. I can't hold this forever. The hurricane's almost on us."

She hesitated for a moment more, but a crash from outside decided her. Biting her lip, she tossed her bag and clothes out of the elevator ahead of her and then slid her legs out of the hole. When she was about halfway out, she began to have visions of the power coming back on and the elevator slicing her in half, and she rushed to slide completely out, not caring that her behind might have brushed against his face or that her wiggling feet couldn't find a toehold.

"Just drop," he told her after a moment.

She did, and collapsed to the floor. Her leg scraped along the ladder as she fell, and she smacked onto the ground with a thud that knocked the breath out of her.

But they were out of the elevator. Thank heavens, they were out of the elevator.

"You okay?" Logan moved to her side, his hands running lightly over her naked limbs, checking for breaks. "You're bleeding."

"Just a scratch. Something broke the skin when I slid. I'll be fine." She sat up, grimacing, and allowed him to help her to her feet. The air was muggy and hot. "What about the hurricane?"

"Sounds like it's getting worse."

"Should we go to the basement? Something?"

"Not the basement. The front lobby's already flooding with water. We need someplace safe." He glanced around. "Someplace with no windows that is off the ground."

"A stairwell?" she suggested.

He nodded and grabbed her hand, dragging her with him. "Come on. I think the stairs are this way."

Surprised that he would grab her hand, Brontë followed him, staring in openmouthed horror at their surroundings as they ran. The hotel looked as if it had been ransacked. Furniture was overturned; papers and pamphlets were strewn everywhere. Doors hung open as if the occupants had simply forgotten to close them in their haste to leave. They raced past the lobby, and Brontë gasped, her steps slowing.

It was flooded. An inch of water had crept across the floor, and more was pouring in by the large glass doors. Large, *broken* glass doors. A quick glance outside showed that the skies were a sickly gray-green, and the closest tree was nearly sideways in the wind. Fear tightened her throat.

"You can sightsee later," Logan told her harshly, tugging on her hand. "Come on."

They ran down one corridor, then another. Every crack

she heard from outside made her heart race, and she was in a near panic by the time they got to the stairwell. Logan flung the doors open and pushed her inside, and she raced up the flight of stairs to pause, breathing heavily, at the landing where they twisted to the next level. It was dark and shadowy, the only light coming from the small, square window of the stairwell door.

"Stay there," Logan said. When she began to protest, he raised a hand. "I'll be right back. I'm just going to check something out."

Brontë slumped to the ground, clutching her bag. She was too winded to bother to put her clothes on now, and too freaked out to do more than stare at the door. What if Logan got trapped out there? What if he didn't come back for her? What if she was going to be stranded in this hurricane alone?

A gust of wind boomed overhead, followed by a crack of a palm tree snapping so loud that she jumped. She didn't like being in the darkness alone. Not one bit. What if the stairwell collapsed in the storm?

To her relief, Logan returned a few minutes later carrying blankets and pillows and a small trash bag. She must have looked a bit shocked, because he immediately dropped everything and climbed the stairs to kneel next to her.

"You okay?" His voice was soft, protective. His fingers brushed her cheek.

She nodded, managing a trembling smile. "I think the noise is messing with my head. Marcus Aurelius said that 'It is not death that a man should fear, but he should fear never beginning to live.' Except I don't think he ever went through a hurricane. I almost prefer the elevator."

"I don't," Logan said. "Wait here. I picked up a few things for us."

He headed back down the stairs to where he'd dropped his haul and then moved it all up to the landing, displaying none of the sheer exhaustion that Brontë was feeling. As she watched in the low light, he offered her a pillow and then a blanket.

"What's all this for?"

"Just in case it gets cold later. We want to be prepared. It's going to be a long night with that storm raging. This is probably the only safe place in the building that we can get to at the moment."

She nodded and examined the pillow, then shoved it behind her back. It provided a bit of relief from the hard wall. "Thank you."

Logan sat down next to her and did the same with his pillow, both of them ignoring the blanket for the moment. It was too hot, too humid to even think about covering up. She was thankful to be in just her bra and panties, since she was feeling sticky and overwarm.

As she watched, Logan dragged the trash bag to his side and pulled out two bottles of water. Her eyes widened, and her mouth went dry. Thirst hit her like a freight train at the sight of that water, and she licked her lips. "Is one of those for me?"

He gave a brief nod and handed her one. It was room temperature. She didn't care. She unscrewed the cap and began to drink, the water tasting sweet and delicious on her parched tongue.

She could have downed the entire bottle in an instant, but she forced herself to drink only half, saving the rest for later. At her side, Logan continued to dig through the bag. "I had to raid the closest minibar. It's not a great selection, but it'll hold us until the worst of the storm passes overhead."

And he handed her a candy bar.

Brontë took it with a smile. "I could kiss you for that."

"You could," he said easily.

She glanced over at him, the breath catching in her throat. Was he flirting with her? Was this—

The wind howled overhead, so loudly that the walls seemed to shake with the force of it. Brontë whimpered in response, pulling her legs close to her chest and hugging them tight.

"Shhh," Logan told her softly. His arm went around her shoulders, and he pulled her closer to him and rested a hand over her hair, as if protecting her head. "I'm here. We're safe."

She huddled close to him, inhaling the spicy scent of his chest and resisting the urge to crawl into his lap like a scaredy-cat. Oddly enough, things didn't seem so bad with him soothing her, and after a minute, she relaxed. Just feeling his large body pressed against hers was comforting and made the storm seem a little farther away.

Her stomach growled, loudly.

A low rumble started in his chest, and she realized he was laughing. "Eat your candy bar."

She unwrapped it with trembling fingers. "Just so you know, in the future, I prefer M&M's. The peanut kind, not the plain."

"I'll keep that in mind. Philosophy and peanut M&M's."

"That's right," she said, taking a big bite out of her candy bar and moaning with pleasure as the taste hit her tongue. "This is really good. Thank you."

She heard the wrapper rustling as he unwrapped his. They snacked on candy, huddled in the stairwell, and waited for the storm to end.

"So how is it that you know Marcus Aurelius by heart, Brontë?"

She shrugged. "My mother loved books, but she especially loved the classics—Brontë, Austen, and Gaskell. The romantic ones." She paused, thinking of her mother. "I graduated from UMKC with a BA in philosophy. Majored in that, minored in history. I like ancient philosophers. I feel like they taught a lot of wisdom that can be applied to modern life."

"Interesting. So you're . . . a teacher?"

Brontë grinned. "Hardly. I'm a waitress at a sock hop diner."

"A . . . waitress." He said the words as if tasting them. "That's a bit of a career change."

"Not really. I started waitressing to pay the bills during school and then kept waitressing while I hunted for jobs after graduating, and, well, two years later, I'm still waitressing." She grimaced. That sounded so . . . lame.

"So you're twenty-four?"

"I am. How old are you?"

"I just turned twenty-nine."

She elbowed him playfully. "Wow, that's ancient."

He snorted.

"Seriously, though, you're doing really good for yourself," she told him. "Manager of a big place like this at twenty-nine? Your parents must be proud."

He was silent for so long that she worried she'd offended him. Then he said, very softly, "Thank you."

She took another bite of her candy bar and wondered at his response.

THREE

⁓

What a lucky streak he'd been on the past two years. First Danica's betrayal, then his father's death, now this. The icing on the biggest fucking cake of his life. His father would've said he'd brought it upon himself.

But then again, his father had always been a huge bastard. He'd disapproved of everything that Logan had ever touched. Not a stretch to think that he'd have disapproved of Logan's latest acquisition.

It had seemed like a simple task. Now that he'd purchased the resort, he wanted to walk through the property and get a feel for it. He had the architect's suggestions for improvements, but he liked to check things out on his own. He never made a firm investment without overseeing the operation himself.

His first walk through the resort prior to purchasing it? That had shown him everything he'd expected. The place had promise; the island was beautiful and central. The hotel itself was old and showing wear, and the rooms were only half full when nearby resorts were packed to the gills.

But it was mismanagement more than anything else that was causing this resort to fail, and that was where he could put together a team to step in and excel. In five years, he could have this property turned into a real moneymaker. The hurricane was doing him a favor, in a sense, because it was going to tear down a lot of the building, and it needed tearing down regardless.

He looked down at the woman curled against his side, her face barely visible in the dim light. She was sleeping, and his arm was wrapped around her protectively. She was an odd one. He had barely noticed her when she'd stepped on the elevator. Beach resorts were full of sexy women, and she hadn't registered attention until they'd been stuck and she'd begun to talk. More specifically, he hadn't noticed her until she'd begun to quote the ancients and lecture him, which he found charming and irritating all at the same time. A philosophy-quoting waitress who giggled when she was nervous. He supposed it could have been worse—she could have been screaming and frightened instead of laughing ridiculously.

Even though he'd barely noticed her when they'd gotten on the elevator, Logan had definitely paid attention when they'd climbed out. He'd seen a hell of a lot of her, especially when she'd slid that pert bottom down in front of his face, her long legs dangling as she'd tried to get out of the elevator gracefully—and failed. Brontë, she'd told him her name was. Like the classics.

Strange that he should feel so protective of her right then, sitting in the stairwell with her. But she'd been brave despite the circumstances, and oddly intriguing. And she had no idea he was rich, which meant that her reactions to him were sincere. She wasn't giving him coy yet lust-filled gazes that promised things if he'd only buy her presents or shower her with money. She was laughing and joking with him, and tartly demanding peanut M&M's instead of candy bars and lecturing him on his attitude by quoting Plato.

He liked that, too. Whoever Brontë was, she was smart and interesting, even if she was just a waitress.

The rain pounded overhead, though it seemed to be less intense than earlier. For a few hours it had raged outside, so fierce that he became concerned that the stairwell wouldn't provide enough protection. Throughout the storm they'd heard the sound of several crashes, and Brontë had huddled closer to him, terrified. He'd remained calm and stoic because, well, that was what Hawkings men did under pressure. They shut down and went into silent mode. His father had been great at that. Brontë stirred in her sleep, her arm looping around his waist and pulling her closer to him. She nestled her mouth in the crook of his neck, sighed, and went back to sleep as if he were the perfect pillow. He could have woken her up, and she would have automatically retreated a few feet, embarrassed at her actions.

But he liked her against him. He liked her warm, curving body cupped against his own. He liked the way she fit in his arms.

And he was as hard as a rock at the moment. Nothing he could do about that. He supposed that if he were a cynical bastard, he'd tell her about his fortune and wait for her to fling herself at him. It never took long. But somehow, he suspected, Brontë would be different.

After all, she thought he was the manager of this place. And for a few days? It was a novelty to just be normal.

He hugged her close. Best to let her sleep. The storm wouldn't be done for a while yet.

———

"Brontë," a low voice murmured in her ear. "Move your hand."

She sighed, licked her lips, and ignored the voice.

"Brontë," it said again. "You've got a rather . . . personal grip at the moment."

Still sleepy, she mentally took stock of where she was. Her butt hurt from sitting on the concrete stairs, and a blanket was pooled around her legs, which were stretched out next to a man's warm leg. One hand was trapped against the man's side, and the other was resting on a thick handlebar—

She snatched her hand away, mortified. "Oh, my God." That was *not* a handlebar.

"My thoughts exactly," he said drily. At least he sounded amused. She was horrified. He nudged her with one shoulder. "How are you doing?"

Other than being humiliated that I woke up clutching your crotch? Just peachy. She rubbed at her eyes and squinted into the dimly lit stairwell. It seemed even darker than before. Jeez, she sure was getting tired of the dark. Her stomach rumbled, and her bladder felt like it was ready to pop. "I'm okay. Is it still raining?"

"It sounds quieter. I think the worst of the storm has passed. We should probably get out and have a look around."

She shifted on the concrete. "Can we find a bathroom?"

"They probably won't be working."

"Yeah, but a nonworking toilet beats a stairwell."

He grunted in acknowledgment and got to his feet. "Come on."

She followed, ignoring the protest of her muscles as she stood. Her entire body felt stiff and achy. Of course, she couldn't complain—she'd gotten through the worst of the hurricane in one piece. Now they just had to wait for the rescue team.

Logan extended his hand for Brontë to take, and she did. Strangely, it was comforting to slip her hand into his bigger one. She wasn't the type who needed a man to make her feel worthwhile. But just having another person here, stranded with her? It somehow made things a little more bearable, made her a little less anxious.

He led her down the stairs in the semidarkness. When they hit the bottom step, their feet splashed into several inches of water.

"Not a good sign," said Logan. "Stick close to me. If the water's come in this far, we don't know what the rest of the building looks like."

"Or the island," she agreed, taking a step closer to him. Her shoulder brushed his, and she blushed, remembering how she'd woken up. Her hand had been on his cock. And he'd been hard.

And she . . . hadn't minded that. He was a stranger, but he was a good-looking, well-built stranger who was easy to talk to, didn't mock her quote-spouting, and was protective of her. She was attracted to him. She hardly knew him, but she still felt dragged inexplicably to his side, fascinated by him.

That was . . . rare. Most guys she met were immature . . . or married. A rogue thought made her flinch. "You're not married, are you?"

"Huh?"

"Never mind. I just didn't want to, you know, fondle a married man."

"So it's all right to fondle a man when he's single?"

"That's not what I meant, and you know it. I was just going to say—"

"I'm not married."

"Oh." She exhaled deeply. It shouldn't have mattered, but somehow it did. This little episode had made her feel somewhat close to him, and it would've been weird and disturbing to think that she'd been cozying up with a married man. "Thank God."

"I'm also not looking for a relationship."

Arrogant ass. She nudged him with her elbow. Okay, more like shoved. "I wasn't asking because of that. This would just be . . . weird . . . if you had a wife."

"We're not sleeping together, Brontë."

"Well, technically, we just did." It just wasn't all that exciting, if you didn't factor in the hurricane.

He stopped in front of her so abruptly that she bumped into his back and stepped backward with a splash of her feet. She could barely make out his expression in the low light of the stairwell. "Why all the questions?"

"I was just curious. You know. If I'd touched single junk or married junk. I think it's a reasonable thing to ask."

His face was tilted as if he were staring down at her, and she could barely feel the hot fan of his breath against her skin. She wished the stairwell were better lit so she could see his expression.

"It only matters if you're planning on grabbing it again, Brontë."

Now, there was a mental image she'd never be able to get out of her head. "Ah. Well. No, I wasn't making plans to do that again."

His chest rumbled in a low laugh. "Well, now I'm disappointed. Come on. I don't think it's safe to see if we can turn the power back on, so let's look for something that we can get some light with."

Logan opened the door to the hall, and they left the stairwell. Brontë was silent. Her mind was abuzz with the conversation they'd just had.

It only matters if you're planning on grabbing it again, Brontë.

Ah. Well. No, I wasn't making plans to do that again.

Well, now I'm disappointed.

Had he been flirting, and she'd just shut him down? He was normally so controlled that it seemed out of place. And yet she couldn't interpret his words in any other way. He did say he wasn't looking for a relationship, though, and she couldn't think of a worse way to start one. Perhaps she was reading too much into simple banter.

As they walked through the hotel back toward the lobby, it became obvious that the hotel was trashed. There was ankle-deep water in the stairwell, but when they took a step down into the hallway, the water rose to mid-calf. They sloshed down the hall, stepping past doors that had been knocked off of conference rooms. There was low purplish light to see by, and Brontë had wondered where the light was coming from . . . until she saw the ceiling. The lobby was set up like a lofting, several-stories-tall atrium with a glass ceiling, and it clearly had not survived the hurricane. Portions of the roof looked like Swiss cheese, open to the sky. Rain splattered inside the building, and the water around her feet felt gritty with sand.

"Wow. Your cleanup crew is going to be working some overtime, I think."

Logan glanced back at her, a hint of a smile on his mouth. "I was planning on renovating the place anyhow. Someone told me I needed thicker walls."

She laughed at that, feeling warm at his regard. "Good call."

"I'm starving," he said. "We should head to the gift shop. We can probably find some supplies there. I'm thinking water bottles, food, and maybe some dry clothes if it wasn't too badly hit."

That all sounded good to her. She paused and thought for a moment, then pointed ahead. "Through the lobby and to the left, I think. Near the restaurant." And then she felt stupid. He worked here—why was she telling him? "But of course, you know that."

"Of course." His hand went to the small of her back, and he gestured at the lobby. "After you."

Brontë felt her body grow warm. He was looking down at her with such an impressed, amused expression that she . . . well, she didn't know what to do with herself. So she offered him her hand.

He took it in his, and her skin tingled in response when his fingers curled around hers. Touching Logan made her stomach quiver deep inside.

At least, she told herself that it was her stomach.

They waded forward, and Brontë struggled to keep up with Logan's bigger strides as they headed into the lobby. It looked as if half of the hotel had been dumped here by the hurricane. There was more water, of course. Furniture was tipped over and scattered, and luggage was everywhere, the contents flung all over the room. Portions of the ceiling had caved in toward the glass doors, and all the glass was gone. She curled her toes, wondering where all that glass had gone. A sodden pillow floated in the water nearby, and a horrible thought occurred to her.

"You don't think we're going to see any bodies, do you?"

"I hope not." He sounded grim. "If we're lucky, everyone else was evacuated."

"Should we check the rest of the hotel? Just in case anyone else was stranded?"

"We will," he told her, and tugged her hand, urging her forward. "After we resupply ourselves. It won't do us any good if you're fainting with hunger."

"Me? You make it sound like I'm some weak flower on my last leg. What about you?"

"I don't faint."

She snorted. " 'Nothing has more strength than dire necessity,' right?"

"Another famous Plato gem?"

"Euripides."

"Of course. That was going to be my next guess."

"Naturally. You're a big fan of Euripides?"

"Who isn't?"

She laughed, shaking her head at his comeback.

They trudged through the massive lobby of the hotel, the weak streams of moonlight brighter the more destroyed the area was. The lobby was dark, but it seemed bright in comparison to the pitch-black elevator. Logan examined the ceiling as they walked, steering them clear of what seemed to be more dangerous areas. "The entire ceiling could collapse," he told her. "We have to be careful."

"Now who's Suzy Sunshine?" she teased, but stayed close.

In the blue darkness, they spotted the gift shop, and Brontë sucked in a breath of disappointment. The security gate was down over the front of it. The glass behind the gate had been destroyed, but the gate itself was intact, with pieces of broken plants and other bits clinging to the metal. There was a large window to the right with a display of toppled mannequins in swimsuits, and through a miracle, it hadn't shattered in the storm.

"Just our luck," she told him. "Do you have the key?"

"No," he told her crisply, and dropped her hand, walking away. "Stay there."

She crossed her arms over her chest, trying to be patient and failing. "What are you doing?"

He returned a moment later, carrying a broken lobby chair. "Getting something better than a key."

"What about the alarm?"

"Either it's not working or we're going to need to hope that the gift shop has earplugs," he told her, and then gestured in her direction. "Stand back."

She sloshed backward a few feet and waited.

Logan heaved the chair up, and she felt that curious flutter in her belly at the sight of his muscles flexing. He had big, broad shoulders that seemed to ripple with strength in the moonlight. And mercy, she liked looking at him.

He swung the broken chair against the glass like a base-ball player up at bat. Part of her expected it to bounce backward, as if maybe the glass were too thick to be broken by a chair if it had withstood the hurricane. But it crashed and tinkled into the water in a shower of glittering pieces.

She shielded her eyes out of instinct, glancing over when the damage was done. Logan stood there looking rather pleased with himself, his body illuminated in moon-light. He looked . . . gorgeous. His hair was tousled, falling over his forehead, and his tall frame seemed all muscles and shadow from this angle. He was definitely easy on the eyes. Too easy. She felt her pulse flutter when he gave her a boyish grin.

"Alarm's dead. Come on."

But she hesitated, trying not to smile at his expression of pride. "What about all the glass? We'll cut our feet."

He glanced down at the glittering shards. "You're right. Stay there."

Again? She did as told, crossing her arms and waiting impatiently as he tossed his broken chair down, then knocked the mannequins into a messy sort of bridge, and disappeared inside. A moment later, he returned and laid a Styrofoam surfboard over the floor of the window front and extended a hand toward her. "Come on."

Stepping carefully forward in the calf-high water, she placed her hand in his warm one, ignoring that funny little jolt that ran through her at his touch. He was just being courteous, she told herself. Nothing to get excited about. She wobbled precariously on the board as it shifted and moved under her feet. "I think I'm going to—"

Her feet slipped out from under her, and she pitched forward.

Strong arms were there to catch her. Logan held her close, her breasts pressed to his chest.

"—fall," she finished lamely.

If she tilted her face up, she'd be within kissing distance, and the thought made her feel flushed with heat.

He helped her stand upright. "You okay?"

"Just feel stupid is all." She pushed away from him, straightening herself and trying to look casual. Brontë glanced around inside the gift shop. "Shoes? We really should have brought ours."

Logan glanced around, then gestured at a far wall. "I see them. Stay there. Only one of us should risk cut feet."

He waded forward, and she studied their surroundings. The gift shop was packed to the gills with a motley assortment of items, half of them on the floor. Racks of ugly t-shirts had fallen over and were currently soaking up water near her feet. A short distance away, there were equally sodden racks of beach towels, and destroyed straw hats floated nearby. Lovely.

"I found you some water shoes. What size?"

"Seven."

"This might be a seven. Hard to tell in the dark." He plucked a pair off the wall and turned to her.

She held her hands up, and he tossed them in her direction. Using one of the fallen racks to support herself, Brontë snapped the string tying the shoes together and slipped them on. Too big. Didn't matter, they'd protect her feet for now. She'd get a better size when they had some light. She shuffled forward. "What supplies do we need?"

"Flashlights, if we can find them. If not, something dry to use as a torch. Lighters. Food and water. Anything else you want." He put on a pair of water shoes and began to move behind the counter.

A change of clothes would have been nice. She glanced at the sodden heap of shirts nearby. Not exactly what she had in mind. Picking through the mess of spilled items on the counters, she was able to locate some plastic-wrapped folded shirts, and she snatched all five of them. Perfect. "I found some dry shirts."

"Good, bring them. I found some lighters."

She moved toward him, sidestepping the mess in the aisles. He took one of the shirts from her and ripped it out of the package, then wrapped it around one of the broken chair legs. Next, he tied it with a shoelace and then flicked the lighter on. When it sputtered and went out again, he cursed, cracked open another lighter and poured the fluid on his torch, and lit it again. That did the trick.

In the flare of the torch light, he gave her an almost wicked look. "Now we can get a really good look at each other."

Her stomach fluttered again.

Logan was handsome, she realized. She'd known that he was clean-cut and well built, and he'd worn a suit when she'd stepped into the elevator with him. She didn't remembered much more, though, and she'd caught glimpses of him here and there, but not a full-on look. The light flickered, outlining the planes of his face with shadows, but he was gorgeous. He had a perfect, straight nose and a gorgeous pair of full lips framed by dark stubble. His jaw was square and strong, and he had dark, arching brows over equally dark eyes. And those big, broad shoulders. A dark, circular tattoo blotted the skin on one biceps, visible through the wet fabric of a white dress shirt that was untucked from his slacks. Somewhere along the way, he'd lost his jacket. Not that it mattered—the disheveled look was working wonders for him.

Logan was handsome, all right. She gave him a weak smile and waved her fingers at him. "Hi there. Long time no see."

The flickering light made his smile in response seem mysterious. "Hello, Brontë."

The way he said her name made her shiver, just a little. "You could have looked at me before. It wasn't totally dark."

"Yes, but now I get to see everything," he said, studying her with a long up-and-down look. "Not just shadows and suggestion."

That very blatant look made her feel fluttery all over again. Frowning, she gestured back at the store shelves behind her, feeling a little flustered and ill at ease. "I'm just going to look for some more stuff."

They continued to raid the store, rummaging through the mess for supplies. There was a cooler in the window display, so Brontë grabbed it and began to fill it with water bottles and sodas from the broken refrigerated drink case. Some had spilled on the floor, and she fished one out of the water at her feet, grimacing at the grit coating it. "I feel like a looter."

He was digging behind the counter for something. "You *are* a looter. You are currently in the act of looting."

"Gee, thanks. Are we going to get in trouble for this?"

"Brontë, I'm the manager. Just consider the tab on me."

She picked up a handful of candy bars and tossed them into the cooler. "How long do you think it'll take for them to get here and save us?"

"I don't know. I've never been in a hurricane before."

She hadn't, either. Brontë chewed on her lip, looking down at the water bottles in the cooler. She counted them. Twelve in there and twenty more still in the case. Handfuls of candy bars. What if that wasn't enough? "What if we're here for a week? Or longer?"

He tossed several lighters on the counter and turned, hands on his hips, checking the wall behind him for supplies. "Then we get to know each other *really* well."

For some reason, that made her blush all over again. Her mind went in an entirely filthy direction with that one single comment.

Part of her hoped they would be rescued very quickly, and part of her hoped that rescuers took their sweet, sweet time so she'd be forced to be around this delicious, half-naked man for quite a little while.

Something sparkled in one of the windows, and Brontë wandered over, her curiosity getting the better of her. One of the glass cases had jewelry in it—she supposed it was for the kind of tourist who wouldn't be satisfied with a T-shirt or a postcard. The necklaces in the window were pretty enough, but one in particular caught her eye. It was a string of diamonds that, when worn, would spill delicately over the wearer's neck as if on an invisible chain. It had a dark gemstone in the center that she couldn't make out and matching earrings.

"Pretty stuff," Brontë commented as Logan moved to her side with the torch.

"You like that?" he asked.

She grinned up at him. "What woman wouldn't? It's really gorgeous, but it probably costs an arm and a leg."

"Want me to loot it for you?"

Her stomach dropped. She shook her head, taking a step backward. "Absolutely not."

"Why?"

"It's expensive, Logan. Don't be ridiculous."

He snorted. "The diamonds probably aren't quality and I doubt that it's worth the markup, but if you want it, I'll get it for you."

"No. We'll get in trouble."

"Brontë, there's no one here. And I'm the . . . manager." He seemed to pause on the word, as if it were unfamiliar.

"I don't want it, Logan," she warned him, feeling anxious. "Looting it is wrong, and you'd be crazy to risk being fired over something like that."

He laughed. "They can't fire me, but suit yourself."

To her relief, he let it drop, and Brontë moved carefully away from the jewelry counter. In her experience, expensive gifts were inevitably the result of lies and betrayal. It made her think of her childhood, and the long weeks during which her father—a traveling salesman—had been gone, and her mother's anxious waiting for him to return. He'd roll back into town after weeks away, with quickly waved-away excuses and a shower of presents for his wife and daughter. Her dreamy mother had always been flattered by the gifts of jewelry and excited to see her husband return home.

Now, as an adult, Brontë knew better. She knew that her father's absences hadn't been due to business as much as they'd been to see another woman, a girlfriend on the side. The presents he'd brought home were apologies more than gifts. She'd learned not to trust impulsive presents, because in Brontë's eyes they were a way of hiding the truth, a distraction. And for some reason she didn't want to put Logan into the same category as her smiling, lying father.

They hauled a bag of candy, the cooler of water, and a few other bags of miscellaneous supplies back to the stairwell that they'd established as their base of operations, since it was currently the only place they'd found that was above water. Once back at the stairwell, Brontë grabbed a water bottle, climbed a few steps, and sat drinking her fill. When Logan sat next to her, she passed the water bottle to him, holding the torch while he drank.

It sputtered and dropped sparks as she watched it. "How long do you think this will last?"

"Not long. We need to find something better."

"We should check the rest of the resort, too. I'd hate to think of someone else trapped in the elevators, waiting for rescue." She chewed her lip, thinking. She felt weak and tired, but someone still stuck in an elevator would feel much, much worse, and she didn't want anyone dying while she sat a short distance away.

He nodded, finishing off the water bottle.

"Should we check the upper floors?"

"I'm not sure it's wise," Logan told her. "You saw how badly the roof was destroyed in the lobby. We don't know that the other floors aren't on the verge of collapse. We can take a look from outside tomorrow and decide then."

"All right," she agreed, then winced as her stomach growled. "I guess we should crack open those chocolate bars?"

"Or we could head to the kitchens," he told her with a

sideways glance. "See if there's anything worth saving now that the power's been off for a while."

"Real food? Sign me up." She got to her feet, feeling a burst of energy at the thought.

There were two kitchens in the hotel, one attached to each restaurant. The first one smelled strongly of dead fish and the roof looked as if it had fallen in, so they went to check the other instead. The second restaurant wasn't nearly as destroyed, but the kitchen had slim pickings. The enormous refrigerators were full of marinating meat that would probably spoil fast. There was a walk-in freezer, and they opened it, both groaning with pleasure as the cool air puffed out and brushed over their heated skin.

"Still cold," Logan told her, and gestured for Brontë to follow him in. "Might be cold for a bit longer if we keep the door closed."

The freezer was full of dinner items—frozen chicken, frozen fish, and myriad packages of sides and desserts waiting to be prepared.

"We should eat some of this," she told him. "Can we build a fire somewhere and cook some?"

"If the stove doesn't work, yeah. Pick what you want to eat."

They grabbed a few packages of chicken from the freezer and a large can of peaches from the pantry, and set about making dinner. Logan tested the stoves, and one of the gas ranges was working. They grabbed a skillet and began to cook the chicken, not talking. While they waited, Brontë found a can opener, opened the peaches, and offered Logan a fork.

He took it from her and speared a peach, and then quickly lifted it to his mouth and popped the dripping slice in.

Her stomach growled at the sight, and she quickly stuck her fork into a peach slice, lifting it to her mouth, her hand cupped underneath to catch the juices. The first bite was heaven—a sweet, sugary rush flooded her mouth, and the taste of peaches was overwhelming to her starved senses. She licked her fingers and leaned back against the counter. "I think that was the best thing I've ever eaten. I didn't realize how hungry I was until just now."

"We've had our minds on other things."

They savored the can of peaches while waiting on the chicken. Though Logan's movements were precise, Brontë found herself ravenously wolfing them down. She didn't care that her hands were sticky or that they were a little too sugary-sweet. It was food, and it was delicious.

Once they got to the bottom of the can, she sighed sadly. "I guess it'd be bad manners to lick it, wouldn't it?"

"I'm sure there are other cans."

"Yes, but this one is right here," she pointed out with a grin.

He watched her for a moment and then leaned forward. His fingers reached for her cheek. "You have some juice in the corner of your mouth."

Automatically, she leaned forward.

Logan's fingers brushed against the corner of her lips. At the light contact, Brontë immediately froze. Her gaze went to his face, and she watched him with a vibrating tension that had suddenly filled her body. She was intensely aware of him all of a sudden, his large presence next to her on the floor, their shoulders barely touching, their legs only inches apart. She was still in her bra and panties.

And he was leaning in.

As she sat there, frozen, his thumb caressed her lower lip. His gaze was on her mouth, and she sucked in a breath at the electric tension that filled the room. He seemed . . . fascinated by her.

Too soon, Logan pulled his thumb away and then licked it, as if tasting her . . . or the peaches.

She could feel the flush cross her face even as her heart sped up. Brontë wasn't quite sure what to make of that tender, intimate action. He'd tasted her.

————

While she watched the cooking food, Logan searched the other elevators and floors for people. No dice—they were the only two that had been trapped.

He'd also found flashlights in a storage closet, which helped immensely in exploring the dark hotel.

Soon enough, they were seated back in the small kitchen. Dinner was ready, and the sexual tension over the peaches was forgotten as they devoured the chicken. Silence fell over the kitchen as they ate their fill. Logan glanced at Brontë from time to time as he ate. There was something so open and trusting about her wide eyes that he found himself instantly responding every time she turned to him with that trusting look. Most women who ran in his circles seemed to be sly and conniving, quietly pricing jewelry in their heads or commenting on the designer labels another woman was wearing. Everything seemed to be a competition, right down to who could snare the richest man.

It was that sort of attitude that turned his stomach, especially after he'd been burned by it. He'd trusted Danica, and she had tried to play him for a fool. He hadn't dated anyone seriously since. No woman could be trusted not to be coldly calculating when it came to his bank account. They all seemed to want the same thing, to the point that their faces blurred together in his mind.

And yet he found himself responding to Brontë's cheerful smiles. To the way her hand seemed to automatically reach for his now. The way she'd curled up against him. Her outrageous—yet apropos—quotes she seemed to pull from out of nowhere.

And she thought he was a manager. A white-collar

worker making a menial salary—well, menial to him. She hadn't cared. Her demeanor hadn't changed when he'd told her what he did for a living, and she trusted him. Liked him, even. He'd noticed the slight tremble of her body when he'd been unable to resist reaching out and brushing his thumb over her soft lower lip.

Her eyes had gone soft; her breathing had sped up. She hadn't turned away, either.

She liked Logan the manager. She couldn't be grubbing for his fortune, because she didn't realize he *had* one. He could flirt with her like any normal man.

Except he wasn't much of a flirt. When your bank account was as big as his, you didn't have to try. All you had to do was look at a woman and suggest she take her clothes off, and she'd be naked at your feet.

It wasn't in his nature to be coy and teasing. Lean over and kiss the hell out of her? Yes. Stage a ruthless takeover? Absolutely. But flirt and tease? Not in his repertoire.

Logan frowned to himself, considering this as he finished off the last bite of chicken. He hadn't come to the island to find a woman. If it hadn't been for the hurricane, this would have been the last thought on his mind. But with Brontë here, warm and pleasant next to him, the two of them completely isolated from the rest of mankind? He wanted to touch her. To feel her melt beneath his touch.

Brontë was definitely attractive. Not his normal type—he went for the more polished, poised sort. Models, ballerinas, and the occasional actress. Women who were aggressive and knew what they wanted. Brontë was a waitress who hadn't found a permanent job since college. But her cheerful demeanor and openness had won him over at once.

The way she filled out those panties helped, too.

He'd have to proceed carefully. Not too aggressively, or she might be frightened away by his interest. But strongly and surely enough that she could not mistake his intent.

"You're frowning," she said quietly. "Everything okay?"

"Just thinking."

When he offered no more than that, she delicately licked her thumb in a movement that fascinated him and made his cock hard. "Thinking that we need more chicken?"

Logan shook his head. "Thinking about rescue," he lied. They had food, they had shelter, and he had an iron-clad insurance policy on this place that would cover repairs. Rescue could wait a bit longer. "It might be days before anyone finds us."

She nodded and gave him a small shrug before reaching for a water bottle, not distressed by this news. "I'm thinking we'll just be really close friends by the end of this."

Friends, or more if he had his way. But he gave a quick nod of agreement. "We don't know enough about each other to be friends," he said, letting the statement hang in the air to see if she'd take the bait.

Brontë pulled her knees up, exposing the backs of her creamy thighs to his gaze. "I guess we could learn, then, couldn't we?"

"We could."

She tilted her head and regarded him. "So how long have you lived here on the island?"

Ah. Damn. One of many lies. "A year," he told her tersely.

"What made you decide to take a job here? Did you live on the island?"

"No. A friend . . . referred me to the owner." Not a lie, not really. "I came here when I got the job."

"Where did you move from?"

"New York City." Seemed a harmless enough truth. Even though he was a billionaire, it wasn't as if his name was splashed all over entertainment magazines, and he was in the news only when he made a sizable charity donation. She'd have no idea who he was. "Where are you from?"

"The Midwest. Kansas City. Have you ever been there?"

"Once or twice. For business."

"You've got one up on me, then. I've never been to New York City."

"You should go sometime. I'll show you around." Direct and to the point, and there would be no mistaking his interest.

She smiled softly. "I'd like that. Have you been to many shows? Visited the Statue of Liberty?"

"No and no." He avoided the shows because he didn't like singing. And he saw the Statue when he looked out the window every day. No need to go visit it.

"That's a shame," she told him, hugging her legs and rocking a little. "If I went to New York, I'd want to visit it. Go get my picture taken and do all the touristy things."

"You and a million other tourists."

"True. I guess it's different when you're there. In Kansas City, those tourists just end up here at Seaturtle Cay," she joked. "Courtesy of 99.9 Pop Fever."

"Pop Fever?"

"Radio station. I won a trip. It's a little out of my price range to go anywhere normally. Too busy making ends meet and all that."

For this trip? He'd thought Seaturtle Cay was a budget hotel. That was one reason he'd taken over the place—to turn it into a luxury Bahamian resort. "Out of your price range?"

She sighed in disappointment, as if she were disgusted with herself. "Remember that I'm a waitress. Pretty much everything is out of my price range."

"You're smart. You can do something other than waitressing."

She laughed. "Actually, I like the waitressing. I like working with people. But the pay stinks. It covers the bills, but just barely. That's why I'd been really hoping to enjoy this trip. It's the first vacation I've had in two years, since I graduated."

"I don't get away for vacation much, either," he told her, trying to level the playing field. "Isn't every day here like a vacation, though? Sun and sand and palm trees—"

"And hurricanes."

She laughed again. "True. Is this your first one?"

He blanked out. Was it the first one Seaturtle Cay had been hit by? Or simply the latest in a long string of storms? "Every one of them feels like the first one," he said, avoiding the question.

"I suppose that's true enough." She grimaced. "I still can't believe Sharon left without me. I shouldn't be surprised, but I am."

"Your roommate?"

She nodded. "She sent me up to her room to go look for her passport that she'd lost. That was how I got stuck in the elevator. I never found it, so I assume she still had it and was able to get off the island." Brontë looked a bit glum at the thought. "If it wasn't for her, I wouldn't be stuck here."

"Then I'll have to thank her," he said, laying his cards on the table. "If I had to be stranded in a hurricane, I'm glad it's with you."

Her lips parted in surprise at his bold statement, and she flushed in the firelight, ducking her head a little. "I . . . thank you. That's very sweet."

"I'm not a sweet man." Most people referred to him as a cold bastard, especially when it came to business dealings. Danica had called him a ruthless jerk the last time she'd seen him, and he hadn't disagreed with her.

"Oh, I don't know," Brontë said in a soft voice. "You've been nice to me."

"That's because I like you. Most aren't so lucky. I barely tolerate almost everyone."

She laughed as if he'd said something truly funny. "Then I'm glad you like me." She nudged him with her shoulder again in that friendly way. "You're just saying that because you're stuck here with me."

"No, I'm saying it because you're smart, and funny, and beautiful. Being stranded with you has nothing to do with it."

She laughed again, but the sound was nervous, and she glanced away. "I imagine work keeps you busy," she said after a moment. "This place is enormous."

He nodded, not adding anything to that.

She yawned, hiding it behind her hand, and then pulled her legs close again. "Do you have a big family, Logan?"

"No," he said in a curt voice. He most definitely did not want to talk about family. "Are you tired?"

"Drained, really." She stifled another yawn and then grinned. "Okay, maybe a bit tired. Not looking forward to getting back to that stairwell, though. It's not exactly the height of comfort."

"I have some ideas of how we can fix that," he told her, and got to his feet. He extended a hand toward her again.

She placed hers in his and then glanced at the stack of dirty dishes and garbage. "Shouldn't we do something about that?"

He reached over and raked the mess into a nearby sink with one arm. "Taken care of."

She laughed, and he felt the sudden urge to kiss her. Her joyfulness was so pleasant. She was the happiest person he'd ever met, which both disturbed and captivated him.

But he didn't give in to his urge to kiss her. He didn't know whether she'd misinterpret his actions if he kissed her right before they went to bed. Though, hell, it wouldn't be misinterpretation: He planned on getting Brontë into his bed. But he wanted her to join him there because she wanted to be with him, not because he was pressuring her. He'd made his interest clear at this point—it was time for her to take the lead.

They headed back to the stairwell, Brontë's steps dragging with fatigue. He was tired, too, but not as much as she seemed to be. He made her wait while he climbed the stairs to the second floor and darted into the first room. It seemed to be untouched, though the room next to it had been hit hard. He didn't trust the stability of the second floor, though, so this would be his first and last venture there. But he was able to haul a mattress and two pillows down to the stairway and slide them down to the landing that he and Brontë called home.

With a bed and more pillows, she sighed happily and curled up in the bed, fast asleep before he'd even sat down. He lay down on the mattress and was pleased when she immediately rolled over and nestled against him, making a content sound in her throat as she rested her hand on his chest.

FOUR

Logan awoke with a raging hard-on and with Brontë's tangled hair across his chest. Her legs were twined with his, and she made soft little noises in her throat as she slept. It would have been so easy to roll her over and show her just how sexy and desirable he found her. To kiss her and persuade her into doing what he wanted.

But he remembered her nervous laugh when he'd told her she was beautiful, and he paused. Was she just humoring him? Maybe Brontë didn't appreciate the attentions of a manager after all. Damn it. His cock was just going to have to wait.

He closed his eyes and focused on his breathing, willing his body to relax. It took a few minutes before he was back under control. It was time for them to get up and face the day. They'd slept long enough, and lying in bed next to her made him want to do things that didn't involve sleeping. He gently shook Brontë. "Wake up."

She jerked away, her hair falling in her face as she bolted upright. "Huh? What?"

"Calm down," he told her. "Nothing's wrong."

Brontë rubbed a hand over her eyes and yawned. "What time is it?"

"My phone's dead. Water must have gotten into it."

She folded her legs under her and pulled out her phone. It lit up for a minute, highlighting her face in the darkness, and then winked out. "Damn it. There goes my battery. It said it's eleven a.m., though."

"We should head down to the kitchens and grab lunch, then."

They headed down to a quick meal of fresh fruit left on the countertop and some wrapped crackers. It wasn't glamorous, but the fridge was starting to smell and even the interior of the freezer was getting too close to room temperature for comfort. Neither of them wanted to risk getting sick from bad food.

Brontë suggested they check the store for any other food items, and then they headed back in that direction since there was nothing else to do with the day. As they walked, though, Brontë stopped in her tracks and stared out through the broken glass of the lobby windows.

Logan followed her gaze. The sun was shining; the sky was blue. A breeze rippled into the building.

"This is the first day it hasn't rained since I got here," Brontë exclaimed, moving forward. Her aqua shoes crunched on the broken glass at their feet, and he noticed that the standing water in the lobby had receded, too. She peered outside and then looked back at him. "Should we check out the beach?"

He shrugged. He'd just as soon go back to the stairwell and wait for rescue, but she seemed to want to explore. "If you like."

Her face brightened. "I would. Do you think the beach is trashed, too?"

"We'll soon find out, won't we?" And he stepped

forward through the broken glass, gesturing for her to follow him.

She did, and they made their way out into the front of the resort, squinting at the bright sun after days of low light. He studied Brontë as she picked her way across the sand-covered sidewalk toward him. In daylight, she was even more beautiful—not in a traditional way. Her hair was wild with tangles and blew around her head like a messy halo, and her face was round, without the well-defined cheekbones of the models he normally dated. But her eyes were sparkling and her skin was lovely and she smiled up at the sunlight as if it were the best thing ever, and he thought she was stunning.

"It really did a number on this place, didn't it?" She raised a hand to her eyes to shield them from the sun and glanced back at the resort. More than half of the windows were blown out, and it looked like one wing of the building had collapsed. He didn't want to think about how much that would cost in repairs. Palm trees that had lined the driveway had been uprooted and fallen over. One had toppled into one of the windows on the second floor. A car lay on its side in the distance, and junk from inside the hotel was strewn across the lawn. A fine layer of sand covered the concrete, gritty under their shoes.

"Come on," he told Brontë. "Let's see what the beach looks like."

They crested a dune, and there was the ocean spread out before them. Rippling and blue and endless, the thin white line of the beach the only thing separating them from it. Birds flew overhead. There was driftwood everywhere, floating in the water, lining the edge of the surf, and piled up on the sand, but nothing could ruin the sight of that beautiful blue water.

At his side, Brontë gasped, her hand going to his upper arm. "It's gorgeous."

It was, though the same could've been said for his companion. He enjoyed her unbridled enthusiasm, too. They slid down the dune and moved toward the lapping waves. At his side, Brontë sighed wistfully.

"What is it?"

"I was just thinking that it figures that we have nice beach weather after my vacation has already been ruined. I would have loved to spend a few days just enjoying the sun and sand."

He waved a hand at the empty beach. "What's stopping you?"

Her face lit up, then fell again. "Shouldn't we be working on making shelter or some other survival sorts of things?"

"We have food. We have shelter. All we need to do is wait to be rescued. If it'll make you feel better, we can make an SOS on the sand."

She stepped forward into the surf, letting it wash over her ankles, and her eyes closed in pure bliss. She tilted her head back, letting her tangled hair whip in the breeze.

He didn't feel the same urge to step into the surf that she did, but his gaze followed her intently as she soaked up the sunshine and enjoyed the water.

Her eyes opened after a minute. "Should we go back and get swimsuits?"

"Why?"

Brontë grinned at him. "To swim?"

Logan picked up a piece of driftwood heading in her direction and tossed it away. He didn't see the point in going back to the hotel just for a change of clothing. "There's no one here but me, Brontë."

She bit her lip, studying him for a moment. "You're right." She took a deep breath, as if steeling herself for courage, and then pulled off her bra. "Last one in's a rotten egg."

Damn. He'd just been suggesting that she could swim in her underwear, not that they should skinny-dip. Of course, now that she was taking the initiative, would he correct her on that?

Hell, no. *Carpe diem*, he told himself, and then grinned. Brontë would have approved of the thought.

———

This was the bravest, stupidest thing Brontë had ever done. She tossed her bra onto the sand, her heart pounding in her breast, and didn't look at Logan as she shucked her panties and kicked off her water shoes. Instead, she concentrated on the water, as if standing naked on the beach were something she did every single flipping day.

The truth was, this was an experiment. And it would either go really well or really badly.

But she'd seen him looking at her. And he wasn't giving her the looks that an uninterested man would give her. The looks he gave her were hot, scorching with interest. As if he were waiting for something to happen before making his move. What that would be, she had no idea.

And she was getting tired of waiting for him. After he'd caressed her lip the night before as they ate, she'd been unable to think about anything but kissing Logan. Sleeping with Logan. Sharing this remote, tropical paradise with Logan and having no one around but the two of them. Granted, a building destroyed by a hurricane wasn't the most romantic setting, but Logan was gorgeous and attentive, and it had been a while since she'd been seeing anyone seriously, so why not grab the bull by the horns?

Standing on the beach, totally naked, she put her hands on her hips and tried to look at this in a positive way. Even if he thought she was a crazy woman, the sun felt warm on her skin, and she was going to enjoy the ocean for today at least. She headed into the surf up to her knees and reached down for a handful of water. It felt colder than she'd thought it would be, and she shivered a little, rubbing her arms.

Something splashed past her. Brontë froze in place, then glanced over just in time to see a pair of white buttocks disappear into the water as Logan made a shallow dive into the surf in a short distance away.

Damn it! He'd been naked, and she'd missed it? She resisted the urge to slap the water in frustration, moving deeper and then sinking into the water to cover her own nudity. He'd accepted her challenge, though. That was a good thing, though she had no idea what to do now that he had. *Flirting really should not be this hard, Brontë*, she told herself.

Logan surfaced a short distance away, flung his wet hair back, and then stood in the water. She noticed the surf went only to his waist. Correction—more like his hips. Low, low on his hips, his privates barely covered by the ripples of the waves.

Her cheeks heated as she couldn't help but look over at him. Okay, the man definitely had a good body. He was toned and fit all over, his body slightly tanned as if he enjoyed the sun, but not too much. There was a tattoo of something on his biceps that she couldn't make out from this distance. He didn't seem like the type to get inked. He was a serious, almost stern sort of man, not a party boy who would get a tat when he was out with his buddies.

Intriguing. That didn't fit the picture she had in her mind of Logan Hawkings, responsible manager. He'd seemed a little stuffier in her mind, but that tattoo added a new angle. She wasn't quite sure who he was, and she liked that.

Brontë moved out a bit farther in the water, feeling extremely exposed without even a swimsuit on. The water brushed against her skin with gentle, silky caresses, and the sunlight touched her everywhere. It was a unique experience, this skinny-dipping thing. She wasn't entirely sure she liked it, though she'd gotten to see Logan's ass, so that was a plus.

His gaze swung to her, and he began to move slowly

toward her through the water. Brontë forced herself to hold her ground, instead of shying away like a nervous virgin. "Well, you're definitely not a man who can resist a challenge," she told him.

Logan grinned in her direction, and she sucked in a breath. The man was sexy when he was stern, but when he smiled? God. She could have sworn her girl parts had just given a squeal of delight in response.

He didn't stop until he was right next to her. It was still only waist-deep, and if she stayed crouched down, she'd be more or less at eye level with his cock. Not exactly a power position. Of course, standing meant she'd show him her breasts, but hadn't he already seen them when she'd stripped down on the beach?

Brontë steeled her courage and got to her feet, water cascading off of her body. She gave him a challenging look as if daring him to say something.

But he didn't. He only stepped closer, his somber gaze intent on her face. He reached out to her, cupped the side of her neck, and she felt him subtly draw her toward him. She was helpless to pull away, fascinated by those dark eyes, and when the tips of her breasts brushed against his bare, wet chest, she gasped.

"For what it's worth," he said in a low, husky voice, "my suggestion was going to be that we swim in our underwear."

"Oh," she said weakly, her gaze dropping to the mouth that was mere inches away from her own. "I wasn't sure—"

His mouth lowered onto hers. She hadn't expected to be kissed with such blatant intensity. He pulled her against him, his wet flesh brushing against hers, and she felt the long heat of his cock against her belly even as they kissed, letting her know exactly what he thought of the situation. Logan's mouth was firm against her own, and he tasted sweet, like fruit. His tongue flicked against the seam of her mouth, urging her to open for him, and she was helpless to resist.

A low mew escaped her when his tongue plunged into her mouth, turning the kiss from an exploration into decadent conquering. It stroked against her own, confident, assertive, and bold.

Each thrust of his tongue told her what he'd be like in a relationship, in bed. He'd take control of her body and make her hum with desire. If she encouraged him even a little, he'd rise to the occasion. He wasn't the type that would take no for an answer.

And she *really* didn't want to say no at the moment.

He tasted so good. Even more than that, he felt good against her, sun-warmed and wet and hard. The waves caressed at their waists while Logan continued to kiss her as if nothing else in the world mattered, and her toes curled in response, desire surging deep inside her.

All he'd done was kiss her, but she felt keenly aware of every bit of his skin pressing against her own: her nipples brushing against the fine hairs of his chest, the press of his cock at her belly, his fingers on her neck as he held her close, his thumb stroking her jaw. His lips caressing her own. His tongue thrusting wickedly, as if suggesting much more than just a kiss.

After what seemed like an eternity, Logan pulled away, and Brontë staggered, her knees suddenly weak and useless. His hand went to her elbow to steady her, and he pulled her body against his.

She gazed down at his biceps, at the mysterious tattoo. It was . . . well, it was rather hideous. The circular blob turned out to be a skull with a twisted two-dollar bill sticking out of the eye sockets. That was not what she'd expected to see on someone like Logan.

He leaned in for one more soft kiss, his tongue grazing her lips and distracting her from her study of his tattoo. "Was that what you wanted?"

That was a rather arrogant question. She blinked

rapidly, trying to focus her mind. "I wasn't sure what I wanted until just now, actually."

"And now?"

"Now I think I'm rather glad we're alone on the beach," she told him breathlessly.

He grinned, his expression confident and self-assured, and leaned in for another kiss.

Just then, a wave rose up. It slapped the two of them sideways, splashing them in the face and covering them with tendrils of seaweed.

They sputtered, breaking apart, and Brontë was hit with a fit of giggles as Logan pulled a handful of seaweed off his shoulder and flung it away from him in disgust. Logan looked over at her with a sour expression. "More nervous laughter?"

"No, this time I'm totally laughing at you," she said, and yelped when he leapt to dunk her.

The spell was broken, and they started splashing each other and riding the waves, or simply floating in the water. It was nice to just play and relax, and even when she dunked Logan, it didn't turn sexual again.

It was as if a question had been answered, and now Logan was content to wait for the right moment. Which made her feel a bit like prey being stalked by a predator. A very masculine, sexy predator that she wasn't entirely sure she wanted to escape. She rather liked being his prey, and what did that say about her?

———

For the first time since going on vacation, Brontë spent a day in the sun and enjoyed every moment of it. She played in the waves, lay out on the sand, hunted for seashells, and laughed her ass off when Logan built the sorriest looking sandcastle ever. They played like children all afternoon, right down to making sand angels and wrestling in the water.

Once out of the water, Brontë put her bra and boy shorts back on, not quite brave enough to run around stark naked. To her relief, Logan followed her lead, and they walked up and down the beach a few times examining debris floating in the water and talking. They were covered in sand and their underwear was more wet than dry, but they didn't care.

Eventually, they grew tired of frolicking in the water, and Logan suggested they make the SOS signal.

"I suppose we should," Brontë said mournfully, looking at the setting sun. She didn't want the day to end.

He must have noticed her reluctance, because he regarded her for a long moment, then said, "There's enough driftwood on the beach that we could build a fire and hang out here a few hours more."

She brightened. "That sounds like a lovely idea." Her stomach, however, ruined it by growling.

Logan's lips twitched with amusement. "How about I work on the SOS and building a fire, and you go and get dry clothes and something to eat and drink?"

Brontë snapped her fingers at him. "Now that sounds like a plan. I'll be right back."

"Take the flashlight," he told her, and picked up a heavy piece of driftwood, dragging it forward into the sand.

She did, and raced up the dune, spraying sand as she walked. She'd seen bottles of wine earlier and thought it might be pleasant to enjoy one on the beach. They had sticks of beef jerky taken from the gift shop, and she could probably find some cheese in the restaurant somewhere. Wine, cheese, and a quasi–beef product. Not bad. Of course, if they were going to have a fire, they should have s'mores. With that in mind, she went to the restaurant and raided the kitchen until she found exactly what she was looking for—graham crackers and marshmallows. With the foodstuff and a few bottles of water to round things out, along with a spare blanket that they'd left out to dry earlier, she headed back down to the beach.

While she'd been inside, the sun had set even lower, turning the orange skies into a deep, smoky purple. On the beach, she could see that Logan had spelled out a SOS in driftwood, and set up a pyramid of wood on the far end of the beach. She headed there and made it to his side just as the fire caught.

He glanced up at her with satisfaction as he got to his feet and continued to feed small pieces of wood into the burning pyramid. "You look great."

She laughed at that, glancing down at her bare, sandy legs, clad only in aqua shoes. She was now wearing a lemon-yellow Bahamas T-shirt that was two sizes too big and went down to her thighs, and she was pretty sure that her hair was one big snarl. "I didn't do anything."

"I know. But you still look great." The look he gave her was appreciative. "I'm glad you're back."

She hefted the wine bottle. "I brought drinks, food, and dessert."

"I'm a lucky man."

"And a flirt," she teased back, but she couldn't help smiling. "But I think that's a forgivable offense."

They spread the blanket on the ground and set up the food, taking bites out of the jerky, crackers, and cheese and drinking straight from the wine bottle.

The sun disappeared below the horizon, and the sky grew dark. Soon, the only light glittering for miles was their small fire. It made Brontë feel very small and alone, and she moved closer to Logan.

He mistook her gesture and passed the wine bottle again, glancing over at her. "Thirsty?"

She took another sip of wine, grimacing at the strong taste of the red. She'd grabbed the most expensive bottle—because hey, why not?—and it was rather strong. She was more of a boxed wine kind of girl anyhow. "Just thinking."

"Thinking about?"

"How there's no one around for miles." She stared off

into the dark skies and uncrossed her legs, stretching them out on the blanket. "And how that can sometimes be a little frightening."

His hand went to her ankle, and he gave her a gentle squeeze before caressing her skin. It was as if he couldn't stop himself from touching her, and Brontë sucked in a breath. After a moment, Logan said, "Don't be frightened. I'm right here next to you."

"I'm glad," she told him softly. "I don't know what I'd do if you weren't here."

"You'd probably still be in the elevator."

She frowned. She didn't like to think about that. If he hadn't been here . . . she shook her head. "I'm glad you're here with me."

His hand remained on her ankle, his thumb lightly gliding over the skin in a way that made her feel nervous and restless and aroused all at once. He wasn't doing anything else, though, just touching her. She stared down at that hand and then blurted, "Do you want s'mores? You know, chocolate and graham crackers and marshmallows? They're the perfect camping treat."

He glanced at the fire, then at her on the blanket. "I suppose this is a lot like camping, isn't it?"

"Right down to the campfire," she said with a grin. "Do you have a stick for my marshmallow?"

As he turned away, she blushed hard, because that sounded incredibly dirty to her own ears. *Do you have a stick for my marshmallow? My God, why don't I just ask him to throw me down on the beach and harpoon me like he's Ahab and I'm a sexy, sexy whale?*

They speared two marshmallows on the same stick, and Logan thrust them into the flames of the fire. "So you're one of those men, are you?" Brontë teased.

He glanced back at her. "One of what men?"

She gestured at the now-flaming marshmallows.

"You're willing to eat a little charcoal as long as it gets done faster."

"Collateral damage," he told her. "One expects that sort of thing when making a bold decision."

"Very bold," she said with a nod. "Could you blow out one of those bold decisions and put it on my cracker so I can eat?"

He did, and she smooshed it with the chocolate, licking her fingers as she nibbled at the treat. He pushed his together and then popped the entire thing in his mouth, eating it in one large bite. The man didn't do anything by halves, did he? She shook her head at him, grinning, and continued to nibble away at hers.

A large dollop of melted chocolate landed on her thumb. She regarded it for a moment and then lifted her hand, intent on licking it clean.

Logan's hand caught hers before she could, and he moved her hand to his mouth and very gently sucked the chocolate off of her thumb. A low flutter started in her belly, and her pulse began to pound as his dark gaze shifted to her face.

"Speaking of bold decisions," he murmured, and then ran his tongue along the pad of her thumb again. "Have you decided?"

"Decided?" she echoed, hating the quaver in her voice.

"You and I keep dancing around our attraction without ever really coming out and saying exactly what we're thinking. I'm not like that, Brontë. I'm the kind of guy that wants to let you know exactly how I feel, but you keep running away."

"I'm not running," she protested, feeling breathless. "Tell me."

"I'll show you, then." His gaze was intense as he watched her, and then it slid to her mouth, and she knew he was thinking about their kiss.

And now she was thinking about that kiss, too.

He leaned in and ever-so-lightly brushed his lips against hers. The movement was delicate but intense, a mere hint at what she could expect from him. And she wanted more, but he moved away and looked down at her, studying her face.

Logan spoke again. "It's your move, Brontë."

She stared at her hand captured in his. Shadows caressed his face, the breeze causing his hair to ruffle over his forehead, and she noticed the heavy beard stubble along his jaw. It had rasped against her skin as they'd kissed, but not hard enough to make her pull away. She could reach out and touch him right now if she wanted. Claim him. Or she could walk away from all of this and they'd just be friends. Camping companions. He was leaving it up to her.

She had no illusions as to what this was—they were alone on the beach. They were spending copious amounts of naked time together. He was handsome, and he must have thought her attractive. They could have wild, passionate sex for a night or two, or however long it took for them to be rescued. Then they'd part ways and she'd go back to work in Kansas City and he'd go back to work managing the hotel and their paths would never cross again.

It was the perfect situation for a no-strings fling. Except Brontë wasn't good at the no-strings thing. That was for strangers, for people she would run into and never see after that night. Logan was different. She already knew a lot more about him than she did a lot of people. She *liked* him. Not that she normally didn't like guys, but most of her relationships seemed to end on an ugly note, and she didn't want that to happen with Logan. But if she turned him down, she'd never get the chance to experience just how wonderful making love to Logan might be.

"I want this," she admitted in a soft voice, "but I don't know how good I am at casual relationships."

"We can worry about that once we're rescued," he told her, and leaned in to close the distance between them.

She was going to do this. *They* were going to do this. She was going to have a ridiculous, exciting, passionate fling with a man. Not just any man. Gorgeous, serious, totally alpha Logan Hawkings, who made her toes curl every time she looked at him. Who kissed like he'd invented it.

And here she was, in an ugly tourist T-shirt, with wild beach hair and not a touch of makeup. Maybe it wasn't Brontë as much as it was that she was the only woman on the island? That was a sobering thought.

He touched his fingertips to her chin, forcing her to look at him. "Should I not have asked?"

"No, asking is good," she said, and gave him a shy smile. "I'm just not exactly at my hottest at the moment."

"Quote me something."

She gave him an odd look and then laughed, blurting out the first thing that came to mind. " 'Happiness depends upon ourselves.' Aristotle."

"See?" He whispered, leaning in to kiss at her neck. "Hearing you say that is so incredibly hot."

She laughed again. "You're a strange man."

"And you're beautiful," he said bluntly. "I haven't been able to take my eyes off of you all day."

And that was enough to bolster her deflated ego. She leaned close to him, her gaze moving to his mouth. "Then kiss me?"

"You have to ask?" He leaned in closer.

"Asking's good," she murmured again, just as his lips met hers.

For the second time that day, she was swept away by his kiss. He had such an amazing mouth. She'd kissed plenty of men, but none of them had ever kissed her with such . . . blatant ownership. Logan's mouth slanted over her own, his lips taking control first, followed by his tongue. She was helpless to resist, and parted her lips when his tongue brushed against her mouth. Then she was lost as his tongue thrust and rubbed against her own, the kiss moving from one of simple pleasure to something deeper. His fingertips played along her jawline as he kissed her, as if ready to hold her steady if they needed to.

His mouth continued to slant over hers, his tongue stroking deep until the world narrowed to Logan's mouth on hers and Brontë was lost in the sensation. She'd barely noticed that she was now leaning heavily against him, his body supporting her weight. When he shifted, she nearly toppled and began to giggle.

"Careful," he warned her. His voice was stern, but there was a crinkling around his eyes that told her he was amused. "It seems my kiss is rather dangerous."

"Extremely," she said breathlessly, resisting the urge to reach up and touch her lips. They felt swollen and soft and wet from his kiss. With her eyes on him, Brontë leaned back on their beach blanket. "In fact, I might need to lie down to get my bearings."

Logan's big body loomed over hers for a long moment, and then he lay down beside her, turning and propping up on one elbow to face her. "Better?"

She glanced over at him. His face was cast in shadow at this angle, but he was still delicious. From the big shoulders to the large hand that lay on the blanket, she loved the look of him. The beach itself made her feel a bit exposed, though. She stared up at the night sky and then turned her head, listening to the gentle sound of the waves as they hit the beach. "Should we go inside?"

"Do you want to?"

"I don't know," she admitted. Part of her wanted to stay out here in the open, by the beach. And part of her was totally panicked at the thought of making love out in the open. "I want to stay out here but it feels . . ."

"Wrong?"

"I was going to say naughty."

One corner of his mouth curved up into a half smile. "And naughty is bad?"

She reached over to him and trailed a hand down his chest, feeling the light sprinkling of chest hair across his pectorals. "Actually, no. Now that I think about it, I rather like naughty. What about you?"

"I don't have condoms out here. Unless you brought them."

She was an idiot. A total, freaking idiot. She should have grabbed them when she was inside. She had her birth control pills . . . somewhere. But she was pretty sure she'd missed a few days and didn't want to chance it. Condoms it was. "No, I didn't bring any."

"Then I can pull out." He lifted her hand from his chest and began to nibble on her fingertips. "If you're okay with that."

His lips danced along her thumb and sent shivers up and down her spine. "I'm good with that. I'm clean, by the way."

"So am I," he said. "Are you sure you wouldn't rather go inside?"

"No, I like it out here."

"Where it's naughty?"

She grinned. "Precisely."

Well, they'd gotten everything out of the way except the actual act itself. He was simply watching her, lightly kissing her fingertips. What had she expected? For him to maul her as soon as she gave the okay? She suspected he was holding back, making sure she was just as interested in this as he was. She had to show him that she wanted him, too, and that she wasn't just saying yes for the hell of it.

So she wiggled a bit closer to him on the blanket and leaned in, pressing her lips to his. His tongue flicked against hers encouragingly, and so she grew a bit bolder, taking more liberties with the kiss and twirling her tongue around his. Her hand slid down his chest, and she twined her fingers into his chest hair, tugging at it.

"Touch me," Brontë told him softly. "Please."

Logan's hand went to her side, and he gently pushed until she rolled onto her back. He immediately followed, flipping over to cover her, his weight braced on his elbows. She could feel his long body settle between her slightly parted legs, and then she was suddenly wide-open to him in a move that felt both shocking and right. She was wearing just her panties under the long t-shirt, and Logan's boxers felt scorching—and far too thin—against her thighs.

Logan leaned in a little closer. "Maybe I want to keep kissing you for a bit longer."

"That's okay, too," she said breathlessly, acutely aware of him.

He lightly ran his fingers over her face, as if memorizing her features by touch. Then he leaned in and kissed her mouth, his lips featherlight against her own. He then kissed her cheek, his lips skimming her skin until he reached her jaw, where he pressed another kiss. Her chin was next, then her nose, and Brontë closed her eyes, enjoying the sensation of his mouth on her skin, his weight over her. She could feel the heavy heat of him cradled against her pussy, and was half tempted to wrap her legs around him. Would that be too much too fast? She wanted to keep enjoying him and his touch. If he wanted to go slow, that was fine with her.

Logan's mouth moved along her jaw, and then she felt him take her earlobe in his teeth and gently tongue it. A gasp escaped her, and she wrapped her arms around his neck.

"Like that?" he asked softly, and repeated the motion.

She bit back the moan rising in her throat and gave a small, jerky nod.

He nibbled on it for a moment longer and then slid his tongue down into the hollow underneath her ear and down her neck, causing shivers to move over her skin. His weight shifted, and she felt his cock press hard against her pussy, then rub up and down against it through her boy shorts. A whimper escaped her throat and she automatically lifted her hips, slipping her panties down and locking her legs around him.

"Like that?" he asked again.

"Just like that," she breathed, rocking her hips against him. He felt so good, and she hadn't had sex in so long. Dear God, if casual sex felt this nice, why wasn't she having it more often?

His hand slid between their bodies, and she felt him tug at her Bahamas T-shirt. "Let's take this off."

She nodded, and he pulled it up to her neck. Then she began some creative wiggling to tug it over her head while still lying on the ground. All the while, she felt him slide farther down her body, and then his mouth latched on to her nipple, tonguing it.

Brontë moaned, a jolt of pleasure moving through her at the touch. Her hands went to his shoulders, rubbing, then digging her nails in as he flicked at her nipple with his tongue before moving over to her other breast and beginning to nuzzle it. A hot ache bloomed between her legs, and she moaned again, unable to bite back her pleasure. His mouth was so skilled. She raked her nails across his shoulders, encouraging him.

He sucked hard on her other nipple and then released it with an audible pop. Dazed, she stared down at him in time to see him lightly flick his tongue over the wet tip, then look up at her. "Your breasts are beautiful. I've been wanting to play with them all afternoon." His hand gripped her breast, thumb grazing her nipple even as he leaned over the other one again. "Watching them naked and glistening with water was driving me mad."

She drove *him* crazy? He was driving *her* mad. At his words, she arched underneath him, thrusting her breasts in the air so he could have full access to them, and was not disappointed when he pinched the tip of one at the same time that he licked the other. A bolt of pleasure shot straight to her sex, and her legs tightened around his torso. Her voice was breathy. "Logan."

"Love it when you say my name," he murmured, his lips moving against her nipple.

"Oh, Logan," she moaned when he nibbled at the tip again. "God, you feel so incredibly good."

"Let's see," he murmured, pressing a kiss between her breasts. His hand left her breast and skated down her belly, then lower, to her mound. A hot, thick finger slid between her folds. "Definitely wet."

She was. She was wetter than she ever remembered being with a man. And she was so turned on that she ached inside, her sex clenching as if she needed something—or someone—buried deep within her. "Oh, God."

"Logan," he murmured, and nipped her breast even as he slid that finger in and out of her pussy. "I want you to say my name again while I'm touching you."

"Logan," she breathed, the word turning into a whimper when his slick finger moved to her clit and began to rub it. Her hips rocked involuntarily, and she clung to his shoulders, her nails digging into the tattoo on his biceps. His touch felt so amazing that her entire body seemed one big bundle of nerve endings, and they were all connected to the clitoris that he was rubbing and rolling under his fingers. Hot tension began to climb through her body, and she moaned low in her throat, her legs tightening around him. "I—I'm going to—"

"Come." He made it sound like a command more than

a question, and as he spoke, his fingers worked over her clit even faster, circling quickly.

She cried out as her entire body stiffened in her orgasm, then bit her lip to hold back as he continued to rub at her clit in slow, teasing circles that made her orgasm seem to last forever. Her entire body was quivering when she finally came down, and she noticed her nails had made half-moons into his shoulder. "Oh," she breathed, removing her hand. "I'm so sorry."

He leaned in and kissed her, hard and possessive. "About what?"

"Y-your shoulder," she said, bewildered. "I'm hurting you."

"You're not hurting me, Brontë," he said, and kissed her hungrily again, making the flames lick through her belly once more. With his hand, he dragged her arms back around his neck and then flexed his hips, surging forward until his cock rested against her naked pussy, and rubbed there. He was incredibly hard and thick, and she made a low whimper at the feel of him through his boxers. "I want you to keep touching me. I don't care if you claw up my back." He tugged at her lower lip with his teeth and then whispered against her mouth, "I like your reactions. They feel real to me."

Another laugh bubbled up in her throat, and she wrapped her arms around his neck again. "I'm not very good at faking these things. Sorry to disappoint you."

"Not disappointed," he said, rocking his hips against hers in a slow, circular motion that made her entire body follow the movement, her legs sliding back around his hips again. "And I know you weren't faking."

That masculine smugness in his voice made her curious. "Exactly how do you know that?"

He pressed a thumb to her clit, and she cried out, her nails cutting into his shoulders again. "Because of that." He slid a finger lower and circled around her opening, then ever so slowly pushed into her, causing her to gasp in reaction. "And that," he murmured. "If I had a finger sunk deep inside you when you came, you'd have clenched all around me, wouldn't you? Milk my finger like you would my cock."

She bit her lip and wiggled her hips a bit, too shy to answer.

"You're sweet, and you're smart, and sexy, and so very real, Brontë. That's what I like about you." He leaned in and gave her another light kiss, his fingers leaving her pussy, and she nearly cried out with disappointment.

"I like you too, Logan," she said softly, her hands moving over his arms and chest, caressing his skin. "I want to touch you."

"I want to fuck you," he murmured against her mouth, and she gasped at his directness. "I promise I'll pull out."

She nodded, and gasped with surprise when his tongue thrust into her mouth, even as he shifted and she felt the head of his cock fit up against the slick opening of her sex.

Logan Hawkings definitely wasn't one to mince words. He told her what he wanted and went after it. Brontë realized this an instant before he thrust deep, and she whimpered at the sting of unused muscles as he seated himself deep inside her.

He tensed over her. "Virgin?"

She shook her head. "Just been a while, that's all. Give me a moment."

He leaned in and kissed her again, his tongue dancing over hers in a way that felt incredibly decadent with his sex buried in her own. When she nudged her hips slightly, he swung his, rocking the two of them in a slow, circular motion that made Brontë instantly aware of every muscle in his body—and hers.

"Oh . . . do that again," she breathed, holding on to him tightly.

Logan did, repeating the motion and exaggerating it for her benefit. It was a subtle roll of his hips, but he pressed forward and pushed enough that it rocked her body with his, and the slow roll of their hips brushed him against her clit, sending sensations pinging through her. She moaned again, her heels digging into his buttocks, encouraging him.

He was not a man who needed much encouragement. This time, when he thrust, he surged deep inside her, rocking her entire body on the blanket and causing her to cry out with pleasure. She clung to him as he began a hard, steady thrusting, pushing deep and hard inside her with every muscle, every sinew in his body. Her world narrowed down to his hips, pushing against hers, the grit of sand on the blanket at her back, the smack of his flesh against hers as he thrust deep again, the bounce of her breasts with every jolt of their bodies. She lost herself in the sensations, her eyes closed, her head thrown back. He was breathing hard over her, every breath a satisfied rasp, as she began to make soft, pleased noises in her throat with each thrust he made.

The elusive orgasmic feeling was rising again, and she focused in on it, moving her hips in time with his to ensure that each thrust was deeper, harder, stronger, and with each push of his cock into her, she got a little closer to coming.

He shifted his weight, adjusting her hips, and with his next thrust, her eyes flew open. That had been . . . different. The almost-but-not-quite orgasm feeling hovering at the edges of her consciousness flared to the forefront, and when his next thrust pushed forward, it happened again. Her pussy clenched around him in response, and he groaned even as he sucked in a breath.

"Wh-what was that?"

Logan's hands moved to her hips, angling her just so, and then he thrust again. When she keened in response, he grinned down at her, the look wicked and triumphant all at once. "G-spot."

Oh, God. She didn't think anyone had ever hit it before. And oh, *God*, she really liked it. Her nails clawed his back again. "I need more."

He gave another brutal surge, shoving their bodies across the blankets with his next push, and she cried out as the orgasm danced so close. Her feet left his hips, and she planted them on the ground so she could better lift her hips when he pushed in again, and thrust just as hard against him, her hips working furiously in time with his. That spot was back, and his short, quick pumps were rubbing up against it in the most incredible way that made her entire body arch with pleasure. She was so close and then—

She cried out as the orgasm rushed through her with force. Her sex clenched tight around him, and she heard him utter a muffled curse before he pulled out. She dropped her hips back to the ground as he stroked his cock with his hand, once, twice, and then he was coming on her belly, hot jets of come splashing over her skin.

Once done, he exhaled heavily and lay down on the blanket next to her, where she was staring up at the sky, dazed and dreamy.

That was incredible. Mind-blowing. She'd totally forgot about being on the beach, though she suspected the sand that had gotten on the blanket would remind her soon enough. "Thank you," she said softly.

"Thank you?" He was still panting. "For pulling out?"

"No," she said dreamily, though that was nice of him, too. "For showing me where the G-spot was. I had no idea. I think I'm ruined for non-G-spot sex now."

He laughed, the sound short and forceful. "I wouldn't be so sure about that."

"Well, okay, it'd have to be really great sex to make up for the lack of the G-spot attention." She sat up and grimaced at her sticky belly, still covered with his seed. "I think I'm going to go take a quick dunk."

"It's probably cold."

"'You will never do anything in this world without courage,'" she quoted at him.

"Is that a challenge?" he asked, grinning. He got to his

feet and curled his hands into mock claws, looking as if he were a predator about to pounce on his prey. "Are you saying I'm not brave enough for cold water?"

"Not at all," she said, turning toward the ocean.

When he took a step forward, she ran for it, a high-pitched squeal of alarm escaping her. Moments later, he had an arm around her stomach and was dunking her in the chilly surf. Brontë screamed and clung to him, dragging him under with her until they were both sputtering and laughing.

"There's your courage," Logan told her between chuckles.

She laughed too, delighted by his mood.

They rinsed off quickly, dumped sand on the fire, and then headed back to the hotel in the darkness. Their stairwell was just as they'd left it, complete with mattress, pillows, and blankets. Before when they'd crawled into the bed, they'd been clothed. When Brontë crawled into bed this time, she was naked and slightly damp, and so was the man who crawled in after her. As soon as she pulled the blanket over her body, he tugged her close and spooned her, his hand sliding possessively over her waist and resting on her breast.

As if he cherished her.

And she thought that maybe, just maybe, Logan was going to ruin after-sex cuddling for her, too. Because being pressed up against his big, strong body as she drifted off to sleep, his hand possessively cupping her breast, felt a little too good to be true.

FIVE

Logan awoke before Brontë did. His body's internal clock was set to 6 a.m. New York time, no matter where he was. He'd also awoken with a stiff cock and pleasant memories of the previous night's sex on the beach with Brontë. Tousled, sweet Brontë, who'd been so responsive in his arms, and absolutely startled when he'd found her G-spot. That look of pleased surprise on her face? That had made him feel like a king in bed.

She hadn't been the most skilled of his lovers—he suspected the Ukrainian ballet dancer would forever hold that spot—but she'd been the most open and honest one. Her expression, totally unable to hide anything, had pointed him to exactly where to please her, and her wide-eyed responses and gasping moans had been an incredible turn-on. She'd been enthusiastic and genuine and pleased to be with him.

Him. Logan the "manager." She didn't know if he had two nickels to rub together, and hadn't cared. She'd just wanted to have sex with him. And he couldn't say that with certainty about any of his former lovers. Had they wanted him? The man? Or just been attracted to the power of his bank account and what he could do for them? It was never easy to tell, and it ruined pretty much every relationship.

And the one woman he'd thought he loved in the past—Danica—had proven herself to be shallow and interested in nothing but money.

A line of sunlight streamed in under the stairwell door below them, giving him just enough light to make out Brontë's sleeping form next to him. She shifted in bed, rolling over and tucking her cheek close to his shoulder. Her hand automatically went to his cock, and his morning wood had turned painful fast. Did she realize how often she reached for him in her sleep? Or was this a calculated move? He remained utterly still, listening to Brontë's evenly spaced breaths.

A light snore escaped her.

He exhaled in relief. That was real. She was real. He was a fucking paranoid son of a bitch, wasn't he? A sleeping girl reaches for his cock, and he automatically thought she had an ulterior motive. It was a good thing she couldn't read minds. Someone as guileless as Brontë would have probably been disgusted. His father and the way he'd treated Logan's mother had polluted his brain.

Logan pulled the blanket off of her inch by inch. She slept on, though she moved a little closer to him as if seeking heat. Carefully, he traced his fingers over her shoulder and down her side, resting his hand on her hip. Her skin was soft and smooth, her hips plump, and her full backside made his mouth water.

She made a soft, breathy moan in the back of her throat and shifted onto her back. Perfect. He could part her legs, slide deep inside of her before she even woke up, and rid his cock of this ache—

Fuck. And then what? Pull out again? That had been sheer torture the night before. They needed condoms. Logan edged out of the bed and down the stairs, slipping on his water shoes and then quietly opening the door. He headed into the lobby, ignoring his nudity. He doubted any rescuer would be here this early. The water on the floor of the hotel had receded, leaving muddy trails on the tile and leftover debris. Rescue would be here soon, he guessed. He and Brontë likely had been lost in the shuffle for a day or two, but it wouldn't be much longer. Someone would notice a missing billionaire, if not a missing waitress.

Logan got a package of condoms from the store, drank a bottle of water and downed a candy bar, and returned to the stairwell. Brontë was still asleep, so he abandoned his shoes at the base of the stairs, kept a condom in hand, and slid back into bed with her.

She was soft and warm against his side, giving a little absent sound of pleasure when he returned as if she'd missed him. He liked that. Logan leaned in and kissed her neck and then her shoulder. They were light, trailing nibbles that teased the skin. A soft giggle escaped her throat, the sound still too sleepy for his taste. Kissing along her arm, he reached over her and cupped her breast, thumbing over the tip and with a touch causing the peak to harden.

The sound she made in response was a low moan.

His cock felt as hard as granite, and it rubbed against her limbs when she shifted in the bed. He wanted to pull her full against him, feel the press of her flesh against his cock, but he was enjoying her unconscious reactions a bit too much at the moment. His thumb skimmed over the hard nub of her breast again, rolling it back and forth as he continued to kiss Brontë's neck.

The woman was definitely a heavy sleeper, Logan thought with amusement. He nipped lightly at her shoulder, and when she rolled onto her back, he leaned down to take the stiff tip of her breast into his mouth.

Brontë moaned again, and her hands went to his hair, digging into his scalp. "Mmm, Logan."

He flicked her nipple with his tongue. "I was wondering what it'd take to wake you up."

"That's a good way," she said dreamily. Her fingers played with his hair.

"It's a shame you woke up before I had to resort to more *insistent* tactics."

"Oh?" She slid a hand down his stomach and played her fingers over his cock. It twitched in response to the light touch. "What did you have in mind?"

"Burying my face between your legs and licking your pussy until you came."

The breath shuddered from her lungs.

He nipped at her breast again. Too quiet. "What are you thinking?"

"I'm thinking I should have slept a bit longer," she said, and then laughed at herself. "I miss all the good stuff."

Logan kissed down her belly, licking at her belly button. "I can be persuaded."

"Oh?"

He dropped his mouth lower, to the curve of her hips, and placed a hand on her inner thigh. He felt her quiver of response, as if his touch simply drove her wild with antici-pation. "You could . . . ask."

"Is that all it takes?" She gave another breathy laugh, and then her fingers dug in his hair again. "*Please*, Logan. I'll be so good to you."

Her breathy, sexy voice made his balls tighten and his cock throb with need. Damn. She was good at that. He lowered his head and, as promised, buried his face in her soft flesh. He felt her entire body stiffen in surprise, and she gave a startled cry when his tongue swiped between her plump labia.

"You don't waste any time, do you?" she said, and her voice sounded nervous.

Too intimate for her, perhaps? He wanted to please her, though. Logan nuzzled her softly. "You taste amazing." She did, too. Like sex and Brontë and a hint of sea salt. He wanted more of her on his tongue, so he parted her pussy lips with one finger and lowered his mouth to lap at her clit.

"Oh." Her fingers twisted in his hair, pulling a little. "Logan, I don't know. I . . ." Her protests trailed off as he continued to lick her clit, hardening the tip of his tongue into a point and circling it around the little bud.

"Do you want me to stop?" He let the words play over her skin. "Are you uncomfortable?" At the end of the last word, he let his hot breath fan over her flesh.

She moaned in response, and he felt her thighs quiver. "Never mind," she told him breathlessly. "Keep going."

Good. She was letting herself relax and enjoy this. It was a shame it wasn't brighter in the stairwell—he wanted to see her expression. He'd just have to go by the sounds she made, and the feel of her body against his.

He continued tonguing at her clit and brushed a finger over the opening of her sex. It was slick and wet, a sign that she was enjoying his attentions. Logan slid a finger in deep and thrust it in time with his tongue strokes.

He could feel her squeeze around his finger, heard the half-sobbed whimper that escaped her throat. His cock throbbed in response, painfully hard and acutely in need. But he wanted her to be ready.

Logan thrust a second finger in with his first, circling them inside her. She was tight, and he remembered that she'd needed a moment the night before. Today, he wasn't going to pull out of her. He'd sink in deep and let her clench around him as she came, because nothing felt better than that.

He tongued her again, faster, and she stiffened. "Logan," she cried out. "I'm so close."

He pulled away, then, ignoring her cry of protest, and tore open the condom. Her hands reached for him, caressing his cock and his chest, stroking him with greedy, desperate motions.

And then it was on, and he adjusted himself between her widespread legs and thrust home.

Brontë gave a keening cry in response, her nails digging into his shoulders in that mix of pleasure and pain he was starting to associate with her. She felt so much that she had to take it out on him, and he'd gladly receive the punishment she doled out.

He began to drive into her, not caring that he was being rough or that his motions weren't fluid. They were brutal and primal, and she clung to him with each forceful push, crying out his name. He concentrated on her responses, waiting for the right moment for his release, because he was so damn close that he ached.

And there it was. Brontë's pussy clenched, and her voice broke on a wild gasp, and then her muscles tightened around him even more. It felt amazing, and he surged again, feeling his own body respond. He came inside her, thrusting hard until he felt drained from his response, and then collapsed onto the bed next to her.

She immediately rolled over and clung to him, her own breathing shallow and ragged. To his surprise, she leaned over and kissed his mouth. "Good morning."

"Morning," he said back.

"Do you wake up all your lovers like that?"

He didn't, but he also didn't feel like sharing that. "Do you always sleep through foreplay?"

"Only if it's not any good," she said, and then broke off into a fit of laughter when he reached out and tickled her sides. "Okay, okay, you win. It was pretty decent."

"Do I need to prove my skills to you?" He found himself teasing back and smiling.

"I might need a little convincing," she said, and trailed a finger down his chest.

"I should get to work, then," he said, moving in to kiss her again.

———

Stark naked, Brontë flipped through the sundresses in the gift shop, looking for one that hadn't been totally ruined in the hurricane. There were a few that had gotten wet and

dried into wrinkled messes but that looked clean otherwise, and she picked through searching for something in
her size.

Her gaze strayed to the glittering diamond necklace,
and she shook her head. Logan was crazy to think about
giving it to her. Thoughtful, sweet, but crazy. It was way
too much money to spend on someone who was more or
less a one-night stand. That's what this was, after all,
wasn't it?

On the flight to the Bahamas, Sharon had talked nonstop about sexy island flings and how she couldn't wait to
have one. And it had made Brontë think, however briefly,
that maybe she wouldn't mind having one, too. Just a little
fun to spice up her life before heading back to Kansas City.
She hadn't expected anything to happen, though.

She sure hadn't expected to meet anyone like Logan.
Much less have the whole resort left to the two of them,
alone. Logan was different from the guys she was normally
attracted to. For one, he seemed to have a stable job. Brontë
always seemed to find herself with men who were "between
careers" or "making a transition," which was code for
"unemployed." Logan was also a bit more . . . dominant,
if she had to put a word on it. She was used to laid-back
guys who let things run their course. And she was pretty
sure "laid-back" wasn't a word that appeared in Logan's
dictionary.

But she had to admit, that was part of his appeal. He
knew what he wanted, and he went after it. He didn't sit
around and wait for someone else to take action—he made
things happen. It had been he who got them out of the
elevator, he who had gotten them supplies, and he who'd
made the SOS.

Brontë picked a dress and tossed the others aside, glancing into the lobby. Logan had gone to see if he could find
breakfast, and he'd left her in the gift shop. For some reason,
she was anxious to see his broad shoulders again. She felt

safe with him around. If she had to be stranded with anyone, she'd take a protective alpha male like Logan any day.

Of course, she hadn't really expected to sleep with her protector. But now that they had? She didn't regret it in the slightest. The sex was incredible.

No, she amended as she put on one of the floral sundresses and ripped the tags off. Better than incredible. Ruined her for other men was more like it. She'd orgasmed more with him than any man she'd dated. Normally they'd be pushing on her head, demanding a blow job before they'd reciprocate, but he'd already gone down on her . . . and had enjoyed it. He'd enjoyed pleasuring *her*.

Not that she wouldn't enjoy going down on him. She paused at the mental image of taking Logan by surprise and knocking him backward into a chair, unzipping his pants . . . then grinned as she slipped on a pair of mismatched flip-flops. Going down on Logan seemed rather appealing at the moment. And turnabout was fair play. Stretching sensuously, she headed out of the broken window and back to the main lobby of the hotel, glancing around.

"Logan?"

No sign of him. That was odd. Maybe he'd gone exploring without her. She wandered through the destroyed lobby.

"Logan?"

Anxiety began to twinge in her stomach . . . and then it rumbled. She was starving. She glanced back at the gift shop, but the thought of eating more candy bars made her sick. It was a bit sad that she was getting tired of chocolate—even M&M's. She headed toward the far end of the first floor, near one of the restaurants, and called Logan's name again.

"In here." Logan's voice sounded distant.

She headed into the restaurant, and paused in surprise. One of the tables in the center of the room had been righted and a water-stained tablecloth spread over it. Place settings had been set down and two chairs slid under the table. As she watched, Logan leaned over a pair of candles and lit them with his lighter.

A slow smile spread over her face as she approached, and a silly, nervous giggle escaped her throat. "What's this?"

Besides the sweetest thing anyone had ever done for her, of course.

Logan looked back at her and smiled, his expression confident. "I thought I'd like to take my date out to dinner. Or breakfast, as the case may be." He reached for her hand and led her to one of the chairs, pulling it out for her with a flourish.

She sat, unable to stop grinning like a fool, especially when he leaned in and kissed the back of her hand. "I hope it's not chocolate."

"It's not. First, we have a fine vintage that I think you'll appreciate." He laid a bottle over his arm and held it out to her as if it were wine.

It was a bottle of water.

She laughed, clapping her hands. "It looks delicious."

"Indeed." He set down a wineglass and began to pour with effortless grace. "The flavor is peerless. I think you'll enjoy the bouquet."

Brontë lifted her glass when he finished pouring and pretended to sniff it. "Very nice." She gave him an appraising look. "You're good at this, you know."

"Waiting tables? Should I be insulted?"

She snorted, ignoring that jab at her job. "I meant with the wine thing." She wiggled her fingers at it. "They teach you how to be classy at manager school?"

He gave her an odd look. "Something like that. Should I bring out the next course?"

She gestured grandly. "Please do."

To her surprise, he pulled out a covered silver dish and placed it in the center of the table, then lifted the lid with a flourish.

A basket of fruit—fruit that looked reasonably fresh, too. She gasped, pleased. "Where did you get this? I thought we picked through everything!"

"I found it in the concierge room while looking for batteries for the flashlights. I thought it'd make a nice breakfast."

It did. Brontë hadn't realized how pleasurable plain, simple fruit could be. They ate their fill of apples, oranges, and bananas, and split a pineapple and a mango. They licked juice from their fingers, sipped water from crystal wineglasses, and had a great time. Brontë couldn't help but grin at Logan from across the table. This entire setup was just . . . perfect. He was perfect.

And she suddenly wanted to reward him.

With a devilish grin on her face, Brontë set down her wineglass full of water and tossed her napkin on the table. One of Logan's dark brows went up, as if he were questioning her.

"Interested in dessert?" she asked in a low, purring voice. "I know just the thing."

"How can I resist when it's proposed to me like that?"

"You can't," she said lightly, and then slid out of her chair and under the table.

He stilled. She watched his legs shift in his chair as she crawled under the table toward him. "Brontë?"

When she got to him, she sat back on her heels and put her hands on his trousers. He was wearing them again today, which was a pity. He even had on his belt, though it was waterlogged and the leather ruined. She pulled at the buckle and began to tug it slowly free. "Just my way of saying thank you," she said. "Thought I'd help myself to a little treat is all."

He groaned, and she felt his knees shift, spreading a bit wider. His hand reached under the table, and he cupped her jaw then brushed his thumb across her cheek.

"You don't have to do this," he murmured from above her.

"I don't *have* to do anything," she pointed out. "However, I want to do this. Now sit back and relax."

He did, his hands moving to the arms of his chair and clenching them. Good.

"Aristotle once said, 'Pleasure in the job puts perfection in the work.'" She leaned in and finished unbuttoning his pants, then lowered his zipper slowly. No boxers underneath, just flesh. That was nice. Brontë grasped his already-hard cock and tugged him free of the clothing, enjoying the feel of his hot flesh against her skin. She hadn't had a chance to really play with him when they were in bed the night before, and this was her time to explore him at her leisure. "Mmm. I see perfection right now."

He was thick and hard, and the crown of his cock was large, the tip already wet with fluid. He felt good in her hands, too. Firm and heavy, his skin hot against her own. She measured her fingers around his girth and found that they just barely met on the other side. Nice.

"I like this," she said in a low voice, running a finger along the length of his cock. He jerked under her touch, and she couldn't contain the chuckle in her throat. It was fun to affect him so much. She leaned in and lightly swept her tongue over the head of his cock, tasting the salty beads of wetness on his skin. So delicious. So hot.

Above her, he groaned, and she felt him grip the edges of the table. "Brontë."

It sounded like he was gritting her name out between his teeth. She smiled and grasped his cock in her hand, circling the base with her fingers before leaning forward and taking him deeper into her mouth. Again, he groaned, and she began to work his thick length with her mouth, rubbing her tongue along the underside as she sucked him deep, pumping with her fist at the base to increase the sensation.

Sucking on his cock was getting her excited, too. She could feel the slickness between her legs, felt the heat of her pulse throbbing through her body, centered low in her hips. She wanted to rock them with every motion she made. More than anything, she wanted to please him, to make him lose control and come.

"Your mouth is amazing," he ground out. She felt one hand slide under the table, felt it tangle into her hair, and then he began to work her head. He was fucking her face, she realized, a little scandalized by that—and a lot turned on. Moaning around his cock, she moved with the force of his thrusts, whimpering when he'd butt up against the back of her throat. He was in so deep, filling her mouth up. His motions were abandoned, as if he weren't quite able to control himself, and she curled her fingers into his pants with excitement, feeling her own sex tingling with need.

"I'm going to come," he warned her. "If you don't—"

She leaned in, sucking harder, letting him know it was okay.

That was all it took. He breathed her name, and his fist tightened in her hair, his hand thumping on the table as he came in her mouth, his hot come wetting the back of her throat. She jerked involuntarily, swallowing and pulling back when he was done. She'd hit her head on the underside of the table, she was pretty sure. She was also pretty sure that neither of them had noticed.

"Brontë," he groaned. "God, your mouth." And he was still hitting the table with that light, rhythmic slap that sounded like a beat. Music?

She smiled to herself, pleased at his reaction.

His hands pulled her up from under the tablecloth, and she realized that the rhythmic sound was continuing. Puzzled, she looked up at him—he had a slightly dazed expression, his hair was mussed and tousled over his tanned forehead, and he was still a bit hazy from his passion. "What's that noise?"

Logan focused, and then his eyes narrowed. A grin spread across his face. "Helicopter."

"Rescue?" She stood, wobbly and leaning against him, her body still humming with need. Lousy timing, that rescue.

He leaned down and kissed her on the mouth. "Come on. Let's get our stuff and see who's here."

———————

Their stairwell went all the way to the roof, and even though there was debris scattered up the stairs and she was pretty sure some of the steps were creaking more than they should, they made it to the top. Once up there, Brontë could see several things at once.

There was a helipad on the roof of the resort. That was handy. There was a helicopter coming in for a landing, too, close enough that her sundress was whipping around her legs and her tangled mess of hair was turning into a tumbleweed around her face.

She could see for miles around up here, too, and she gasped at the sight of the island. There were cars washed off the road in the distance, in ditches. Trees were uprooted everywhere. Boats were overturned at a distant marina. On the far side of the hotel's roof, it looked like the hotel had crumbled away. The east wing hadn't fared nearly so well as where they'd been staying. She was thankful their elevator hadn't been there.

"Come on," Logan shouted over the deafening *chop chop chop* of the helicopter. He put an arm around her shoulders possessively, and she put her hands to her sides to keep her dress from flying up. He leaned over and yelled something at her that sounded like, "I think I recognize that chopper."

They ran forward, and to her surprise, a man jumped out of the helicopter and ran across the helipad to meet them. He was wearing mirrored sunglasses and a khaki shirt and shorts, and laughing as if this were the funniest thing he'd ever seen. He raised a friendly hand in greeting, and Brontë was surprised when Logan gave it a high five, clasped it, and then brought the man in for a hug.

That was rather . . . friendly.

The man in the sunglasses gave her a rather knowing up-and-down look and then turned back to Logan. "I should have guessed," he shouted over the helicopter's blades. "You looked entirely too happy for a man who's been stranded for a few days, but I guess the company was good, right?"

"This is Brontë," Logan told him. "She was stuck in the same elevator I was."

"You picked a good elevator to get stuck in," the man agreed amiably and then thrust his hand toward Brontë. "Nice to meet you."

She shook his hand, noticing that it was very big and sturdy, and covered in calluses. Small scars crisscrossed his dark tan up and down his arms. The newcomer looked wild and just a bit dangerous. Handsome, she supposed, but Logan was more appealing to her. Still, it was odd that Logan would be such good buddies with the resort's pilot. Maybe the manager of a resort had to fly around in a helicopter a lot? She had no idea what his job entailed.

"We're so glad to see you," she told the newcomer as they moved toward the helicopter. "I guess I picked the right hotel to be stranded at if it's the one with the private helicopter."

They got into the helicopter, and the men buckled her in. The seats were plush leather and incredibly nice. Not what she'd expected from a rescue copter. It seemed almost luxurious. Someone handed her a headset with a microphone, and she put it on. Thank goodness, no more shouting at each other. The *thwack thwack thwack* of the helicopter blades was so strong it vibrated in her belly, but at least it wasn't making her eardrums want to burst anymore.

The new man was giving her a confused look, though, as he sat back down in the cockpit again. Next to . . . a pilot. Strange. "Does this dump of a resort have a helicopter, Logan?" the new guy asked.

Logan's response was crisp over the headphones. "It does not."

"Huh." The newcomer grinned, then turned back to Brontë. "I'm Jonathan, by the way."

Something wasn't adding up. "You don't work for the hotel, Jonathan?" she asked.

He laughed as if she'd said something hilarious. "Hell, no. And if anybody asked, this is a Red Cross helicopter. Or Coast Guard. Or something."

"It's not?"

Logan fixed her with a meaningful look. "We'll talk about this later, Brontë."

That sounded like he was trying to quiet her down. She narrowed her eyes at him, her jaw set. "What's going on?" She turned back to Jonathan. "Who are you, exactly?"

"Just an old friend," he said, flashing her a white smile. "And somehow I'm thinking Logan's in trouble, isn't he?"

That depended on what exactly was going on. She studied Logan's clenched jaw, his slacks. The shirt he'd casually pulled on, hiding his tattoo. The luxury helicopter they were currently sitting in that wasn't Red Cross or Coast Guard. The laughing man who looked as if he were enjoying her confusion way too much.

It wasn't adding up.

She gave Logan a curious look. "You're not the manager of this place, are you?"

"I'm not." His words were clipped and displeased.

"Then who are you?"

He said nothing.

Over his shoulder, Jonathan grinned. "He's the owner, baby."

He what? Brontë stared at Logan, betrayed. It didn't

make sense. And yet . . . it all made sense. The expensive necklace he'd offered her. His lack of knowledge of how the hotel worked. All of it. Logan wasn't a manager. He was some rich asshole who'd decided to have a good laugh at her while lying about who he was.

And to think that she'd *slept* with him!

The entire thing was a lie. Just like her mother, she'd stupidly fallen for a man's smooth words and let her heart get carried away. Just like her father, he'd turned around and betrayed her.

SIX

Brontë didn't speak during the entire helicopter ride back to the mainland. Instead, she seethed quietly.

She felt like an idiot. A huge one. How could he not tell her the truth? Did she matter so very little to him that he'd hide his identity from her? Was his name even Logan Hawkings? She couldn't trust a single word that had come out of his mouth over the past few days.

And she'd slept with him! Oh, *God*. She wanted to hide her face in her hands, but that would give away too much of what she was feeling at the moment. Instead, she pasted on her best friendly-waitress smile and tried not to think about how she'd cuddled with the man the night before, or had gone down on him under a table that morning because she was goofy for him.

She'd thought she'd been so lucky to be stranded with someone like Logan. Handsome, take-charge, intelligent, sexy, and strong. Well, she could add a few more adjectives to that list. Words like "liar" and "jerk" and "untrustworthy."

How he must have laughed at her, Brontë thought

bitterly. Every time she'd mentioned how he ran the hotel, he'd been silently *laughing* at her. A waitress. Had he let her assume he was the manager so she wouldn't be so intimidated by his job, thus ensuring that she'd sleep with him? Ugh.

Well, she'd wanted this to be a weekend fling, hadn't she? Mission accomplished. If she never saw the man again, it would suit her just fine.

They landed some time later on an unfamiliar roof, and everyone began to unbuckle their seatbelts as the helicopter blades slowed to a stop. Brontë removed her headset when the others did, and she couldn't help but ask as Logan hopped out of the helicopter, "Where are we?"

He didn't answer her but simply extended a hand to help her out of the helicopter. She took it and waited for him to reply as she stepped down. When he didn't, she turned to Jonathan and repeated the question.

He grinned over at her. "One of my summer homes in Miami. You can stay here until we get things sorted out."

One of his summer homes? *One* of? She glanced around at the massive roof she stood on. It was probably bigger than her apartment building. Exactly how much money did Logan and his buddy have? She narrowed her eyes at their backs, following them down the stairs and into the house.

Inside, her suspicions were confirmed. The house was an enormous mansion. White walls that had never seen a speck of dirt were artfully decorated with expensive light fixtures and framed art. Her dirty sandals flapped on marble tiles, and she had to fight to keep her mouth from going slack at the sight of the expensive carpets and furniture. It looked like a showroom of some kind. Except this was someone's house, which was bizarre.

Jonathan led them down a long hall and then gestured at one of the doors. "You can stay here, Brontë. I only have a few guest rooms in this house, so if you don't like it, we can switch your room."

"I'm sure it'll be fine," she told him with her polite waitress smile. She didn't plan on staying here any longer than she had to. Of course, he didn't have to know that.

"She stays with me," Logan said in a firm voice.

Her eyes narrowed at his confident tone. "I want my own room."

He glanced down at her and gave her a small shake of his head. "You're staying with me."

"Is that so?"

Jonathan gave her an appraising look. "In that case, I guess you can stay with Logan." He nodded at his friend. "It's your usual room."

Logan grunted in acknowledgment.

So it was decided? Just like that? She gritted her teeth. "Care to show me which room that is? I think I'd like a shower."

Jonathan grinned, as if remarking on her barely contained fury. "I'll let lover boy here do the honors. I need to make a few calls. Feel free to head downstairs when you're up to it." He put his hands in his pockets and whistled, heading down the long marble staircase at the end of the hall with a jaunty confidence that bespoke years of familiarity with the place.

She turned to look at Logan and crossed her arms over her chest. "You have some serious explaining to do."

"I know, and we'll talk about it later. I promise," he said, putting a hand on her shoulder and steering her down the long hall to a different set of doors.

Brontë waited for him to explain, but he paused in front of the door and said only, "This is our room." He pushed it open, and she gaped at the room before her. Thick, plush red carpet covered the floor. A massive wooden four-poster bed dominated the room, along with a bay window that overlooked an enormous swimming pool. A Pre-Raphaelite painting hung over the bed. The entire thing screamed money.

And Logan had a "usual room." Ugh again. Everything he'd told her was a lie. What was the point in lying to her about his job, though? It didn't make sense. It only hurt her feelings that she hadn't mattered enough for him to tell the truth.

"Make yourself comfortable," Logan told her. "I need to meet with Jonathan to discuss a few things and then call my assistant. I've been out of pocket for too long."

She stiffened, then turned to give him an incredulous look. "I thought we were going to talk."

"It can wait."

"No, it can't. You lied to me."

"The lie ended up being to your benefit."

She gasped. "My benefit? Since when is lying to someone to their benefit?"

"I'm wealthy," he said. "I'm sure that'll make up for a lot of things. Take a shower, and you'll feel better. I need to talk to Jonathan."

He leaned in to kiss her, and she turned her face away, still stewing. She didn't realize that he'd left until she heard the door shut and she was left all alone in the gorgeous room.

He wasn't who she'd thought he was. He had money, and he obviously thought that having money made his opinion more important than hers.

The lie ended up being to your benefit.

Brontë wanted to punch him for saying that. She kicked off her sandals in a fury and crossed her arms, heading over to the window to stare out at the pool below. After the hurricane, it was odd to see a pool that wasn't full of broken deck chairs. Jonathan's pool was, of course, full of sky blue water. A large waterfall cascaded down some rocks on the far end of the pool, and to the side she saw a white linen tent fluttering in the breeze, with cushioned wooden deck furniture underneath.

Wooden deck furniture. She wanted to laugh at the

ridiculousness of it and that white linen tent. Of having a pool with a freaking waterfall. She glanced around the room she was standing in. The carpet must have been two inches thick. She eyed the massive bed and expensive-looking coverlet, the painting with the plaque underneath that told her it was legit and not a copy. She went to the bathroom and flicked the light on.

The bathroom was bigger than her apartment. There was a sunken marble tub, a glass box shower, and three sinks. A wall full of mirrors on one side. A toilet and a bidet. Naturally.

This wasn't just big money. This was ridiculous, stupid money.

And here she was, just a diner waitress who had gotten stuck in the elevator with a rich guy on an island.

No, she amended, a rich guy who *owned* the island.

She frowned, glancing back over at the bed. A telephone sat on an antique nightstand next to it. She went and picked it up, thinking hard. Brontë pulled out her wallet. Her credit card was intact, the few dollar bills she had in there a bit soggy but serviceable.

So she dialed information and got the number of a local taxi service. "I need a car to take me to the airport, please."

"No problem. What's your current address?"

"I have no idea. Can you do a reverse lookup on the number?"

The woman on the other end of the line agreed, then a moment later, said, "I've got the address. Someone will be there to pick you up in fifteen minutes."

Brontë hung up and crossed the room, sliding her shoes back on. She'd wanted a harmless weekend fling that she could leave behind, no strings attached. She'd gotten one. Logan might have wanted to continue their little island affair now that they were on the mainland, but he should have thought of that before he'd lied to her and then dismissed her concerns.

In her mind, she'd left Logan behind on the island. She'd liked the playful, fun Logan. Manager Logan. She had no interest in the rich asshole Logan, she thought sadly. The *real* Logan.

The one she'd fallen for was a fake.

———————

Logan appropriated Jonathan's study and made a few important phone calls that couldn't wait another day. He called his assistant and asked her to order a new phone to be shipped to him overnight as well as to cancel his credit cards since he'd left his wallet somewhere at the resort. Then he called a few business partners to let them know he was indeed alive and that meetings should be rescheduled.

When he'd finished with the calls, he hung up the phone and found that Jonathan had reentered the room at some point during his last call. He'd brought a bottle of whiskey and sat down directly across from Logan, placing it between them. "Need a drink? You look like you could use one."

He waved away the offer. "The only drink I could use right now is water. Alcohol just dehydrates you."

Jonathan rolled his eyes. "You never loosen up, do you? It's a wonder that your little gal pal didn't run away screaming as soon as you opened your mouth."

Funny. Brontë hadn't thought he was a stiff-necked jerk. He scowled at Jonathan. His adventurous friend got on his nerves with his laissez-faire attitude. Jonathan would move mountains—or destroy companies—to help his friend out, but sometimes the man needed to learn to shut up.

"We got stuck in an elevator."

Jonathan snorted, knocking back his drink. "Is that how you got left behind? I was wondering if that shit manager of the place had neglected to tell anyone that you were there."

"I fired him a few hours before the evacuation." So no, Logan hadn't been really surprised that no one had come looking for them. "How'd you figure out I was still there?"

"Oh, Hunter's assistant's been trying to get a hold of you for something, and when he couldn't contact you for a couple of days, he set Hunter on it. Hunter didn't have a chopper, so he called me." Jonathan shrugged. "Wasn't hard to figure out where you were at."

Huh. Logan supposed he should thank Hunter next time he saw him. "Thank you for the rescue."

Jonathan grinned. "I figured I'd come after you. It might have taken anyone else a few more days."

Yet another thing to tick off on his list of items to improve at the Seaturtle Cay resort: evacuation plans. From what he'd seen, he wasn't impressed. He and Brontë could have been in serious danger. Damn useless manager. Logan was glad he'd fired the guy.

"So . . . the girl. You said her name was Brontë?"

Logan nodded absently, thinking of her wind-tossed hair and her brilliant smile. Her crawling under the table, her lips around his cock.

"Cute girl. She's with you, I take it?"

His eyes narrowed and a possessive surge rocketed through him. "Why?"

Jonathan raised a hand. "Down, boy. I was just going to comment that she wasn't your regular type."

Logan's jaw clenched. Was this another Danica comment? "What exactly do you know about my regular type?"

"They're friendlier, for one. That girl looked like she was ready to chew you up and spit you out once she found out you owned the place. You lied to her?"

"She saw my suit and assumed I was the manager. I decided not to disabuse her of that assumption. Seemed easier."

"Well, I guess she's not a gold digger," Jonathan commented. "She did look pretty pissed, though."

"She'll get over it. The lie was to her benefit."

"Shit, man, that's cold. I hope you didn't tell her that."

Logan fixed his narrow gaze on Jonathan. The man wasn't a player like Reese; he was constantly traveling or in some sort of adventure, and he had yet to find a woman to keep up with him. Ironic that he was giving Logan advice on a woman's feelings. But if he was saying that Brontë would be offended, he might be right. "She's not like other women. She'll realize that I was protecting my identity and be fine with it."

It had been an utterly pleasurable experience, too, he had to admit. Being with a woman and not having to worry whether she was thinking about what he could buy her? It had been freeing. He hadn't realized how much so until he'd met Brontë.

"If you say so. You know her better than I do. What did you say she did for a living?"

"Nothing."

Jonathan frowned and then leaned forward to pour himself another drink. "What do you mean, nothing?"

"I mean she does nothing for a living. She's a waitress at a sock hop diner." He tried hard not to let his lip curl at the thought. "She worked there during college and never really left."

"Ah. I'm starting to see why you kept your identity a secret. Afraid she's going to look to you to keep her in the lifestyle that she needs?"

Logan thought about that for a moment, frowning to himself. Actually, he didn't see Brontë like that at all. She'd been so pleased with the smallest of things—like this morning's breakfast. If anything, she seemed uncomfortable with wealth. She'd been looking around Jonathan's beach house in pure dismay. It would take her a while to get used to this lifestyle, he figured.

He imagined bringing her with him to his penthouse in New York. Imagined dressing her in the finest silk lingerie and getting to strip it off of her body as she showed him how pleased she was with it. Introducing her to his friends and seeing her radiant smile light up her face. Coming to bed and having her roll over and snuggle close, her hand going automatically to his cock to grasp it even in her sleep.

He rather liked the thought of Brontë in his life. Low-key, unassuming Brontë in his arms, snuggled up next to him in the car, in his home . . . in his bed. He liked that visual very much. And she was a waitress, so it wasn't like she'd be giving up a career to be at his beck and call. An inward smile curved his mouth.

"She's not like that, Jonathan. She's different. Trust me."

"If you say so. She seems nice enough, the few minutes she wasn't glaring at you." His friend shrugged and picked up the liquor bottle, moving back to the cabinet by the window.

"I'll make it up to her," Logan decided after a long minute. Maybe he'd take her to another beach resort. A real one, not that rundown rat trap at Seaturtle Island.

But Jonathan was still staring out the window. His lips twitched, and he glanced back at Logan. "You said she won't hold a grudge?"

Logan shook his head.

"And that she's different from most women?"

"Where are you going with this, Jonathan?"

Jonathan grinned and thumbed toward the window. "She's definitely different, I'll give her that. I'm thinking she was so overcome at the news of your wealth that she felt the need to run. Your ladylove just escaped in a cab."

Logan jumped to his feet, moving to the window. Sure enough, there was a cab pulling away from the house, heading east. Damn it. She'd run away. Why? He didn't understand. "Where do you think she's going?"

"Away from you?"

He glared at Jonathan. Bullshit. His lovely, laughing

Brontë? Running? Something was wrong. "Go tell your driver to follow them."

Jonathan gave him an incredulous look. "You're joking, right? She's a free woman. She's allowed to leave. Why don't you call her and apologize?"

Logan didn't have anything to apologize for, damn it. He scowled as he picked up the phone, then dropped it again. "I don't have her number."

Jonathan shrugged and glanced back out the window again. "So call your private investigator and ask him to look her up. There can't be that many Brontës running around, can there?"

Logan watched the cab disappear into the distance with hard eyes. The time they'd spent together on the island had been perfect. Why was she running now that they were back on land? Was this punishment because he'd lied to her? A challenge of some kind? Did she want to be chased?

Little did she know that Logan Hawkings never backed down from a challenge. And her leaving without even saying good-bye? That was definitely a challenge.

Except she likely didn't realize that it only made her more attractive to him, Logan thought. If there was any further proof needed that she wasn't after his money, it was this. Brontë had wanted him when he was a nobody. Now he needed to find her again and prove to her that she'd still want him, regardless of the fact that he was really Logan Hawkings, billionaire.

And he could be very convincing when he wanted to be.

———

When Brontë entered the diner on Monday, Sharon approached her with a happy little squeal. "You're home!"

"I am," she said wearily, returning the enthusiastic hug with a halfhearted one. "Did you get home okay?"

"I did! Did you know that my passport was in the bar? Silly me. Anyhow, a nice man found it and gave it to me just before I got on a bus. I ended up spending the rest of the trip in some low-rent hotel on Miami Beach. It was free, but it wasn't great." She shrugged. "I tried calling you, though. You never answered and I couldn't find you, and I couldn't stick around. Which bus did you get on?"

Brontë moved to the break room and unlocked her locker, then tossed her purse in, all the while Sharon was at her heels. "I didn't get on a bus. I got stuck in an elevator when the power went out."

Sharon's eyes went round. "The power went out?"

"Misfortune shows those who are not really friends," she quoted to herself. Aristotle had certainly been right on that account. Sharon hadn't even stuck around to see if Brontë was coming back? What a pal.

Brontë pulled her frilly white apron out of her locker and tied it around her waist. "That's right. I was stuck in there for almost a day."

"By yourself?"

She hesitated a moment. "No, there was a guy in there."

Sharon's look went from shocked to sly in an instant. "Was he hot?" She paused, and then grinned. "You're blushing. He *was* hot, wasn't he? Did you two hook up?"

"Island fling," Brontë said, keeping her tone casual. "Just like we talked about."

"How totally romantic!" Sharon clutched her notepad to her breast and gazed at the ceiling. "So it was just you two, all alone in a big resort. . . ."

"Don't forget the hurricane," Brontë said drily. "And anyhow, it was just a momentary thing. It's done. Over with. I didn't even ask for his phone number." She'd been too busy fleeing Jonathan's house in Miami.

Sharon gave her a knowing look, reaching over and shutting Brontë's locker. "Hound dog, huh? Maybe he only looked good in the middle of a hurricane."

"I said he was good-looking." She headed out to the front of the diner, which was already packed due to lunch hour. It was a themed restaurant, sock hop style. They served malts, burgers, and played fifties songs. Very kitschy. Her waitress outfit was retro, too. Sometimes it was fun. Sometimes it wasn't. Today was one of those days when she would've rather been anywhere but the narrow little diner, since it meant she'd be bumping elbows with a very curious Sharon all afternoon.

"If he's so hot and studly, why didn't you bother to get the digits?" Sharon's eyes widened, and she followed Brontë behind the bar. "Was he bad in bed? Is that why you ran?"

"I didn't run," Brontë gritted out. "And this is none of your business."

"Bad in bed," Sharon pronounced triumphantly, sauntering off to a table waving her down.

Brontë tucked a pencil and pad in her apron with extra care, determined to ignore Sharon. She was just trying to bug her, Brontë reasoned. And what exactly could she come back with? *Actually, Logan was very sexy, and great in bed. Why did I run? Because he was loaded and he didn't tell me. I felt like he lied to me.*

Sharon wouldn't understand that. She'd hear the word "loaded," and her brain would stop functioning. And she'd insist on Brontë either hooking up with Logan again, or giving Sharon his number. And she wasn't sure she wanted to do either.

She'd had a weekend to stew on her strategic retreat. All the way to the airport, then on the flight home, she'd half expected to turn the corner and see Logan waiting for her. The fact that he hadn't bothered to come after her made her feel . . . well, she wasn't sure. Part of her was disappointed that he'd let her walk away and part of her was relieved.

Brontë had searched for him on the Internet when she'd gotten home. He wasn't just the owner of the resort, she'd found out. He owned that and an airline. And another hotel in Vegas. And a castle in England. And a private island in

Fiji. And a dozen other companies that she didn't even know what they did.

Logan Hawkings was not just rich. He was obscenely rich. Billionaire rich.

And that scared the hell out of her. It was just as well that he'd lied to her, or she would've run away. Guys like that had the ability to ruin someone's life. That was a little too much power, in her opinion.

And sure, he'd been handsome and flirty . . . on the island. Then, it had been just the two of them. As soon as they'd gotten to Jonathan's swanky house (which apparently was small compared to Logan's sixteen residences), everything had changed. He'd gone from being the manager to being some foreign creature with tons of money, and she hadn't known how to handle that.

So she'd run away.

It was for the best, she told herself. People like Logan moved in entirely different circles from people like Brontë. Besides, he wasn't really interested in her. She could just imagine how he'd sneered to himself when he'd found out what her job was. A waitress was good for a fling, but that was about it. And he'd told her that he didn't want a long-term relationship. Fair enough.

Someone raised an empty glass of water, and Brontë grabbed a pitcher, heading over to the table.

She was a waitress, and she had a small, simple life. Someone like her had no business being in someone like Logan Hawkings's life.

As soon as Logan returned to New York, he contacted his private detective to get an update on Brontë.

"Found her," the detective said into the phone. "I'm sending the information over to your personal e-mail address. Let me know if you have any questions."

"Excellent work," Logan told him, and hung up. He hit

refresh on his e-mail and waited, staring out the window at the New York skyline. Gorgeous night. Gorgeous weather.

But he was restless as hell.

He blamed Brontë and the island. He'd woken up from a dream about her the night before and had found himself alone in bed with an aching erection. When he rode the elevator to his office, he automatically thought of Brontë curled up on the floor in the darkness in her bra and panties, and the way she'd slid her ass into his face as she'd escaped. When someone laughed, he thought of Brontë's nervous giggle.

He . . . missed her.

It was pointless and a bit stupid, of course. He'd only known her for a few days. He'd spent more time with other women. But there had been something so easy and likable about Brontë. She hadn't required anything of him but his attention. She hadn't asked not-so-innocent questions about investments or properties. She'd been relaxing. Adorable. Charming. Sexy.

And she'd run away from him.

The e-mail dinged, and Logan swiveled in his chair. He ignored the meeting invite that popped up on his calendar and opened the e-mail attachments instead, pleased to see the info he'd requested.

His private investigator was thorough, he'd give him that. Enclosed were several scans of Brontë's personal documents. Her driver's license showed a woman with smooth, silky brown hair, but the wide face and beaming smile were his Brontë. *Brontë Dawson*, it read, and it had her home address. Age twenty-four. Kansas City, Missouri. He studied the picture of her, then moved on to the credit report. Some credit card debt, a few late payments, but nothing egregious. Very normal middle-class American. He moved to her employment history next. She currently worked at Josie's Diner. The private detective had even taken a few photos from afar and attached them to the e-mail, and Logan's breath caught at a picture of Brontë in a short pink waitress costume with a frilly apron. Her head was tilted, and she looked like she was laughing at something someone had said. A man? His gut churned with jealousy.

The next item was a brief history of the diner and financials on it. The place was months away from going out of business. There was a list of prior addresses that Brontë had lived at, along with roommates. Female names. Good. She didn't have a live-in boyfriend. Not that he thought she would. She didn't strike him as the type to lie about her relationship status when she'd been so very offended by his lie about his financial status.

His gaze fell on her phone number. He called and listened to it ring.

"Hello?"

Her voice was soft and pleasant, just like he remembered. "It's me, Brontë."

He heard her suck in a breath. "Don't call me. Please."

"I wanted—"

"You're a liar." She hung up.

He stared down at the phone. He wasn't going to call and beg her to see him. That wasn't his style. But he wanted to talk to her. To see if they could connect like they had on the island. He needed to find a way that she'd be unable to avoid seeing him.

Logan picked through the information the private investigator had sent him and paused on the diner's financial info. And he smiled.

———

"Hello?" Brontë picked up her phone, yawning and glancing at the clock next to the bed. It was seven thirty in the morning on her day off. This call had better be an emergency.

"Hey, Bron, it's me." Sharon's voice. "You're not going to believe this."

She rubbed her eyes, trying to wake up. "What is it?"

"The diner was sold."

"Sold?" Brontë sat upright, her heart pounding. "Do we still have our jobs?"

"As far as I know. But the new management has called a meeting this morning at nine, and they want everyone to attend."

"Gotcha. I'll be there."

Brontë dressed in jeans and a T-shirt and drove down to the diner. The diner sold? She knew that being a waitress wasn't a permanent sort of job, but she didn't have the savings to make a career transition at the moment. Plus, if your résumé showed nothing but waiting tables, people wouldn't hire you for much else. Turned out that a philosophy degree didn't really get you places in Kansas City. She hadn't planned on being a waitress for so long, but now that she was in danger of losing her job, her stomach was tied in knots. She needed a paycheck.

When she got to the diner, the sign was flipped to CLOSED, unusual given that it was breakfast rush hour, but maybe the new boss didn't care about that. She slipped inside, noticing a cluster of employees seated at booths at the far end of the diner.

"Hi," she said, casting a worried look at Sharon, Angie, and Marj, fellow waitresses. The cooks sat at another table, and the old manager was nowhere to be seen. "Did I miss anything?"

"Not yet," Angie said, pushing a piece of gum into her mouth and chewing nervously. "You think the new boss is going to shut us down?"

"Surely not," Brontë said.

"Then why call us all in here?" Marj asked, worried.

Brontë didn't know. "Maybe he just wanted to meet us all personally?"

Sharon smacked her lips. "I caught a good look at him. I'd like to meet him up close and personal. Rowr. He's sexy."

"He's your new boss," Marj snapped. "Keep your hormones under wraps."

"You saw him?" Brontë asked. "Does he seem nice?"

"I don't care if he's nice," Sharon said, grinning. She smoothed a hand down her ruffled apron. "I told you he was cute, didn't I? I think he likes me. He keeps looking over here."

Brontë turned around, glancing back at the kitchen, only to have Sharon tug on her bushy ponytail.

"Don't look!" Sharon hissed. "You're being too obvious."

She pulled her hair free from Sharon's grasp. "Is he in the kitchen?"

"Yep. Oh, here he comes now."

A pair of men in suits emerged from the kitchen. One was an older man wearing a suit and carrying a briefcase. The younger one was tall and chiseled, his hair effortlessly perfect. At the sight of him, all the blood drained from Brontë's face.

Logan.

Her eyes narrowed as she studied the two men. She leaned over to Sharon. "Which one did you say was the new owner?"

Sharon snorted. "It's not the old geezer. The hot one. He bought the place. Seems he's an investor of some kind. Likes to buy businesses and turn them over for a profit."

Just like he had with the hotel. But this silly little diner seemed too tiny to be on the radar of someone as important as Logan Hawkings. There could only be one reason he was here personally. Brontë's jaw clenched. He'd bought her place of work because she'd hung up on him.

And now she was trapped.

That *jerk*.

SEVEN

⟡

She didn't look pleased to see him.

Logan had expected that. He'd guessed when Brontë had hung up on him that she was holding a grudge of some kind. That was his reason for buying this hole-in-the-wall diner. He wanted to find out what the problem was so he could fix it.

And then he wanted her back in his arms and in his bed, laughing as he kissed her skin and quoting Plato when he undressed her.

But she was seated with the other waitresses, arms crossed over her chest, and she looked furious. Even furious, though, she was lovely. Her smooth brown hair was twisted into a messy knot at her neck, and she wore a slick of lip gloss that made him wonder what she tasted like with it on. She wore a plain blue T-shirt, jeans, and sneakers, but even in the casual clothing, she appealed to him more than the last model he'd dated.

"Mr. Hawkings is the new owner of Josie's Diner," the consultant he'd hired began. "Over the next few weeks, we're going to be looking carefully at every aspect of the business to determine where the most profit can be made. This means an inspection of purchasing, cooking, hours clocked in, and anything else you can think of. Mr. Hawkings is simply here to show you his commitment to the business."

As Logan watched, Brontë's lips thinned into a line.

Logan stood then, straightening his suit and casting a dispassionate look over all of them. "I'd like to meet with each of you individually so you have nothing to fear in regard to your job." He picked up a clipboard and ignored the name on the top of the list, calling out the only one he was truly interested in. "I'll start with Brontë Dawson."

She got to her feet reluctantly, her jaw set firmly.

"Please follow me." He gestured toward the kitchen.

She stomped through the door, letting it swing behind her, and he resisted the urge to smile.

Logan followed her in a moment later and gestured at the metal folding chair that had been set up in the center of the floor. "Please, have a seat."

She glanced at the door and then moved in a few feet, as if making sure that no one could hear their conversation. "You can drop the charade, Logan. We both know why you're here."

"Oh?" He raised an eyebrow at her, keeping his expression cool.

"You're doing this to get back at me."

Get back at her? Nothing could have been further from the truth. But Logan kept his expression neutral. "Perhaps you are not aware that my business excels at purchasing small, failing companies and making them profitable?"

For a moment, she looked uncertain of herself. "Is that why you bought this one? Because it was failing?"

"No," he said, keeping his voice light and playful. "I purchased this one because I knew it was the only way I could speak to you again."

"So I was right. This is about me and you." She gave him a sharp look. "It seemed like a bit too much of a coincidence that you showed up here."

"You got me," he said, and stepped a bit closer, wondering if she'd back down or hold her ground.

Brontë put her hands on her hips and stared up at him with a defiant look. "I did get you, didn't I?" Her tone was half flirt, half challenge. "The problem is, you seem to think I want more of you."

"I think you do," he said in a low, seductive tone. She hadn't backed down when he'd moved closer. They were so close now he could reach out and touch her, but he wouldn't until she indicated she wanted him. "I think the real problem here is that you're mad at me."

"Mad at you?" She gave a small, sharp laugh. "How can I be mad at you? I don't even know who you are. Remember?"

She *was* mad at him. Interesting. "If you're not mad at me, then why avoid my phone calls?"

Brontë ruined it by giggling. That high-pitched, nervous giggle told him volumes. "Because I went to that island to hook up with someone. You were nothing more than an island fling. I'm not interested in carrying on something off the island"

"You're lying."

"You should know what it's like. You're a liar."

"Am I?"

"You didn't tell me who you were." She crossed her arms over her chest again. "You let me go on and on about the hotel, all because I thought you were the manager. Except you weren't. You were the *owner*. And you never bothered to share that with me. You just kept it from me and laughed behind my back."

"Is that what you think of me?" His voice was husky now. "That I lied to you because I was laughing at you? Truly?"

"I don't know what to think of you," she said in a soft voice that trembled just a little. "I don't know you, remember? You made that very clear."

"I had my reasons for keeping my identity a secret from you, Brontë, and none of my reasons involve laughing at you."

She cast him another hurt look, and he began to realize just how much that secret had wounded her. Was it truly such a big deal to her? He'd been protecting himself, but it seemed that it had come at the expense of her feelings.

And he needed to fix that.

Logan stepped closer to her and brushed his fingers over her cheek. She slapped his hand away, but he supposed he deserved that.

"You know who I am now, don't you?" he asked.

"The entire world seems to know who you are," she said bitterly. "Stupid me was the only one that didn't clue in to it."

"You're not stupid," he told her. "Don't speak of yourself like that. I doubt you'd be familiar with my face unless you read the *Wall Street Journal* or followed the business section in the papers. And I'm not even sure then. Just because you have a lot of money doesn't mean you're a celebrity." He shrugged. "It does change how they react to you, though."

The tension in her shoulders eased just a little. "Oh?"

"Most women I meet are more interested in my wallet than who I am. I thought I was going to be stuck in an elevator for God knows how long. I didn't want it to be with someone who only saw dollar signs when she looked at me."

She crossed her arms over her chest once more. "You should have had more faith in me."

"I didn't know you," he corrected gently, throwing her words back in her face. "We spent days together, and I feel like we still don't know enough about each other. The time we had? It wasn't enough. I want more time with you, Brontë. I want to learn about you, and you to learn about me."

Brontë looked up at him, chewing her lip as she thought. She shook her head. "How do I know that's not a line you tell all the girls?"

He flipped out his phone and offered it to her. "Call my assistant. She'll tell you how many women I've dated in the last year. And then ask her how many women I asked to see again. The answer is none."

She wavered. "How would she know about your dating life?"

"She schedules my reservations," he said with a hint of a smile curving his mouth. "She knows my personal business because it's her job to."

Brontë stared down at the phone for a minute, then back up at him. "Why me? You can have anyone you want. Why waste your time with a waitress from Kansas City?"

"Because you treat me like a regular guy," he told her. This time, when he leaned in to stroke her cheek, she didn't pull away. "Because you make me smile. Because you light up when you find a perfect quote for the situation, and I love to see that. Because you're smart and funny and down-to-earth, and that's a rare combination in a pretty woman. Because you thought I was no one, and you still took your top off to swim naked with me."

A hot blush stained her cheeks. "I was trying to have an island fling, thank you very much."

"But now we're off the island," he told her. "And I'm still interested in flinging with you."

"Logan, I don't know. You're not the guy I thought you were. I wasn't intimidated when I thought you were some guy with a hundred grand a year salary. Now you're some guy with two hundred million dollars in businesses."

"Actually, it's more like two billion."

She looked sick.

"Technically."

"And you bought this diner just to meet with me again?" Her voice rose a squeaky octave.

"Do you want this place? It's yours."

She threw her hands up, shaking her head quickly. "No, absolutely not. I don't want it. I don't want my friends to lose their jobs just because you want me to date you, though."

"Your friends are safe. I don't plan on interfering with business. Improving it, yes. Shutting it down, no. I wouldn't hurt you like that."

She sighed with evident relief. "Thank you."

For some reason, that irked him. It was as if she didn't believe him when he said that her turning him down wouldn't affect her job. "Don't thank me. It has nothing to do with your decision. I'm not a monster."

"So if I told you that I never wanted to see you again, you wouldn't close the diner out of revenge?"

"I would not. Even I can take a hint, Brontë."

She challenged him with a look. "You haven't been very good at it so far."

Time to be direct, then. He took her hand in his and raised it to his lips, kissing the knuckles gently. "I liked what we had before. I liked waking up with you beside me. I liked wrapping my arms around you." His mouth twitched with amusement. "I liked watching you play naked on the beach."

"Boy, you sure are focused on the naked—"

"I also liked just talking with you, and laughing with you. Just being normal Logan with normal Brontë, having a dinner of M&M's and scavenged crackers."

This time, her mouth curved into a smile. Her gaze went to his lips, and he continued to hold her hand close, ready to kiss the back of it.

"Will you give me another chance, Brontë? A chance to get to know you better?"

She nodded slowly. "But I want things to be normal

between us. No more buying companies just to get close to me."

He grinned down at her and kissed her knuckles again, then flipped over her hand to graze her palm with his lips. "No more buying companies. Got it."

She leaned in, and he felt a surge of triumph when he saw her tilt her head back as if waiting for a kiss. Lust surged through him, and he leaned in and claimed her mouth, wrapping his arms around her and pulling her in tight against him. His mouth conquered hers, their tongues slicking together and when they parted, she was breathless as she gazed up at him.

"Logan, I—"

He leaned in to kiss away any sort of protest she was about to make. When they parted again, she looked up at him, dazed.

"I missed you," she blurted, and then blushed. "Wow, that just sounded stupid."

"Not to me." He found himself grinning down at her. "Was that Plato?"

She rolled her eyes, but was unable to stop the beaming smile that spread across her face. "You think everything is Plato." She smoothed a hand over her hair and gave him an awkward little smile. "So, um, do you live in Kansas City, too? I thought the articles said you live in New York City."

"I do."

Confusion swept over her face. "Then how are we going to see each other?"

"I thought you'd come back with me," he told her. "Stay with me for a few weeks. See if we still click."

Her mouth worked in silent protest.

He moved in, wrapping her tight in his arms. His mouth descended on hers once more, taking her in a hard, relentless kiss that promised so many things. By the time he released her, she staggered and had to cling to him for support. "Say you'll come with me."

"I don't know. I—"

The words died in her throat as he kissed her once more, his tongue stroking against hers in a rhythmic, suggestive fashion that sent curls of heat licking through her body. When he released her that time, he repeated the same command.

"Say you'll come with me, Brontë."

"I—"

Logan leaned in to kiss the protest out of her again.

"Okay," she said quickly, putting a hand to his chest. "You don't have to convince me again. This'll just be vacation two-point-oh or something." Brontë peered up at him suspiciously, still dazed from the kisses. "I don't suppose you have a nice, low-key little flat in Manhattan?"

"I own several nice, low-key little high-rises."

She rolled her eyes. "Forget I asked. So when are we doing this?"

He glanced down at his watch. "Now?"

"Now? Don't you have to interview the other employees?"

"The consultant'll take care of that. I hired him for that reason. You and I have other plans."

Brontë stared up at him, her expression a mixture of wonder and consternation. "You're not good at people telling you 'no,' are you?"

He pulled her close again, his hands resting on her lower back. "I'd rather hear you saying 'yes.'"

Her breath caught in her throat as his intentions were made clear. And she slid her hands up the lapels of his suit and then tugged on his coat, lowering him down to her mouth. "I'm definitely more of a 'yes' girl."

"So this is a yes, then?" Logan leaned in close.

"Do you need more proof?" She ran a finger down the front of his tie, and his nerve endings lit up at the brush of her fingertip. "I told you I like you. I'm not exactly sure that we're a good fit, but I'm willing to see where this goes. 'Fortune favors the bold' and all that."

His hand slid to her ass, cupping it. "I love it when you talk Plato to me."

"Virgil, baby. Virgil." Her lips brushed his.

"Mmm. I wish we were somewhere private right about now."

She grabbed him by his tie and began to drag him to the back freezer. "Come with me. I'm wanting to test that 'fortune favoring the bold' thing right now."

He allowed her to lead him in by his tie. They entered the walk-in freezer, and he immediately felt the chill through his jacket and clothing.

"Cold in here."

"I'll warm you up," she teased. "Come here." And she gave him a slight push, knocking him against a large box of frozen burger patties.

A crate shifted nearby, and he sat down on it, dragging her down with him. "You sure you want to do this here, Brontë? Once I start kissing you again, I'm not going to stop."

She wrapped her arms around his neck and pretended to consider it for a moment. "Think anyone is going to follow us into the kitchen?" Her fingers lightly trailed along his ear, distracting him.

"Not if they value their jobs," Logan said. "I made it quite clear to the consultant that we were not to be disturbed."

"Then we don't have anything to worry about," she said in a sultry voice, and leaned in to kiss him.

He tilted his head back in anticipation of the kiss, but she stopped just before her lips met his. "You don't have anything else to tell me, do you? Secret marriage? Bodies in the backyard?"

"I'm afraid that I am alarmingly dull," he said in a dry voice. "No kids. No wives. No bodies in the backyard."

His hands rubbed up and down on her round ass through the seat of her jeans. He loved her curves. She was so damn sexy and vibrant.

"Seems like I'm getting the raw end of this deal," she said teasingly, nipping at his mouth. "You sound terribly boring."

"Terribly, terribly boring," Logan agreed. He grabbed that messy bun of her hair and dragged her mouth to his. She'd been intending on a light, teasing kiss, but he made it slick and deep and wet. He was determined to show her just how much he wanted her.

Brontë whimpered low in her throat. "Your mouth makes my panties so wet."

God, that was erotic. He groaned. "Plato again?" he asked between kisses.

"Brontë Dawson," she replied huskily. "I hear she's got a thing for tall, dull guys."

"It's a lucky day to be a dull guy." He took her lower lip in his mouth and sucked on it, enjoying her moan in response and the way she arched against him, straddling his lap as he sat atop the crate.

She rocked her hips against his, rubbing deliberately over his rock-hard erection. "I don't suppose you brought condoms?"

He had brought one, just in case. "We're good." His hands slid to her front, and he cupped her breasts through her T-shirt, his thumbs stroking her hard nipples. She had such high, perfectly curved small breasts. He loved them, and loved that she was confident enough in her body not to change a thing.

Her gasp of pleasure was a thing of beauty . . . and incredibly loud in the small, cold room.

Logan kissed her hard again. "We'll have to be quiet unless we want to broadcast to your coworkers exactly what you're doing with your new boss."

"I'm thinking they've already guessed," she said

between kisses, groaning as his fingers continued to skate over her nipples. "And I'm thinking I don't care that much. I just want you."

Her words made his cock ache with need. He groaned against her mouth, letting his hands slide to her jeans, and he paused there, waiting to see her reaction. They were in a walk-in freezer, after all. He wouldn't have blamed her if she wanted to continue this some other time.

But she brushed his hands aside and undid the buttons of her jeans, shoving them down her hips even as they continued to kiss, her lips moving over his with the same desperation he felt.

She broke the kiss after a moment, then slid out of his lap and shucked her jeans, tossing them to the floor. Skimpy panties cupped the curves of her ass, and he couldn't resist running a hand up the bared flesh of her smooth thighs. So beautiful. So sexy.

"I want you, Brontë," he told her in a low, husky voice.

"I want you too, Logan," she breathed, stepping in close and straddling his hips again. "Make love to me."

Before she could sit down in his lap again, he undid his belt and unzipped his slacks. He shoved his boxers down, freeing his cock from the restraints that were making him ache. The bite of the cold air was bracing, but not so cold that it was disturbing. But when she moved in close and slid into his lap again, her warm thighs hugging him and the hot cradle of her sex cupping his cock, he groaned. She felt so good. Strange that he'd missed being with her this quickly. He could take or leave most women. Relationships were time-consuming and not worth the effort. But Brontë was different.

He pulled the condom from his wallet and tore it open, shifting the warm, delicious woman in his lap so he could roll it on. She pressed her breasts to his face in response, and he bit at her nipple through the fabric of her shirt.

She whimpered, the sound making his cock throb in response.

And then the condom was on. Thank God. He needed to be in her, now. Logan ran a finger up the seam of her sex—she was already wet and waiting for him. With a groan, he pushed aside the fabric of her panties, exposing her slick pussy. He rubbed a finger along her folds, watching her reactions until she was moaning against him, her fists clutching his lapels.

"Please."

He sank home inside her.

She cried out softly, and he inhaled at the sensation of her, so tight and hot around his cock. She felt so good. "Brontë," he murmured, his hands going to her hips and dragging her upward and then slamming her back down again. "My Brontë."

"Yours," she whispered, her hips following his lead. She began to buck and ride him, increasing the motion of his thrusts with her own hip movements, until he was pounding into her, and she squeezed her eyes shut tight with pleasure, gasping with every thrust. "Yours, Logan."

He came with a groan, unable to hold back. The fucking had been quick, brutal. And she hadn't come, he realized, even as his own release flooded out of him. But she only kissed him and rubbed her body against him, still rocking even though he was no longer thrusting. Telling him that it was all right, that she'd enjoyed herself even if she hadn't come.

But he was going to make this good for her, too. He slid a hand between them and stroked down her belly until he felt the damp nest of curls. Then he pushed his thumb deeper until he hit her clit, and began to rub.

She stiffened against him, her fingers digging in, her eyes going wide. His other hand moved to the back of her neck, and he pulled her in for a searing kiss, silencing her cries even as he began to rapidly flick her clit with his thumb, bringing her over the edge.

She didn't last long, either. Her tense body began to shudder almost immediately, her groan of his name swallowed by his kiss. Her pussy spasmed around him, clenching him tight like a vise.

And then she was falling against him, replete.

He pressed a kiss to her forehead, and she absently trailed her fingers over his jaw.

"Can I make a suggestion to my new manager?" she asked in a drowsy, sated voice.

"Ask away."

"I recommend tossing out this food," she murmured. "I don't know that I could serve it to anyone after knowing what we just did in here."

He chuckled. "I'll take that into consideration. But you're not going to be here to serve it, Brontë. You're going to be with me."

"I shouldn't go with you, but I'm going to anyhow. The others are going to talk a mile a minute if I leave with you for a week."

He wanted to tell her that it'd be more than just a week, but there was no sense in alarming her if she was still skittish. "You can tell them you're doing training at my corporate office if anyone asks."

"I'm not sure they'd approve of that kind of training," she said with a wry smile.

"They wouldn't dare say anything to you," Logan said. "Not if—"

"Logan," she said in a warning tone.

"You're going to the corporate office to represent your company for a few business meetings," he told her, smoothing a hand down her backside. "A few friendly, intimate business meetings."

And night after night in his bed.

———

Getting out of the restaurant was more embarrassing than Brontë had imagined. Her cheeks were flushed a bright red as they left the kitchen. Logan had raked a hand through his hair and straightened his clothes, and he looked fine. Her? Her mouth red from his kisses, and her hair was loose around her shoulders. She was pretty sure her jeans were dirty from where she'd tossed them on the floor, too, but she supposed that didn't matter.

Everyone was staring at them as if they knew exactly what they'd were doing. Sharon was giving Brontë a highly suspicious look; the other waitresses were giving her mystified glances, and only the consultant was acting as if nothing were out of the ordinary.

The consultant turned to Logan. "The next employee on the list is Marj Davis."

Logan straightened his tie, barely glancing at the woman that stood nervously. "I've got another appointment to get to. I trust you'll be able to handle it from here?"

Brontë studied her nails, positive that her cheeks were lit up like a string of Christmas lights. She peered at Marj's face, but Marj seemed relieved that she wouldn't be meeting with Logan after all.

Sharon was still staring at Brontë, though.

"Everything's under control, Mr. Hawkings," the consultant said. "I'll send you my full report in the morning."

"Excellent," Logan said, adjusting a cuff link as he turned toward the door. He paused, glanced at Brontë, and turned back to the watching group. "I'll be taking Miss Dawson with me."

And there it was. The looks of the other waitresses turned from confused to knowing. Brontë gave them all a hesitant wave and then bolted for the door as soon as Logan opened it. Everyone knew she'd just made a 'special' arrangement with the boss. Everyone. Her cheeks stung with embarrassment. Her earlier bravado about not caring what they thought vanished instantly.

"Well," she told him as soon as they stepped out on the street. "That's going to make things awkward when I have to go back to work."

He frowned down at her, as if just now realizing what she meant. "Should I have the consultant speak to them?"

"What? No!" God, she could just imagine how that conversation would go. "Let's just forget about it. I'll give it a few days to die down before I come back. I'll talk with the manager about clearing my schedule."

"I'm clearing it." He put a hand on the small of her back, directing her to a waiting black sedan.

She stopped, looking up at him. "For how long?"

"Indefinitely. I want you with me."

Her mouth opened, and then she snapped it shut again. Hadn't she been so excited to take a vacation? To get away for a few days? This was just an extended one, really. "And I'll have my job when I get back?"

"You will," he agreed.

Of course, if she and Logan didn't work out, that would make returning to work doubly awkward. She tried not to think about that. *"A happy life consists in tranquillity of mind,"* she reminded herself. If that philosophy worked for Cicero, it would work for her.

Logan moved to the door of the sedan and opened it for her, gesturing for her to enter. Brontë eyed it. Black, shiny, and brand-new. It screamed money. Totally not her kind of ride. She pulled her keys out of her purse and jingled them. "I drove myself here."

Logan extended his hand, palm up.

She gave him a curious look. "You want to drive to my apartment?"

"No." He grimaced and looked at his watch, clearly torn. "I wasn't lying, Brontë. I do have a meeting I have to get to back in the city. We don't have time to go back to your apartment. I can have someone drive your car back safely."

Her jaw dropped. "You want me to go with you? Right now? I don't have any of my stuff."

A hint of a smile curved his mouth, and he slid on a

pair of Oakley sunglasses. "I need to go, but I'm not letting you out of my sight again. So, yes, I want you to come with me."

"I'll need clothes," she warned him.

"I have credit cards."

Yeah, so did she, but they were pretty much maxed at the moment. Brontë crossed her arms and studied him. "So you're going to buy me a plane ticket, put me up in a hotel, buy me clothes, and pay me a salary, all so I can spend time with you?"

"That's right."

"That puts all the power in your hands, don't you think?"

The smile he gave her was feral. "I didn't get where I am by letting others have control."

Yes, but what did that mean for a relationship, exactly? "I don't like being a kept woman."

"Think of them as necessary expenses for my new . . . philosophy consultant."

She snorted.

He grinned, and for a minute, he didn't look like the confident, aloof billionaire. He looked like a mischievous little boy. Her heart melted, just a little.

"All right," she grumbled and stepped forward, handing him the keys. "But if you start picking out my clothes, I'm leaving."

"I don't know a thing about women's sizes," Logan told her, pocketing the keys. "You're safe on that count."

Brontë slid into the sedan, noticing the plush black leather seats. The windows were heavily tinted, the interior immaculate. A man in a black suit and sunglasses nodded at her from the driver's seat.

Logan slid in beside her and shut the door.

"Where to?" The driver glanced at the mirror, his gaze on Logan.

"Airport." Logan rested a hand on Brontë's knee, the gesture intimate and possessive. He looked over at her and that arch smile returned to his mouth. "Ever ridden on a private plane?"

"Never. You have one?"

"Two, actually."

"Naturally," she said. "Let me guess. Two, just in case the other needs an oil change?"

He chuckled.

That wasn't a no. Brontë laughed and shook her head. He was impossible.

Soon enough, they were at the airport and crossing the runway to a large plane. She'd thought he'd have a tiny plane, but this seemed like a regular-sized one. Just for one person?

The interior was like nothing she'd seen before. Thick, beige carpet covered the floor. On one side of the plane was a wet bar of some sort. On the right, two enormous leather chairs sat across from a table and two additional chairs. A large flat-screen TV was set into the wall, and the entire back of the plane was closed off, with a door barring it. She gawked at the interior, clutching her purse close. This was so not what she was used to.

"Have a seat," Logan told her, brushing his fingers over her lower back again. "If you're tired, you can take a nap in the bedroom after we take off."

"Bedroom?" She looked at him incredulously. "You have a bedroom on this thing?"

He shrugged. "Sometimes I have to take late flights. It makes things easier."

No kidding. She supposed having your own flying apartment did make things easier. Brontë sat down in one of the chairs, trying not to seem too intimidated.

EIGHT

W arm lips brushed her cheek. "We're here."

Brontë stirred, embarrassed that she'd fallen asleep in the car. "We are?"

"Yes. We have just enough time to get you situated upstairs, and then I have to head off to my meeting."

Yawning, Brontë blinked her eyes rapidly, trying to wake up as she followed him out of the car. She stood on a wide sidewalk, the street lined with cars up and down both sides. All around her were tall, elegant buildings. Nearby was an awning and a doorman stood below it, waiting.

Logan leaned over the car and spoke into the window. "Wait here. I won't be long." Turning back to her, Logan took her by the arm and began to guide her toward the building with the doorman. "I'll show you my place, and you can get comfortable."

"Do you have to go?" she asked, glancing uncomfortably at the doorman as he opened the door for them.

Logan ignored the doorman and headed into the lobby,

then toward the elevator. "It's a meeting I've rescheduled twice already. I won't reschedule it again." When the elevator dinged, they stepped on, and Logan pushed the button for the forty-fourth floor. "When I get back, we can go out to dinner."

She nodded, stepping closer to him when the elevator doors opened again and an older woman in a red suit carrying an enormous designer handbag stepped onto the elevator. She smiled at Logan, though her gaze frosted over at the sight of Brontë in jeans and a slobby T-shirt.

Brontë crossed her arms over her chest. Well, now she felt awkward. She smoothed a hand over her sleep-rumpled hair.

The woman got off the elevator ten floors later, and Logan gave her a curious look. "Uncomfortable?"

"Nah," she lied, drawing the syllable out. "Just thinking that everyone in this building pays more in rent per month than what I make all year. What would make a girl nervous?"

"Don't worry about what other people think," he told her, a hint of a smile on his lips. "You're gorgeous just as you are."

"Easy for you to say."

"It is, yes."

How was it that he managed to defuse her anxiety so easily? She shook her head, unable to stop smiling. "It's just going to take a bit of getting used to for me."

The doors opened on the fourty-fourth floor, and they stepped out. Brontë glanced down the hall, surprised to see only one set of doors. "Is this your apartment?"

"It's the only one on this floor." He moved forward and slid an electronic key out of his wallet, pushing it into the lock.

"You have an entire floor? For one person?"

He chuckled. "Would you prefer I had a studio?"

"Studios are cozy," she pointed out, uncomfortable. Why did one person need an entire floor?

"I prefer more living space. A studio doesn't exactly set the right image for a billionaire." The door opened with a click, and he gestured for her to enter.

She did, a bit stunned at her surroundings. She knew Logan had money. Lots and lots of money. But it was hard to visualize that. Even the jet, as ridiculous as it had been, hadn't really made things sink in for her. Walking into his apartment, though, she realized just how much of a strange world she was entering. It was like nothing she'd ever seen before.

For one, it was enormous. Wasn't the joke that apartments in New York City were the size of closets? This man's living room was three times the size of her Kansas City apartment. Brontë stared around her in awe. His entire apartment was a showplace. He had vaulted ceilings, delicate crown molding accenting a chandelier in the center of the room. Across from where she stood, the entire south side of his apartment was nothing but windows looking out on the city. In between her and the windows, designer couches were strategically placed on plush Persian rugs over the most gorgeous oak floor she'd ever seen. Nearby he had a fireplace with a marble mantel, and over it was a painting she was pretty sure should have been in a museum somewhere.

She turned to look back at Logan, who was casually tossing his keys and wallet onto a small nearby table. "This is where you live?"

That charming half smile that made her insides melt slid across his face again as he turned to look at her. "When I'm in the city, yes."

Which was a totally vague nonanswer that she could have asked a million more questions about. But she didn't, since that seemed nosy. "How many rooms is this place?"

He shrugged. "I don't recall. Four guest bedrooms? Five?"

"Naturally," she teased. "Every bachelor needs at least five guest bedrooms."

Logan moved forward and wrapped his arms around her waist, tugging her against him. "Are you uncomfortable?"

"I'll be fine," she lied. Since he was good at evading, she supposed she could be, too. "How long will you be gone?"

He glanced down at his watch. "Three hours, depending on traffic, of course. If you need anything, dial nine on the phone. That'll forward your call to my assistant, and she can get you anything you need."

"Gotcha."

"What do you want for dinner? I'll make reservations."

She had no clue. Brontë had never been to New York City in her life, so she had no idea what was in the area. "You pick."

He nodded and then glanced at his watch one more time. "I should go so I'm not late." He hesitated again, watching her.

"I'll be fine," she assured him, straightening his jacket. "Seriously. It'll probably take me three hours to figure out how to work the remote on your TV. Or discover where the TV is. You'll be back before I know it."

"If you need anything, call," he said, then leaned in for a kiss. "Or if you're thinking of me, call. Actually, think of me anyhow. I know I'm not going to be able to take my mind off of you here in my home, waiting for me."

This was the part of Logan that she'd never be tired of. His lips met hers, the kiss starting out featherlight and sweet. His tongue brushed over the seam of her mouth, requesting entrance, and she opened for him. He swept into her mouth with a possessiveness that made her knees weak, and when they finally broke the kiss, she was dazed, and bitterly regretting that he had a meeting.

Logan gave her one last kiss. "I'll be back soon."

When he let go of her, she staggered, her legs wobbly. "I'll be here." She gave him a small wave as he left, and when the door shut, she sighed and stared around her like she'd been dropped on another planet.

But since she was alone, she decided to explore and count rooms. Sure enough, there were five bedrooms, six bathrooms, a game room with a pool table, a patio with trees and grass on it overlooking the city, a media room, and a study. She stopped in the study, delighted and wondering what kinds of books a billionaire would have. Of course, she was disappointed to find that the too-uniform books lining his shelves were nothing more than false fronts. Either he'd had a decorator just fill in the room with whatever or Logan didn't read at all.

The bathrooms were exciting, though. The master bathroom had a sunken marble tub with jets that she was dying to try out, and a glass-walled shower. It was also lined with windows, and overlooked a distant Central Park. She wanted to see the park, but not today.

After wandering around Logan's ridiculous apartment, she was a little bored. She would've liked to sit out on the patio for a time with a good book, but there weren't any in the apartment. So she headed to the media room instead. Logan had a desk and a laptop set up in the corner, and she was tempted to play around with it, but she avoided it. Computers were personal. Instead, she sat in one of the enormous leather chairs and tried to figure out which of the six remotes on a nearby table turned the TV on.

When she gave up on that, she returned to the master bedroom and examined it. The bed was neatly made and a pair of Logan's shoes tucked under one side of the bed. Either Logan was a very neat person or he had a maid come in and clean house. She suspected the latter. Unable to resist being nosy, she opened his closet and examined his clothing. Row upon row of suits on dry cleaning hangers hung before her, each one with a more impressive label than the last. Armani. Versace, Domenico Vacca, and others she'd never heard of but was pretty sure were equally pricey.

Yeah. His socks probably cost more than her entire wardrobe. A little disturbed by that, she took off her shoes and lay on the bed. It seemed like the only safe thing to touch at the moment.

She woke up later to find that the sun had set and Logan was lying on the bed next to her. He'd pulled her close and spooned her body, still dressed in his suit. Brontë sighed and rolled over, snuggling close.

"Tired?" he asked in a low voice.

"More like bored," she told him with a yawn. "Did you know that you have six remotes? And none of them turn on the TV?"

"It's voice-activated," he told her with a chuckle. "I can show you how to use it."

"I'm afraid to touch it. Actually, I'm afraid to touch most everything in here."

"Why?"

"It's expensive. All of it."

He snorted. "My home is your home while you're here."

But that was just it. This wasn't her home. Her home had a big comfy easy chair with duct tape over a cushion rip and mismatched throw pillows. Her home had a mattress that sagged on one side, so she slept on the other. Her home had a few paintings and mismatched plates that she'd picked up at yard sales. If anything broke, it didn't matter. Here, she was afraid to leave fingerprints on anything for fear that a maid would come by and smack her hand for daring to touch the great Logan Hawkings's expensive furnishings.

He began to kiss her neck, nibbling on her skin. "Do you not want to be here?"

She sighed, his touch sending feelings skittering through her and making her nipples hard. "No, I want to be here. I think I'd just feel better if this didn't look like a museum. You need a puppy to dirty this place up or something."

Logan chuckled, the sound muffled by her hair. "I have you."

"Gee, thanks." Her hand slid up to twine in his hair, and she closed her eyes, enjoying the feel of his lips on her skin. "I'm glad you're back. Did your meeting go well?"

"Well enough," he said. "We have a cocktail party to go to tomorrow night. I want you to meet some of my friends."

She stiffened at the thought. "I don't have clothes for that."

"Tell my assistant your size. She can pick out something for you."

"I'd like to buy my own clothing, thank you."

He sat up in bed, gazing down at her. "I suppose you should change for dinner, too."

Brontë groaned. "Logan, I don't have anything to wear."

"We can stop by a store and pick something up on the way out."

She grimaced at the thought. It was nice just lying in bed, their legs tangled together. When his hand slid down to her stomach and began to slide under her shirt, Brontë burrowed closer to him. "Can't we just stay in bed tonight? Surely you can get a pizza delivered or something."

His thumb skimmed over her belly button. "Chinese?"

"Sounds delicious." She leaned up and nibbled on his chin, enjoying the scrape of his stubble.

Logan pulled out his phone. "I'll get my assistant—"

She pulled the phone away from him and continued to kiss along his jaw. "Or we could just order it ourselves. You know, like normal people. You don't have to call your assistant for everything."

"You win," he said, leaning in and capturing her mouth. "You order, and I'll pay?"

"Deal." But she didn't get up. Instead, she curled her fingers in his shirt, wishing that she could feel his skin underneath the layers of clothing. She kissed his mouth lightly again, her lips brushing over his, and when his parted, she began to lightly suck on his upper lip.

A low groan escaped him, and his hands began to rub up and down over her body. "Exactly how hungry are you?"

She shifted, her thigh moving between his legs. "Mm, not so hungry just yet."

"Good," he told her, and lifted her arm over her head. Her shirt was pulled up, revealing her belly, and he leaned down to kiss the exposed flesh. "I thought about you through my entire meeting."

"Oh?" Her voice was shaky, just a little tremulous with desire.

"I liked the thought of you in my house, in my bed. Though, in my daydreams, you were naked."

Brontë laughed. "In my daydreams, your library had real books."

He grinned up at her, then kissed her belly again. "If you want real books, buy some. Buy as many as you want."

She rolled her eyes. This man was constantly trying to get her to go shopping. "I didn't come here to shop. I came here for you."

"So you did," he said in a husky voice, and pushed her shirt up farther, exposing her bra. He cupped one of her breasts through the fabric, skimming his thumb over her nipple. "I find that very . . . arousing."

"I find your touch very arousing," she told him, running her hands over his shirt. She tugged on his tie, slowly undoing the knot. "Though you're wearing entirely too much clothing."

Logan peeled back the cup of her bra, adjusting the fabric so it clung to the underside of her breast and pushed her exposed skin up. "I could say the same of you," he murmured.

Brontë cried out when he leaned in to suck on her exposed nipple. His mouth moved against the tender flesh, his tongue circling the areola in a teasing gesture that made her want to writhe on the bed. His teeth grazed the tip in a light scraping motion that was quickly soothed away by his mouth once more.

Her hands went to his hair, and she clung to him as he lavished attention on her breast. His hands were roaming over her body, too, smoothing over her skin as he eased her fully onto her back and then began to pull down the other cup of her bra until both breasts were exposed. Then, with a nip, he left one breast and began to pay attention to the other, working it with the same maddening precision.

The feeling of his mouth on her breasts was driving her wild with need. Her breath was coming in small pants, excitement and arousal pulsing through her body. When his knee pressed her legs apart, she rubbed up against him, a small whimper escaping her.

"I want you, Logan," she whispered. "I need to feel your skin against mine."

His hands went to her jeans. "You first."

Within moments, they had her jeans undone and were working them down her thighs. He groaned seeing she had no panties on. "I think you forgot something."

"I had a rendezvous with my lover in a freezer earlier, and I had to discard them."

He kissed her inner thigh. "Lucky man."

A knot formed in her throat. "He is," she agreed, wiggling when he continued to kiss up her leg. She slid her bra and T-shirt off over her head while he kissed a trail over her belly. "He's also still wearing entirely too much clothing."

Logan grinned up at her and pressed a kiss to her mound. Her breath caught in her throat, and she watched, entranced, as his tongue crept out and slicked through the folds of her sex, his gaze on her. Desire rocked through her, and she shuddered.

"I want you naked on top of me," she moaned when he continued to ignore her words, leisurely spreading her pussy with his fingers and continuing to lick her in a measured, leisurely fashion that drove her mad with need. She whimpered, her hips bucking as his tongue circled her clit over and over again. He continued the slow, deliberate motions, not speeding up or slowing down despite her writhing beneath him, and the unhurried torment brought her to a screaming release when he casually thrust two fingers deep and began to work her.

When she'd recovered from the sudden orgasm, she leaned in and kissed him, laughing and panting. " 'Short is the joy that guilty pleasure brings.' "

He studied her, a smile on his lips. "Are you using Plato to criticize my techniques?"

Brontë laughed at his smug expression and pushed on his shoulders. "Not at all. Just sad that it didn't last longer." She leaned in and bit his earlobe. "And I'm pretty sure that was Euripides."

"Ah. Good old Euripides."

"Mmmm." She ran a hand over his chest. "You are still wearing entirely too much clothing."

He rolled over on his back, grinning at her. His cock had formed a hard tent in his pants.

He looked so delicious that she immediately rolled on top of him, straddling him there. She grinned down at him playfully. "Now I have you right where I want you." She finished undoing his tie and tossed it aside, then began to work on the buttons of his pants. "And I want you naked."

Logan groaned, his hips thrusting up against her wet sex, driving his cock against her. "I think I like you on top of me."

"Do you, now?" she teased, exposing his pecs and breathing a sigh of pleasure at the sight of his chest hair. It felt like it had been forever since she'd seen him naked. The quickie in the freezer this morning had been nice, but it hadn't been enough. She tugged at his clothing, exposing his chest, and ran her fingers over him even as he bucked his hips under her again. "I love looking at you."

"It's mutual," he told her, and his hands reached out to cup her breasts.

She gasped at the sudden surge of pleasure, then batted his hands away. "Clothes off."

He sat up then and leaned in to kiss her as she straddled him. She slid her hands under his shirt, and they were able to push it off of him, and then his torso was exposed and beautiful and, my, she loved staring at his skin.

Brontë gave a little wriggle over his hips, a deliberate tease. "Now we need to get rid of these pants."

He flipped her down on the bed in a quick motion that surprised her, and got up, ripping his belt off and flinging it aside. His pants and boxers quickly followed, and then he was lying down naked. But to her surprise, he grabbed her and rolled her back on top of him, settling her hips over his erect, straining cock. "I like you there," he told her, and thrust again.

This time, she could feel his cock slide through the slick lips of her sex, brushing against her clit, and she moaned at the sensation. He palmed her breasts again, and she held his hands there, closing her eyes and enjoying the feel of his body against hers. "You're right," she breathed. "This definitely has merit."

"We need a condom," he told her, tweaking her nipples. "In the nightstand."

She leaned over him and reached for the drawer of the nightstand, laughing when he nipped at her breast as it dangled too close to his face. She opened the condom and gave him a challenging look. "Shall I do the honors?"

"Please do," he said in a courteous voice that was ruined by the husky growl low in his throat.

Brontë moved to the side and took his cock in her hand, working it with a few teasing squeezes. He thrust against her fist, and she leaned in and gave the head a quick lick, tasting the pre-come that slicked the crown.

"Tease," he growled.

"You like being teased," she told him, rolling the condom on quickly. Her own desire had escalated, and she was feeling aroused and needy again. She desperately wanted him inside her and was done with teasing.

She straddled him again, and his hands went to her hips, steadying her as she grasped his cock and pressed it to the entrance of her sex. She ached for him, she needed this so badly. But she wasn't used to being on top, and so she sank onto him with small, careful motions, rocking her hips a little to take him deeper and deeper. His hands on her waist guided her down until she was seated on top of him and full of his cock.

It was a delicious, overwhelming sensation. Every nerve ending felt alive, and he felt enormous inside her from this angle. Brontë bit her lip and rolled her hips a little, experimenting.

He groaned beneath her.

That was encouraging. She repeated the motion, rolling her hips even more, and was pleased when he rocked with her. She began a rhythm, moving over him and working her hips in a way that made him brush up against that spot inside her that drove her so wild. His movements echoed hers, and before long, she was increasing the pace, needing more and needing it faster, harder, than what she was doing.

His hips began to buck hard against hers, so that when she bore down, he thrust upward roughly. Brontë cried out each time he did, and when his hands moved to her breasts, teasing the nipples as she bounced on top of him, she lost control. She rode him wildly, lost to the sensation, until her entire body stiffened and began to quake with her orgasm.

"Brontë," he growled, and she felt him clasp her hips

again, grinding her down on top of him as he pushed to his own release. A moment later, he bit out a curse and shuddered, and she knew he'd come too.

She fell on top of him to catch her breath, twining her fingers in his chest hair. It was ridiculous that one man could make her feel so very good. Her entire body was one big bundle of pleasure right then.

He wrapped his arms around her, holding her on top of him.

Her stomach growled, ruining the moment.

Logan chuckled, pressing a kiss to her hair. "Why don't you jump in the shower, and I'll order the food?"

"You know how to sweet-talk a girl."

They stayed in the rest of the evening. Brontë borrowed one of Logan's T-shirts to wear. The Chinese food was excellent, and they ended up watching a movie in the media room with their takeout. She wanted to cuddle next to him on the couch, but the media room had only big, overstuffed recliners, so she was thwarted. He promised to put a couch in for her, though, and she simply rolled her eyes.

After dinner, they made love again, and she curled into his arms to sleep. All in all, not a bad day. When she was in Logan's arms, she forgot about everything else.

———

The next morning, she woke up to see Logan off for the day. He kissed her at the door for several minutes, then sighed. "I have meetings all day, but I'll be back in time to pick you up tonight."

"Gotcha. Is there a bookstore nearby I can hit up once I find some pants?"

Logan chuckled. "You have all of New York at your disposal, and you want a bookstore?"

"Pretty much." She wrapped her arms around his neck. "But it comes second to pants."

He leaned in and kissed her again. "Tell you what. I'll send my assistant over in about an hour with some clothes for you. She can escort you around town."

She wasn't sure that she needed a chaperone, but it might be wise until she got her feet under her. "All right." She wrapped her leg around his and clung to him in a way that left nothing to the imagination. "You're going to think about me today, right?"

Logan groaned, his hands moving to cup her naked ass under his shirt. "I couldn't stop if I tried."

"A wise man once said, 'We strive after the forbidden.' "

"More Plato?"

She rolled her eyes. "Everyone's Plato to you. That was Ovid."

"If you find a bookstore, buy me some Plato. I hear he's interesting." Logan leaned in and kissed her one more time, then reluctantly pulled away. "I'll call when I'm on my way home."

That felt . . . domestic. But she nodded, a hint of a smile on her face as she closed the door behind him. They were clicking so well it was almost scary. Scary, but enjoyable. Was it too good to be true? She supposed she'd see when she met his friends.

Just the thought of it made her stomach knot up. She was a waitress. He was a billionaire. They were going to think she was after his money, when the truth was his money just made her downright uncomfortable. Money was nice, but it wasn't the reason to have a relationship.

Of course, she doubted anyone would believe her if she said that.

Brontë took a quick shower and had just combed her hair into a damp ponytail when the doorbell rang. She bounded to the door, pulling on her dirty jeans. "Coming."

When she opened the door, a woman about her age stood on the other side holding a Saks Fifth Avenue bag. She was about the same height as Brontë, but her figure was radically different. Where Brontë was lean everywhere except her behind, the woman in the doorway seemed to be all softness and curves bundled up into a stuffy brown suit and tight bun. Her makeup was minimal, her skin pale, and she wore a pair of oversized sunglasses that she removed as Brontë opened the door.

She gave Brontë a friendly, efficient smile and stepped inside. "You must be Brontë Dawson." She held out her hand. "My name is Audrey Petty, and I'm Logan's assistant. He asked me to come by and see if I could help out today."

Brontë shook her hand enthusiastically. "Hi there. Yes. I'm Logan's girlfriend."

The look on Audrey's face remained professional. Her smile could have been painted on. "Well, Logan told me to come by with some clothes so you could go shopping today. It seems he didn't give you time to pack?"

"That's right." Brontë crossed her arms over her chest, feeling a little awkward. "Sorry to be such trouble."

She gave Brontë an odd look. "Trouble? Logan once asked me to drive to Pennsylvania to pick up floor plans because he didn't like the way they looked faxed. Taking someone shopping? That is not trouble in the slightest."

Brontë relaxed a little at that, even as Audrey moved past her and began to unpack the contents of the bag she'd brought. "Does Logan often make you run strange errands?"

"I don't know if they're strange," Audrey said. "But he does sometimes ask me to run favors for him. It's my job as his assistant, of course. He has a secretary for other business needs."

Brontë stared. "So wait. He has an assistant and a secretary?"

Audrey turned and gave her a puzzled look. "Of course. Now, Logan told me that he had no idea what your size was, so I bought a sweater and some pants in every size.

We can just return the ones that don't fit. I also brought some panties and bras in some common sizes. If you don't have shoes, I can go back out and get some."

"This is fine," Brontë said, reaching out to touch one of the sweaters. It was plain black, cashmere, and extremely soft. "This is nicer than what I normally wear, actually. You could have brought me a T-shirt and jeans."

"Not if I wanted to keep my job," Audrey said cheerfully. "I know Logan, and if he thought I was cheaping out on you, he'd have my head."

He'd never seemed to mind what Brontë had worn before, though. She picked up the sweater in the right size and grabbed the closest slacks and panties. "These'll work."

"Super. You go change and I'll pack everything else up, and then we can get started. We've got a lot of shopping ahead of us."

She gave Audrey a dismayed look. "We do?"

"Logan's instructions are, and I quote," she said, pulling out her BlackBerry and reading from the screen, " 'Make sure that she gets a few weeks' worth of clothing, along with some evening wear. You know my events calendar.' " She looked up from the screen. "I do, and it's a doozy." She looked back down again and continued to read. " 'Also, take her to the best bookstore in Manhattan. My library needs restocking.' " She looked up at Brontë in surprise. "He has a library?"

"Not really," Brontë admitted, her lips twitching with her efforts not to smile like a lovesick idiot. "And I really don't need that many clothes. Just a change or two."

Audrey shook her head and waved the phone. "I have my orders, and I'm afraid they trump yours."

Brontë didn't disagree. She just took the clothes and went to change. She emerged a few minutes later, fully dressed. The clothing was elegant and yet casual. The price tags had been removed, so she didn't know what they'd cost, but she had horrible visions of exactly how much everything had set Audrey back. "Thanks for the clothes. How much do I owe you?"

Audrey gave her a look. "Very funny."

"I can write you a check."

The other woman stared at her. "Are you or are you not aware that you're dating a billionaire? He has a little cash to throw around. This is coming from his wallet, not mine."

Brontë flushed. "Just because he has the cash doesn't mean that I want him to spend ridiculous amounts on me. I'm a grown woman. I can buy my own clothes."

Audrey arched a brow at her. After a moment, she said, "Well, that's something I don't hear very often from women in Logan's circles. Huh." She shook her head, as if not quite believing her ears. "Anyhow. Today, the shopping is on Logan. You can argue with him when he gets home. As long as you're with me, though, his card is the one we're using."

Fair enough. She'd go light on the shopping today to please Audrey and go back later for more stuff if she needed it. "Sounds good. Where are we heading?"

"Fifth Avenue and Madison Avenue," Audrey said promptly. "That's where the best shopping is. Do you have a preference?"

"Someplace with reasonable, comfortable clothing?"

Audrey stared at her for a minute. "Oh, honey. No. We'll start with your dress for the party tonight. I'm thinking Bergdorf's or Saks. And shoes. We'll definitely need some shoes. This could get a little pricey, so I just want you to close your eyes and remember who's buying, okay?"

Brontë crossed her arms. "Audrey, this makes me . . . really uncomfortable. I don't know that I can spend someone else's money like this."

"I know you can't," she said with a reassuring pat. "That's why I'm in charge. And may I just say that this is a refreshing change? Usually I have to pry his girlfriends away from the Centurion card."

"I thought he hadn't dated much in the past year?"

"He hasn't. I've been with him for several." Audrey gave her another tight, efficient smile. "Shall we go?"

They headed out, Audrey chattering a mile a minute as they walked the few blocks to the shopping district. Brontë tried to pay attention to Audrey's nonstop stream of conversation, but she was too busy soaking in the atmosphere of New York. Skyscrapers rose all around her, and the streets were crawling with pedestrians, the curb lined with cars. Awnings hung over the front of apartment buildings, and nearby someone pushed a street cart. Taxis were everywhere.

She'd never seen anything like it. It was crazy . . . and vibrant. The city was alive with people and business, and it was like being in the center of a very slick, industrious anthill. She could see why so many people loved living there. Standing on the street, surrounding by endless tall buildings, it truly did feel like the center of the universe.

Audrey continued to chatter as they walked, barely paying attention to other pedestrians or traffic. She'd been working for Logan for three and a half years, Audrey told her. He was a very fair boss, though he could be demanding of her time. And even though she'd been asked to buy presents for occasional girlfriends or to manage his calendar for his personal life, she confessed that she did not shop for many women, which made Brontë feel better.

At least it did until Audrey added, "Especially after Danica."

Danica? Brontë swallowed, feeling a sick knot in her stomach. "Who's Danica?"

Audrey chewed on her lip, looking chagrined. "I shouldn't have said anything. Except . . . the party tonight? You're going to be there, and the other guests on the list? They all know about Danica, and someone's sure to bring it up even if she doesn't show up."

Brontë gritted her teeth and repeated herself. "Who's Danica?"

The assistant sighed. "I really shouldn't tell you. My number one loyalty is to Logan, and this feels disloyal. It's not my place to speculate—"

"Audrey," Brontë interrupted. "Who is Danica, and why do I need to know about her?"

The other woman wrung her hands, clearly torn. After a moment, she said, "Danica is Logan's fiancée. Ex-fiancée."

Brontë stared at her. He was engaged? He'd never told her. "Exactly how ex of a fiancée is she?"

"They broke things off about two years ago. He hasn't really dated anyone seriously since."

Her stomach clenched uncomfortably. Logan had *had* a fiancée. Past tense. She wasn't sure how she felt about that. He'd almost been married. That was a little different from dating. "Why did they break up?"

Audrey shrugged. "I can't speculate. That's Logan's business and not something he shared with me. But I do know it was ugly. They're not speaking. That's why you have to look stellar at this party tonight. Odds are that she's going to be there, and you can't give her any reason to pick you apart."

She swallowed uncomfortably. "I'm a waitress. I'm dating a billionaire. You don't think that's reason enough for her to want to tear me apart?"

"It is. You just don't want to give her any more."

" 'The wise learn many things from their enemies.' "

Audrey paused to stare at her. "Huh?"

"Oh. Um. Aristophanes. Never mind."

Audrey pointed to a store they were passing. "We can start here. They have some really nice selections. Sophisticated and moneyed. Nothing that screams streetwalker." The assistant looked at Brontë's clothes, and then added, "Not that I think you would have trouble with that, but you never know. Some women think that if they're spending a lot, the clothes should have a lot of flash. It's just the opposite, really."

"I'll keep that in mind," Brontë murmured.

The store was like something out of a movie, complete with marble floors and soft music piped in. They wandered through some of the racks, Audrey leading the way. She seemed to know exactly where she was going, and Brontë was content to let her take charge.

As they walked, a pretty blouse with a delicate ruffle along the neckline caught her eye. All right. If she was going to be staying with Logan for a few weeks—maybe more, maybe less—she needed clothing that wouldn't embarrass him. She paused and examined it, admiring the pale silky fabric, then flipped over the tag. Her breath seized in her lungs.

That blouse cost more than two months' rent of her Kansas City apartment.

Brontë put it back on the rack, hoping desperately that her fingerprints hadn't smudged anything, and followed Audrey with wide eyes.

The assistant began to pick through a rack of dresses. "You have such lovely dark hair and pale skin that I think you could probably look great in a nice jewel tone. Maybe blue? Green? Do you have a preference?" She glanced up at Brontë and noticed her expression. "What's wrong?"

Brontë reached for a nearby tag and winced. "I really don't feel comfortable with the prices here."

Audrey gave her an exasperated look. "Are you still going on about this?" She shook her head and turned back to the rack of clothing, flipping through dresses. "You are dating a billionaire. Wearing T-shirts and jeans is fine for at home, if that's your thing. But if you go out? People are going to look at what he's wearing, and they're going to look at what you're wearing. You have to convey an image. The functions that Logan attends? They frequently make the society pages. The last thing you want is for someone to point out fabulously wealthy and handsome Logan Hawkings and his thrift store girlfriend. Understand?"

Brontë said nothing.

Audrey gave her another disappointed look. "Do I need to call Logan? Because if we don't get you outfitted appropriately, I'm the one who's going to be in trouble, Brontë. As his assistant, it's my job to make him look good. And if you look good, he looks good. And I really like my job and would hate to lose it."

"That is totally emotional blackmail."

"Yes, it is." Audrey pulled a dress off the rack and held it up to Brontë's chest. "Now, green or blue?"

Several hours later, Brontë returned to Logan's apartment with sixteen shopping bags. Once Brontë had caved in, Audrey had been a determined shopper, and Brontë now possessed several pairs of designer shoes, matching jewelry, four designer handbags, two clutch purses, four cocktail dresses (for starters, Audrey had said), and multiple sets of everyday clothing. Since Audrey had been determined that she be fashionably beautiful from the inside out, Brontë now had bags of designer unmentionables from Agent Provocateur and La Perla.

The lingerie, she admitted, she rather liked, since she knew Logan would appreciate them. The rest, though— well, it bothered her. But since she didn't want to get Audrey in trouble, or embarrass Logan, she'd caved in to the pressure and bought it. She'd stopped looking at price tags since that just seemed to slow everything down, and she felt sick at the amount they'd spent on clothes that day.

All she kept thinking about was that it could have paid her rent for a year. Fed a family of four for a year. Purchased a small car or two. Instead, it was just sweaters and skirts and matching earrings. For the amount of money they'd spent on her shoes, they should have been gold-plated and given her a foot massage as she put them on.

She and Logan hadn't discussed closets, and she didn't want to be presumptuous, so she filled a closet in one of the spare rooms. Once her things were put away, she took a long, luxuriant bath, pulled her hair into what she hoped was an elegant upsweep, and began to apply her makeup.

A half hour later, she was ready, and anxious. Brontë examined her appearance in the mirror. The designer dress she'd chosen for that night was a deep wine shade. It was made of gathered jersey that clung to her curves and outlined her figure in an elegant drape. The back was a low, daring cowl that swooped all the way to the base of her spine and made her feel just a bit scandalous. She'd paired it with dangling silver earrings and nude Manolo Blahniks (since Audrey had insisted) and examined the final picture.

Not bad. She didn't look a thing like herself, but she didn't look bad.

Brontë slipped off her shoes and sat on the edge of one of the couches in the living room, waiting anxiously for Logan to return. When watching the door didn't work, she moved to the window and watched the skyline slowly light up. She was fascinated by the city. It was more interesting viewing than TV.

The sun was setting behind the sea of buildings when she heard a click at the front door. She turned just as Logan entered, a bouquet of flowers in his hand.

He stopped at the sight of her, his gaze sweeping up and down over her body. A grin crossed his face. "You look gorgeous, Brontë."

She smiled at him. "I look expensive, you mean."

"You do, but it's perfect for the party tonight." A slow smile curved his mouth, and his gaze again roamed over her body approvingly. "You're perfect."

Brontë flushed under his scrutiny, secretly pleased. Audrey had been right after all. She made a mental note to hint that his assistant needed a raise. "I didn't know you were going to work so late," she began, feeling awkward as he continued to admire her.

He grimaced and held the flowers out to her. "Note my apology. I had a few meetings that ran late. If I'd have known you were so incredibly gorgeous while waiting for me, though . . ." He leaned in and pressed a kiss to her neck, his hand sliding down her naked back. "I like this part."

She took the flowers and slunk out of his grasp. "What time does the party start?"

"About a half hour ago."

Her eyes widened, and she gave him an anxious look. "So we're late? Please tell me this isn't a dinner party."

He shook his head, moving to the bedroom. "Just a mixer," he called back to her. "Some close friends and business associates. Nothing to worry about."

It didn't exactly sound like nothing to worry about. The whole "business associates" part was exactly what she was worried about.

His eyes gleamed as he gazed down at her. "I think your dress needs something."

"Does it?" She glanced down at the material, then twisted to see the back—or lack of back—on her gown. "I thought I looked pretty good, myself."

He reached into his jacket pocket and pulled out a long, blue velvet box, holding it out to her. "See if you like this."

Brontë's tongue felt glued to the roof of her mouth. "Oh, Logan. You shouldn't have. Really. Whatever you spent, it's too much."

"Look at it," he said, a twinkle in his eye. "I tried to find one like in the gift shop. Now that you know that I have money, I can give you these things."

She gave him a skeptical look but opened the box. And gasped.

The necklace in the box was way more expensive than

the one at the hotel gift shop. Where that one had been a delicate chain of diamonds, this one was a thick wreath of dripping jewels. The matching earrings were encrusted. It looked as if it had cost more than her college education.

It was gorgeous. And it made her incredibly uncomfortable.

She snapped the box shut and tried to hand it back to him. "I can't take this, Logan."

"I want you to wear it, Brontë. You'll look beautiful in it."

"It's too much. I'm already wearing stuff that's way more expensive than it should be. You're spending too much money, Logan. I don't like it."

Ignoring her protests, he flipped the box open again and pulled the necklace out. "Turn around."

She made a frustrated noise in her throat, but it died with Logan's smile of pride and the gorgeous sparkle of the necklace. "Do you always get your way?"

"Always," he told her with a pleased expression. "Turn around."

She did, and put a hand to the necklace as he clasped it around her neck. It was heavy, decadent. "Thank you, I think."

"You're welcome." He leaned close and nibbled at her ear. "I think."

————————

A half hour later, they emerged from Logan's sedan in front of an unfamiliar building. Brontë gave a nervous smile to the doorman who held the way open for them, but she couldn't avoid the sick feeling in her stomach. This was like high school all over again. No, worse. It was like those nightmares she had where she was pushed out onto stage and didn't know her lines. A thousand worries flew through her mind. What if someone asked what she did for a living? Should she lie? Act coy? Would the truth embarrass Logan? What if they had to eat something and she had no idea which fork to use? A small giggle escaped her at the thought of their horrified faces if she used a salad fork on her dessert.

"Are you all right?" Logan asked as they entered the elevator and waited for their floor. He was dressed in a gorgeous suit with nearly invisible pinstripes that had been tailored to fit his handsome form. He wore an equally dark gray shirt underneath it, with the collar slightly open and no tie. It wasn't a super formal event by his standards.

"I'm okay," Brontë told him. "Just nervous."

"I know."

She looked at him. "How do you know?"

"You have this strange giggle that you do when you're nervous." His eyes glinted down at her in amusement. "That, and you've got a death grip on my sleeve."

She released his arm with a flush. "Sorry."

"Don't be." He put his arm around her shoulders and drew her close. His mouth began to move over her neck and jaw, pressing whispering little kisses over her skin. "You look utterly delectable. If we weren't heading to this party, I might be convinced to stop this elevator and see what you're wearing under that dress."

"I'll spoil the suspense for you," she said flirtatiously. "Nothing."

He groaned, pulling her hips against his own. "No tan lines, either?"

"Nope. I spent my day at the beach totally nude." She wrapped her arms around his neck and grinned. "I had good company, if I recall."

"The best." He leaned in and lightly kissed her lips.

The elevator chimed, and the doors opened. A sea of people stood before them, and a wave of laughter and light applause erupted at the sight of Logan Hawkings and his date wrapped around each other. Logan simply smiled, releasing Brontë and extending a hand to hold the elevator open for her. "Very funny," he said to the few people clapping nearby.

Mortified, Brontë stepped out of the elevator, her hand automatically going to touch the expensive necklace at her throat. Not the entrance she'd wanted to make. She wanted to look good, but she also wouldn't have minded blending in with the scenery despite her backless gown. That hope had flown out the window, though. She'd shown up kissing a billionaire, and judging by the looks some of the women were casting in her direction, that was an unforgiveable offense.

It was going to be a long night.

A hand went to the small of her back, and Brontë jumped, relieved that it was Logan. "Come on. We should go say hello to our host."

She nodded, allowing him to steer her through the party, mentally noting everyone. The room was glitzy, strings of lights hanging from the ceiling and chic decor. There was an ice sculpture in the center of the room that looked like a skyscraper of some kind, and soft music played from a band in the corner of the room. No one was dancing. Instead, everyone was dressed in suits or cocktail dresses, clutching glasses of wine and chatting in small, close-knit groups. Small party indeed.

Making conversation and drinking. Okay. She could do that. *"Not even the gods fight against necessity."*

They approached a gray-haired man and his silver-haired wife. Both were kitted out in black, the woman's neck sparkling with a thick choker of diamonds. Both lit up at the sight of Logan and turned toward him.

"Brontë," Logan said. "I want you to meet my newest business partner, Doyle Bullet, and his wife, Rita."

Her eyes widened at the name. The only Doyle Bullet she knew of was an oil tycoon who was sometimes mentioned in the news. She thrust her hand out. "Pleased to meet you both. I'm Brontë Dawson."

Rita took her hand, smiling. "How lovely to meet you. Such an unusual name, too."

"Thank you," she said, noticing how Rita's fingertips had barely grazed her hand. "It's not after any Brontë in particular. Or rather, any or all of them. Pick a Brontë, any Brontë." A high-pitched giggle escaped her.

Logan cast her a knowing look.

Oh, hell. She'd just done her nervous laugh again. She quickly shook Doyle's hand, humiliated.

"Thank you for inviting us tonight," Logan said smoothly. "And for letting me bring a friend on such late notice."

"But of course," Rita said generously, smiling at Brontë and then at Logan. "Would you excuse me? I just want to make sure that the caterers have everything under control."

She slipped away, leaving Brontë and Logan with Doyle.

Doyle turned to Logan. "Don't suppose that you saw what the Dow closed at today? It was a bloodbath in there."

"I was in meetings all afternoon." Logan casually snagged two glasses from a passing waiter and handed one to Brontë. "What happened?"

"News report about more banking scandals, of course," Doyle said with a chuckle. He turned to Brontë. "Do you dabble in investments, my dear?"

She clutched her wineglass, resisting the urge to touch the necklace at her neck to make sure it was safe. "No, I don't. I'm sorry."

He gave her a friendly smile. "Well, you should consider it. You'll never make any money if you don't risk any money."

"Of course," she said, flustered. This was really not going well.

"Logan, you old dog. When did you get back?" A man's cheerful voice boomed behind Brontë, making her jump.

She turned, and to her surprise, she saw Logan clapping hands and slapping backs with a large blond man.

"Cade," he said in the same easy voice, "I'd like you to meet my date. Brontë, this is Cade."

"Pleased to meet you," she said in a small voice.

"Cade is also a business partner of mine," Logan said smoothly.

"I prefer the term 'friend,' " Cade said with a grin. "You know, like regular people."

She laughed, feeling instantly more comfortable at Cade's words.

"As I was saying, Logan . . ." Doyle's reedy voice rose a bit. "I wanted to talk to you a bit more about the meeting this afternoon."

"Of course," Logan said, and glanced at Cade. "Would you mind introducing Brontë to a few people? I'm sure this won't be interesting for her."

"I would be delighted," Cade said, offering her his arm. "Shall we?"

"Sure," she said, placing her hand in his arm and letting him lead. She gave Logan a reluctant wave good-bye and allowed Cade to pull her away and into the mix of the party. She looked up at her escort. He seemed friendly enough, and the expression on his face was kind. Handsome, she supposed, if she were looking, but everyone paled in comparison to Logan's cool, austere good looks. "How do you know Logan?"

"We go way back," Cade said easily. "College. Dartmouth. We studied business there together. Same frat and everything."

She smiled at the thought. "Same frat? Logan doesn't strike me as the party boy type."

"He's not. Even back then, he'd glare at us over our drinks and remind us that we had a test in the morning. He's always been excessively responsible, I'm afraid. He tries to keep everyone in line."

She laughed. "That sounds like Logan."

"So how do you know Logan?" he asked her. "It's been a long time since he's brought a date to one of these sorts of things."

"We met under inauspicious circumstances, I'm afraid. Did you hear about his trip to Seaturtle Cay resort?" At his interested glance, she filled him in on the details—their meeting in the elevator and how they'd been stuck there for nearly a day, their nights spent curled up in the stairwell as the hurricane raged around them, their day spent on the beach, and Jonathan's timely rescue. She omitted her own subsequent return home due to hurt feelings. That seemed a bit too personal to share.

"I suppose we can credit Hurricane Latonya for bringing you both together, then. Logan seems happy enough."

Brontë took a sip of her drink, smiling politely. "Does he?"

"Indeed." Cade seemed amused. "From what I've heard, he hasn't been at work nearly as much since returning, and we were speculating as to why. It seems I've found out the answer."

"We?" she couldn't help but ask. "Who is we?"

"Logan's closest friends. Would you like to meet a few?"

"Please." She was intrigued.

"Hunter's not here tonight. He never attends these sorts of functions. But he and Logan are very close. I'm sure you'll meet him at some point. Griffin's over there, by the ice sculpture. The one with the glasses."

She turned, studying the crowd until she located a man with glasses. He was tall and lean, almost lanky. His face was handsome, his style and poise suggesting he was at ease in these surroundings. The expression on his face betrayed sheer aristocratic boredom.

"He seems . . . nice," she lied.

"Oh, Griffin? He's a snob," Cade said easily. "His family's British aristocracy. Very old money. Grew up with a silver spoon in his mouth and a polo pony at the ready. He's extremely intelligent. Good guy, once you get to know him, though."

"I'm sure," she said in a noncommittal voice.

"He doesn't take kindly to strangers, though, which is why we're standing over here talking about him instead of introducing you. If you were on a committee or wanted to discuss funding for a university project, I imagine he'd talk your ear off. Most of us run in fairly exclusive circles, you understand."

She was beginning to understand, all right, she thought with a sinking feeling. Did all of Logan's friends have money and success? How on earth would she fit into his world?

"Reese is also here tonight. See the man to Griffin's left with the women hanging off of him?"

Brontë scanned the room and spotted a well-built, dark-haired man with a rakish look. Two gorgeous women were laughing at something he said, and as Brontë watched, he reached out and brushed a lock of hair off of one of his companion's shoulders in a very intimate move.

He glanced up, as if noticing Brontë's stare, and winked at her.

She blushed in response, turning back to Cade. "I think I found him."

"Reese is a bit of a ladies' man, which is why we're standing way over here. If I take you over to Reese, Logan will probably charge over to protect his territory."

That wouldn't be such a bad thing, Brontë thought with another sip of her wine. "And you? Where do you fit into the picture? You've shown me the professor and the playboy. Where do you fit into all these neat little categories?"

He grinned at her, flashing white teeth. "I am a Lancelot at heart, I'm afraid. I like nothing more than to be of service. You're looking at the world's largest Boy Scout. Show me an old lady who needs to cross the street, and I'll show you a man who will trip over his own two feet to assist her."

She laughed, shaking her head. "That's a rather interesting picture you paint of yourself."

Cade shrugged. "I find that most people fit into basic archetypes if you think about it."

"Oh? Where do you see me?"

"I don't know enough about you yet." He studied her for a moment. "What do you do for a living?"

It figured that he'd ask that. She bit back her grimace and kept her face deadpan. "I'm a waitress. Does that change things?"

His eyebrows rose, but he nodded. "I'm still forming my opinion. You're definitely more of a Mary Ann than a Ginger, though."

"Can't argue with that. Unfortunately, it feels like this party is full of Gingers."

"These sorts of shindigs always draw a lot of Gingers," he said sympathetically. "Luckily for me, I've claimed the one Mary Ann in the bunch. Much better conversation."

He was such a sweetheart. She couldn't help but smile at him. She took another sip of her wine and then pointed at Logan's broad back as he stood commanding a small group that was hanging on his every word. "And Logan? What is he?"

Cade grinned. "He's the boss, of course. Just like everyone wishes they could be."

"Mmm. 'He who owns a hundred sheep must fight with fifty wolves.'"

He gave her an impressed look. "Who said that?"

Another man moved to her side, and to her surprise, she found it was Griffin. The snob. "Plutarch," he told Cade with an arch smile. "And you're keeping Logan's new friend all to yourself tonight. I'm wounded, especially when I come and find that she's quoting Greek philosophy to you."

She put her hand out in greeting. "I'm Brontë."

"Of course you are," Griffin murmured, his voice

cultured and smooth. He took her hand and lifted it to his lips, kissing the back of it. "Anne, Charlotte, or Emily?"

"Take your pick," she said lightly, feeling a bit more comfortable. If he could name all three Brontë sisters, he was probably well educated and would be interesting to talk to.

"I'm chaperoning while Logan has to do the rounds," Cade said. "Brontë didn't look as if she was enjoying the stock market conversation, so I was put in charge of her rescue."

"Wise choice," Griffin agreed. "So you quoted Plutarch. Are you a big fan of his work?"

"Actually, I don't know that I am. While I enjoyed his *Parallel Lives*," she said, tilting her head to study Griffin's expression, "I find them rather biased toward his own particular philosophy, which is ironic considering that he castigated Herodotus for doing the same in his works."

Cade chuckled. "And this is the part where both of you lose me. I think I'm off to get a refill while you two discuss dead Greek guys. Would you like more wine, Brontë?"

"Please," she told him with a smile. "That would be lovely."

Griffin stepped closer to her as Cade moved away. "So how did Logan end up with a woman who quotes philosophy? You'll forgive me if I say that most women he dates don't seem the type to be able to read anything beyond a fashion magazine, much less ancient history."

"Well," she began, smiling at Griffin. "We got stuck in an elevator together in a hurricane."

The party continued on throughout the night, and Brontë caught occasional glimpses of Logan, but every time he paused to speak to her or pull her close for a stolen moment, someone else would appear and steal him away from her. Brontë took it all with good humor. It was fascinating to see just how many people wanted to talk to Logan and seemed to hang on his every word. It wasn't his party, but he was the star of it.

Cade had courteously remained at her side throughout the night, chatting with her and making her comfortable, introducing her to people. She suspected that Logan had had a conversation with him in advance of the party itself to ensure that she was taken care of when he couldn't be at her side, but she didn't mind. Cade was charming, and he shielded her from uncomfortable questions. Griffin had turned out to be extremely pleasant and knowledgeable, too, and she had a standing invite to attend a philosophy salon he was holding at a local college.

She'd even met playboy Reese for a brief moment. He'd approached with a seductive look on his face, kissed her hand, and then backed off when Cade introduced her as Logan's date. He'd given her a reluctant grin, as if to say "next time," and moved on to a group of supermodels.

Cade excused himself to meet up with an old friend, and Brontë took the opportunity to escape out onto the balcony. Her head was swimming from all the wine she'd drunk, and she'd eaten very little due to nerves. Fresh air helped, though, and she leaned against the railing of the near-empty balcony breathing in the night air. At the far end of the balcony, a smoker finished his cigarette and returned to the party. Brontë remained, though, staring down at the view with something akin to wonder. Definitely not Kansas City. New York seemed to be a magical place. There was something about it that thrilled her. It was a place where things happened, and she liked that.

"Well, hello there," a sweet, almost musical voice said at her shoulder.

Brontë turned and smiled faintly at the woman standing before her. She didn't look familiar. She was gorgeous, though. Long, pale blond hair rippling in the night breeze, a thick fringe of bangs over her forehead. Her body was sheathed in a tight white bandage dress, and she towered over Brontë in platform sandals. She looked like a beautiful, cold ice queen.

She gave Brontë an assessing up-and-down glance. "I was wondering if I'd get a chance to talk to you. They're keeping you well guarded, aren't they?"

Brontë smiled politely. "What do you mean, well guarded?"

The woman waved a hand. "His little friends. The band of billionaires or whatever they call themselves. Logan wants to make sure that you avoid people like me at this party, so he's assigned his buddies to shadow you."

Realization hit. Brontë kept the smile on her face with effort. "You must be Danica. I was told you'd be here."

The woman looked impressed for a moment. "Not told by Logan, I imagine." Her gaze dropped to Brontë's diamond-encrusted throat. "Nice necklace. Present?"

Brontë said nothing.

Danica cocked her head. "Did he tell you that we were engaged? My guess is no. He's very closed off emotionally. I suppose you can blame his father for that. The elder Mr. Hawkings was a real asshole, but at some point, Logan has to take responsibility for himself. Not everything in life is a business transaction. Of course, Logan hasn't learned that lesson yet. He thinks everything has a price. The old man taught him that."

That sounded uncomfortably close to Brontë's experiences with Logan. Hadn't he bought the diner just so she'd have to talk to him? He used his money like it was power, and by using it, he got what he wanted. She studied Danica for a long moment, not responding. The woman was gorgeous, elegant, everything that Brontë was not. "I take it that you and Logan are not on friendly terms?"

Danica looked sad. "I wanted to be on friendly terms. Our breaking up was not my choice, you know. He dumped me."

"Why?" As soon as the word escaped her lips, she wanted to bite it back, but the damage was done.

Danica's beautiful smile turned hard. "Logan likes for everyone to stay in the neat little box he's created for them. If you try to escape the box, he'll try to push you back into it. And if that doesn't work, he's done with you. He's ruthless." She stared out into the night sky, then glanced over at Brontë again. "He wanted me to be the perfect little stay-at-home wifey. My schedule didn't matter as long as I was available for him. And when I tried to have a life outside of him, or to assert my freedom, he cut me off at the knees." She shrugged. "The next thing I knew, I was being removed from the apartment we shared and all of my belongings were put into storage. He didn't even give me a warning before tossing me into the trash."

Brontë's stomach clenched painfully. It wasn't true. It couldn't be. Logan wasn't like that. Danica was just trying to crawl under her skin. "Why are you telling me this?"

Danica touched her arm, a pitying look on her face. "Because you look like a nice girl. And you're out of your depth with Logan. You're just his type."

"I am?"

"Of course. You look soft and just a little bit shy. Intimidated. That's the kind Logan likes, you know. He plucks a girl out of nowhere and molds her into the woman he wants at his side. If you don't have a life, that makes it perfect for him, because he needs you available at his beck and call. He's a great guy . . . for a time. He'll make you the happiest woman on earth until you cross him. And if you try to be independent, be ready for him to send you packing. I don't want you to be caught off guard like I was. I thought I loved him and he loved me. It turns out that he doesn't know how to love. He just knows how to succeed at business."

Brontë stared at the other woman, saying nothing. What could she say? Could this possibly be true? It didn't sound like Logan—cold, emotionless. And yet . . .

He was ruthless.

Not everything in life is a business transaction. Of course, Logan hasn't learned that lesson yet.

"Logan's not like that," Brontë protested.

"Isn't he? Have you told him you love him?"

Brontë said nothing.

"Try it. See how he responds. That'll tell you everything you need to know." She nodded as if agreeing with her own words. "I did, and he totally ignored me. Logan doesn't know how to love. All he knows is how to make money."

"Thanks for the warning," she said softly.

"I'm sorry I had to be the bearer of bad news. But it's best if you're prepared for the eventual heartbreak." Danica glanced at the door of the balcony. "And if anyone asks, we didn't have this conversation, understand?" She gave Brontë's hand a little pat and returned to the party.

Her head swimming with Danica's bitter words, Brontë turned back and stared at the skyline before her. Millions of lights dotted the nearby buildings and crawled through the streets below. Yet it was surprisingly quiet out here compared to the party inside, and she found it peaceful.

Perfect for gathering her thoughts.

Danica had to be lying. She'd been so incredibly vague about why she and Logan had broken up that her word couldn't be trusted. And yet some of what she'd said had a ring of truth to it. When Brontë'd left Logan, he'd followed her and taken ownership of the diner simply because he'd wanted to talk to her. That wasn't a man who was used to being told no.

And yet . . . Brontë liked him. She tried to picture him as the brutal tyrant that Danica had painted, as a man determined to push her into a box and mold her into what he wanted. Instead, all she could think about was Logan bringing her flowers when he'd come home late. Logan curled up against her, spooning in bed. Logan naked on the beach with her.

She didn't want to believe it. She was already in love with the man, and she didn't want to think that he wasn't who she'd made him out him to be. Sick at the thought, Brontë clung to the railing and stared up at the black sky overhead.

That's the kind Logan likes, you know. He plucks a girl out of nowhere and molds her into the woman he wants at his side.

Is that what he was doing with her? Had he done the same with Danica? Made her into the woman he wanted, and when Danica had tired of being his plaything, he'd gotten rid of her?

Logan doesn't know how to love.

If that was the case, Brontë had fallen in love with the wrong man.

Big, warm hands cupped her shoulders, and she smelled Logan's aftershave a moment before he pressed against her back. "It's cold out here."

"I hadn't noticed," she said softly.

He rubbed her arms, sending shivers of pleasure through her. "Is everything all right?"

She smiled up at him. "Yes. It just got to be a bit too much, and I drank more than I should have. I thought this would help clear my head."

Logan pressed a kiss to her shoulder, and she felt her nipples harden in response. "Would you like to go home? I'd love to peel this dress off of you."

She pressed back against him, molding her body to his. "That sounds good to me."

"If there weren't two hundred people in the other room, I'd bend you over the balcony and make you mine right now."

She shivered at the intensity of the mental image. A wave of heat pulsed through her, centering on her sex. A whimper escaped her throat. "Logan."

"You're lovely in that dress, Brontë, but I can't wait to

see you out of it. Every man here is jealous that you're going home with me tonight. Your smile and your laugh are so charming that half the room turned around every time they heard you."

She gave him a wry smile. "I think that's your imagination."

"It's true. Why do you think I asked Cade to keep you company?"

Her smile faltered. *They're keeping you well guarded, aren't they?* "I suppose. Let's go home. I'm tired."

They extracted themselves from the party and soon enough were in the limo, the driver steering them through the streets of New York. She grew sleepy, laying her head on Logan's shoulder, and made a soft sound of pleasure when he pulled her close, his hand around her waist.

"Did you enjoy the party?" he asked in a soft voice, his mouth a breath away from her ear.

She thought about her response for a moment, then said, "I met Danica."

He stiffened against her. "Oh?"

"She wanted to warn me about you. And how you treat everything like business."

He cursed under his breath.

Brontë glanced up at him. "When were you going to tell me you had been engaged?"

"I didn't think it was important. We were only engaged for a day or two. Never set a date. It was over two years ago." He laughed, the sound mirthless. "Apparently she's still quite upset over it."

"She tried to warn me off of you. Said you'd dump me like so much trash the moment you got tired of me."

He pulled her closer against him, then tugged her leg over his lap and turned her until she was straddling him in the backseat of the limo, her hips riding his. "You know that's not true, Brontë."

"I suspect she told me a lot of things that weren't true,"

she admitted. Danica didn't have a motive other than to fuck with Brontë. Still, there was nothing that hurt like the truth, so she suspected she'd been told just enough truth mixed with the lies to make her mind work in circles. "Why did you two break up?"

"I had my suspicions that Danica was with me for my money and not for me. I asked her to sign a prenuptial agreement. She refused, and that told me everything I needed to know."

Brontë thought for a moment, then leaned in and wrapped her arms around Logan's neck, her mouth a breath away from his. "She told me that she was trying to be independent and you didn't like that."

He gave her another humorless grin. "Danica's version of independent was going on vacation with her friends without me. Repeatedly, and on my dime. When I suggested we take a trip together, she accused me of trying to smother her."

"Boy, she sounds like a real winner," she muttered.

Logan leaned in and kissed her softly. "She's nothing like you, if that's what you're worried about. And our relationship is nothing like the one I had with her. Don't let her lies get to you."

"I won't," she said, and moved her hips on top of him, pressing against his erection as she straddled him. "But you should have told me."

He groaned and reached over to the door to push a button. Behind her, the barrier between the driver's seat and the backseat went up, shielding them from the driver's eyes. "Trust me when I say she is not in my life anymore. Hasn't been for some time. There's only you." His hand slid up to her hair, grasped the loose knot that threatened to fall apart. "Only you."

Warmth curled through her, and she leaned in to brush her mouth over his skin, to run her tongue across his parted lips. "I want you, Logan."

He groaned low against her mouth. "As soon as we get home, I'm making you mine, Brontë."

That seemed like forever to wait. She flexed her thighs, clenching over the seat of his pants and feeling his erection press up against her. Her slinky dress had ridden up high on her thighs, and an inch or two more and she'd be exposed to him. She hadn't been lying about her lack of undergarments, either, and right now she was feeling rather thankful for it.

Her hand slid between them, and she rubbed against his cock. "I don't want to wait until we get home, Logan. I want you now." Maybe it was the wine talking, or Danica's bitter words that had dug into her skin . . . or her own desperate need for this man, but she needed him like a drowning woman needed air. "I don't want to wait."

Logan thrust up against her hand, his mouth sliding over hers desperately. "I don't have a condom, Brontë."

"I'm on the pill," she said between frantic kisses, and then rubbed her hand over his cock again, stroking his length. "Please, Logan. Take me now."

His hand slid between them, and she stilled, expecting him to unbutton his pants. Instead, she felt his hand slide over her sex, already wet with need. "Ah, Brontë," he murmured. "Your skin feels like silk. Wet and ready for me already?"

She bit her lip and nodded, pressing her forehead to his, lost in sensation as his fingers danced over her needy flesh.

When his fingers grazed her clit, she cried out, but the sound was swallowed by his mouth. He kissed her, his tongue thrusting slow and deep into her mouth in a steady, maddening motion. Her hips rose and fell, echoing the stroke of his tongue, and his fingers continued to work her clit. She spiraled higher, reaching for her orgasm, only to whimper when he slid his hand away and began to undo his pants. Her fingers moved to help, frantically working to free him from his clothing and get him inside her.

Then he was lifting her hips, just a little, and she felt his cock against the hot well of her sex. He sank deep inside her, and she sucked in a sharp breath, her eyes widening at how fully he filled her. Another whimper escaped, and she began to rock furiously over him, her movements just as jerky as his. Hard, fast, and frantic, he pumped into her, wild with need. Her moans were swallowed by his mouth as she rode him with abandon, her hips slamming down over his.

The orgasm that ripped through her was almost violent in its intensity, and she cried out at the feeling of it, her entire body shuddering. He slammed into her again, and his mouth took hers roughly, and then she felt him coming inside her, too.

Her arms wrapped around his neck, and she clung to him, still astride his lap, her breathing rough. He was hers. Danica was wrong. Bitter, envious, and wrong. "I love you," she blurted out, the words escaping before she could stop them.

Logan's arms wrapped around her waist and held her tight in his lap.

But he didn't say anything back.

And a little part of Brontë died.

NINE

⌒

"This meeting of the brotherhood is called to order," Logan said around the cigar in his mouth. He handed the deck of cards to Hunter at his right. "Deal."

The scarred man took the cards and gave Logan a wary look, but said nothing. That suited Logan just fine. If his mood was a bit black at the moment, he didn't give a shit if his friends knew it or not. They could all be in pissy moods for all he cared. A table full of cranky assholes suited him at the moment, since he was one.

Brontë had been sad and listless for the past two days, and he didn't know what to do about it. Fucking Danica. He still suspected that she'd gotten her claws into Brontë despite the talk he'd had with her. Something had changed between them that night. The lovemaking was just as intense as ever, but her smile seemed somewhat faded, and he could have sworn that when he came in the room sometimes, her eyes were red as if she'd been crying. She always said nothing was wrong, but he could tell.

She'd told him she loved him, and he'd given her a hug.

He wasn't the kind to declare his love, though. Not before a prenup was signed and he could be sure of her feelings. He'd traveled down that road once before, and he wasn't going to be taken again. His father had been a tough buzzard, too. Just before he'd died, he'd mocked Logan for being so upset about Danica's reluctance to sign the prenup. What had Logan expected after spouting off about feelings to her? Of course she wasn't going to sign, his father had sneered. Logan had declared his love for her. She had him by the balls. Hawkings men didn't declare their feelings, because it gave power to someone else.

Logan wouldn't make that mistake again. So he had said nothing when Brontë had confessed her feelings to him, even though he'd felt a surge of satisfaction at her admission. She loved him. His beautiful, sweet Brontë loved him.

Brontë had common sense—it was one of the charming things about her—but he didn't know what to do with her sadness. Common sense told him to ignore it. But her melancholy bothered him. It bothered him even more that she was trying to hide it. Hence, his foul mood.

The door opened, and Cade walked in, the last to arrive. "Sorry I'm late," he said. "Hold up at the office. Someone deal me in?"

"'Bout fucking time," Logan said, tossing the cigar in his mouth into the ashtray on the table. "We can start now."

Drinks were passed in his direction, as well as chips. Cade was giving him a scrutinizing look but said nothing as Hunter dealt the cards. After a moment, he looked over at Logan again, and said, "I enjoyed meeting Brontë the other day."

Logan grunted a response.

"Charming girl," Griffin said, tossing a chip into the pot to start the bidding. "Very interesting education. She's a step up from your normal airheads, Logan."

"She's a waitress," he growled. "Don't get too attached to her."

This time, it was Reese who frowned as he tossed his chips into the pot. "What does her job have to do with anything?"

Logan said nothing.

But Cade's gaze was sharp, knowing. "She's not another Danica. You don't know that she's after your money."

"He doesn't not know it," Hunter said in a grave tone, folding his hand.

"Do we have to talk about this right now?" Logan asked.

"Well, clearly it's affecting your mood," Reese pointed out. "Is the problem that she's a waitress or that you like her enough that you're worried you're being taken for a ride?"

Logan's temper flared. He forced himself to be calm, pick up his cigar, and stare at his cards. "She's not like Danica."

"No? She's female, isn't she? That means she's interested in your wallet. Face facts, Logan."

He ignored Reese and clenched his cigar. He would not get angry. These were his friends, after all.

"Well, if she's just a fly-by-night, let me know when you're done with her," Reese began. "Because I saw her ass in that little red dress and—"

His words cut off with a yelp as Logan jumped across the table to grab him.

Chaos erupted. The men jumped to their feet, and hands pried him off of Reese's collar. The other man smirked knowingly, pleased that he'd gotten a rise out of Logan. Cade stepped between them, staring at the two with narrowed eyes. "No fighting during a meeting, remember? Do we need to take this outside?"

"I'm fine," Logan said, flexing his hands and taking a step back. The red was receding from his vision, but he was now more furious with himself. Furious that he'd come so close to punching Reese, and furious that he'd shown his thoughts as clear as day by jumping on him.

Hunter's hand went to Logan's shoulder. "Come," he said. "Let's go walk for a bit." He looked back at the others. "Play on. Logan and I will be back shortly."

Logan had half a mind to tell Hunter to fuck off, but he needed to get away from the table. Casting another furious look at Reese, he stormed away, heading up the cellar stairs.

He didn't speak until he and Hunter were up on the roof of the bar. Hunter pulled out a fresh cigar and offered it to Logan, who declined. The scarred man pulled out a lighter, clipped the end of his cigar, and lit it as casually as if two of his friends hadn't just gotten in a fight. "So. You do realize that Reese was just busting your balls?"

"I realize that now," Logan said with a snarl. *Fucking egomaniac.*

"I've never seen you this stressed over a woman. Even Danica, and we both know she left her mark."

Logan said nothing. Hunter knew him better than the others. The quiet, scarred billionaire had been Logan's closest friend in college. Logan had led, and Hunter had followed. They shared a tight bond. And it was that friendship that kept Logan from storming off of the roof and heading home to see Brontë's sad eyes.

"I agree with Cade, for what it's worth," Hunter said quietly. "She doesn't sound like Danica. Griffin likes her. Griffin doesn't like anyone. He says that Brontë's very intelligent and can hold a conversation. How many of your supermodels has Griffin ever said that about?"

"I bought her a necklace. She didn't want it."

"But she accepted it, didn't she?" Hunter's gaze was cynical.

Damn. Logan stared out at the night sky. He thought of Brontë's sweet smile. The curve of her lips when she leaned in to kiss him. Her fury when she'd found out that he owned the resort.

But how did he know it wasn't simply a masterful act

by a consummate actress? Danica had had him fooled, after all, and she wasn't half as clever as Brontë. "I need to know for sure," he told Hunter.

"Then test her," his friend said. "It's the only way to be sure."

———————

The next evening, Logan tucked a manila envelope under his arm and strode down the hall to his apartment. An odd sense of anticipation curled through him, much like the adrenaline rush he got from a lucrative business deal. This was it.

This was how he'd see if Brontë was after him or his money. Hunter had suggested a test, and Logan thought it was a brilliant plan. He'd give her something valuable out of the blue, something that would be important to her, and watch her reaction.

If she was pleased with his gift, or demanded more, he'd know that she wanted it more than him. If she refused his gift, he could feel more confident in how she felt about him. She'd been upset when she'd found out he was rich . . . but she'd also been quick to cave in to his demands to go to New York. And every time he told himself that Brontë wasn't like that, he saw Danica's face again. Danica, who'd had him totally fooled.

And maybe, just maybe, if Brontë passed this test, he'd feel comfortable telling her how he felt about her, too.

Logan entered the apartment, pleased to find Brontë curled up on one of the couches, an open book spread across her breasts as she napped.

She was beautiful. Her long, chestnut hair was tousled around her face, her small nose pointed up in the air, her lips slightly parted in sleep. She wore her favorite T-shirt and jeans: Audrey had complained to him that she couldn't persuade Brontë to part with them, no matter what lovely clothes she was bought. He liked seeing Brontë in jeans, he had to admit. Her ass filled them out nicely, and the T-shirt showed off the rounded swells of her small breasts to perfection. He pulled the book off her chest, and her eyes opened slowly.

Brontë blinked and focused on him, then smiled, her expression sleepy. "You're home early, aren't you?"

"I am. I canceled the rest of my meetings." He didn't tell her that it was because he'd been unable to concentrate on anything but her that day. They'd made love fiercely the night before, but when she'd come, she'd been utterly silent. She didn't whisper words of love anymore when they had sex.

And for some reason, he wanted to hear her say it again.

Logan smoothed a lock of hair off of her cheek. "I have a present for you."

She sat up on the couch, frowning, one leg tucked under her, and ran a hand through her hair. "Present? Why?"

He forced himself to be indifferent and held the envelope out to her. "No reason. I just wanted to give you something."

"You've already given me enough stuff, Logan." But she obediently took the envelope and opened the clasp, pulling out the contract inside. She stared at it, puzzled, then looked back at him. "What's this?"

"It's the paperwork for the diner. There's three of them, actually. One in Kansas City, and the other two are in Dallas and Atlanta. They're yours."

Brontë looked down at the paperwork in her lap, then back to him. "Why?"

Her reaction didn't tell him anything. "What do you mean, why?"

"I mean, why give me a diner? What's the point?"

"It's a gift. Income. You can live off of the profits, if you want, or you can work on improving the chain. I've set up a meeting with the consultant so he can go over what he's learned so far and suggest improvements. You—"

She held up a hand, giving a small shake of her head to stop him. "Logan, I don't understand."

"It's an expensive gift," he pointed out, frustrated by her mulish responses. "Most people would say thank you."

"I guess I'm confused. Why do you think I'd want the diner?"

"So you can make something of yourself."

She stiffened. "You mean, so I can be something other than a waitress?"

"Something like that," Logan said.

The papers smacked his chest. Brontë leapt to her feet. "Keep the diner."

She didn't want it. Didn't want his money. Elation surged, and Logan watched her get up and cross the room. "You don't want it?"

She didn't answer him.

She was . . . angry? Logan got to his feet and followed her down the hall. She stormed into one of the guest rooms, and when he followed, he noticed she was emptying one of the closets. He noted her stiff shoulders, her furious movements.

And that she had a suitcase open.

"Where are you going?" he asked, frowning.

"You said I could stay as long as I wanted," Brontë said, her voice tight. "This is as long as I want. I'm done here."

"Why?" His voice was harsh. Anger rocketed through him. This was completely irrational of her. "You're mad because I tried to give you a gift?"

"No," she cried, turning to face him. "I'm mad because you think I'm not good enough for you. Are you embarrassed that I'm a waitress? Is that why you're trying to turn me into some sort of diner tycoon?"

"What? No. Don't be ridiculous."

"Then why would you do such a hurtful thing?" Her eyes shimmered with tears.

"Brontë," he said, his voice soft. He moved to draw her

into his arms, but she stiffened and pulled away. He'd made a mistake, then. "I'm sorry if I hurt your feelings. I'm not embarrassed by you."

"Then why give me the diner? I never said I wanted it."

"It was a test," he confessed.

"A test?" Her voice rose an octave in response. "A test? What sort of test?"

He remained silent at that.

Her eyes widened. "Oh, my God. You think I'm after your money. Like Danica. Is that it? You're testing me to see if I want it."

Logan's jaw tightened. "It's not like that."

"It's exactly like that," she said bitterly.

"I love you, Brontë."

"You do now," she bit out. "Now that you realize I don't want your money. Well, news flash, Logan. You can't withhold love as a reward. You either love someone or you don't. Money plays no part in this."

"Money always plays into things, Brontë. That's not fair—"

"You're not being fair," she said, viciously slamming her suitcase shut. "And I hate to say it, but Danica was right."

"Danica doesn't have anything to do with this—"

"No? She told me that you treat everything like a business transaction. And silly me, I thought she was wrong." Tears spilled down her cheeks, driving a knife into his gut. "It turns out she was right after all."

She moved to the dresser and pulled out a blue velvet case—the necklace case. She looked at it and her lip curled, almost in disgust, and she held it out to him. "Take this."

"It's yours."

Brontë shook her head. "I don't want it. I told you I didn't want it, and you pushed it on me." When she held it out again and he didn't reach for it, she tossed it on the bed as if it were garbage and pulled out the handle of her suitcase.

"Brontë," he said, trying to take the suitcase from her. "We need to talk about this—"

"No," she said, and her voice broke a little. "We don't need to talk. You've said enough. Good-bye, Logan."

She pushed past him and headed out the front door, rolling the suitcase behind her.

"Brontë—"

"No," she repeated. "Don't make this ugly, Logan."

And she turned and left. He watched her go, his mind seething with turmoil. She wasn't willing to listen to reason right now. She was furious—and she had every right to be, he supposed—but he wasn't going to give up. Somehow, he'd get her to talk to him again. He'd explain his side of the story, and then they'd hash things out. Kiss and make up.

And then he could tell her he loved her like he should have—with no strings attached.

He went back to the room she'd emptied and stared at the discarded necklace box. *I told you didn't want it, and you pushed it on me.*

It seemed like he'd pushed and pushed until she'd finally broken. Damn it. There had to be a way to fix this.

TEN

Brontë dashed down the street, ignoring the people around her. The suitcase dragged behind her on tiny wheels, slowing her down, but she didn't care. Hot tears splashed down her cheeks, and her heart felt like a burning hole in her chest.

Logan wanted her to *make something* of herself.

The words made her sick. He didn't like who she was. He thought she was a joke. Worse, someone to be embarrassed of.

Well, screw that, and screw him, she thought, dashing the tears from her cheek with the back of one hand. A subway station appeared down the street, and she headed for it, needing a sense of purpose. Somewhere to go. Anywhere.

Of course, when she got into the station itself, she swiped the MetroCard she'd gotten with Audrey while shopping and then realized that she had nowhere to go. She frowned and took a seat on one of the benches, staring in dismay at a nearby map of subway interchanges. She'd been so content, wrapped up in her little cocoon that Logan had created for her, that she hadn't even bothered to sight-see in the city she'd been so excited to visit. No Statue of Liberty, no Guggenheim, nothing. All she'd done was go shopping and attend a party.

And spend hours in Logan's bed, being pleasured out of her mind, she corrected herself.

Except he didn't want *her*. Not really. Brontë the wait-ress was embarrassing. He needed her to be Brontë the small business owner so he could retain his billionaire street cred or something. She sighed in humiliation and hugged the suitcase closer to her as someone sat down on the far end of the bench.

And here she was, stranded all over again. Except this time, there wasn't an elevator or a hurricane or a handsome man to keep her company. This time she was stuck in New York City with nowhere to go and no one to talk to, her heart broken into a hundred pieces.

She could always go straight to the airport. Call this little vacation quits, admit defeat, and return home. Of course, then she'd have to find another job. Logan was her new boss, after all. She wouldn't be able to stay at the diner knowing that at any moment he could come through that door and insist that she talk to him again. So. New job. It was a shame. She liked her coworkers.

Despair threatened to overwhelm her. She'd lost the man she loved, lost her job, and was stuck in a strange city. Had she ever been lower? Tears welled in her eyes.

Music began to play at the far end of the station, and she automatically looked up. A man stood by a pillar, his violin case open, his soft song echoing in the tunnel. Some-one passed by and dropped a dollar, barely even looking, but Brontë was entranced.

She was sitting in New York City, and she hadn't even explored the place. *"Adventure is worthwhile,"* she told herself. Aristotle had it right. Why not visit all the places in New York City that she wanted to see before going home? A thought occurred to her, and she pulled out her phone, flipping through the list of numbers. She dialed a recent one.

"Audrey Petty," the woman on the line answered promptly.

"Audrey? It's me, Brontë."

"Brontë?" The other woman sounded confused for a moment. "Why are you calling me?"

"I need a place to stay," Brontë said, her eyes on the subway map. "I've left Logan."

Just saying it out loud made her chest ache. They'd had a whirlwind courtship. She'd fallen fast, and she'd fallen hard. Logan Hawkings was going to be a difficult man to get over, she realized. She felt raw, completely shredded on the inside. Part of her wanted to turn around and hear him explain, to have him soothe away her hurt, and to return into his arms. She would've done anything just to curl up against him again.

Except he didn't love her, did he? She'd told him that she loved him, and he'd given her a polite pat on the back. And then he'd tried to *fix* her, which rankled. Danica had been right. She'd blindly trusted him, and he'd tried to shove her into the mold of what he thought she should be.

"You . . . huh?" Audrey paused. "Wait. You *left* him, and you're calling me? His assistant?"

A weepy little laugh escaped her. "You're the only person I know in this town."

"Oh." Audrey got quiet. Then she sighed, as if resigned to her course of action. "Where are you?"

"The subway."

"Yes, but where?"

Brontë curled up on the bench, feeling a little foolish. The subway map looked like a bunch of scribbly lines to her, and she'd never even taken as much as a bus in her life. "I honestly have no idea. It's by Logan's building."

"Okay. I'm pretty sure I can guess what station that is. Just wait there, and I'll swing by to get you. We'll talk."

"Thanks, Audrey," she said softly. "I appreciate it."

"You bet," the assistant said, and hung up.

The violinist began to play a sad tune, and Brontë's heart sank with every sorrowful note.

Logan didn't love her. She'd given him everything he'd asked for—her time, her attention, her affection—and he'd still thought she wasn't good enough. A fresh onrush of sadness rippled through her, and she swiped at her eyes again, frustrated with her own emotions.

Crying didn't do any good. She was sad and hurt— okay, more like devastated—but she was also angry with herself. She'd let Logan control how their relationship had gone, and she'd gotten burned. If she ever dated someone like him again, she wouldn't make the same stupid mistake twice.

———

Audrey showed up a short time later, a rounded bundle in a stylish gray peacoat. She was always dressed as if about to head into the office, Brontë realized with a sniff. "Hi, Audrey."

"Hi," she said, immediately offering a small packet of tissues to Brontë. "You look rough."

Eyes watering, she nodded. "I don't seem to be taking this well."

"No," Audrey said, a little troubled. "I don't think you are. I suppose I should be offering you condolences, but I'm mostly just mystified. You broke it off with him? Are you aware he's a billionaire? A really good-looking one? Was it truly that bad?"

Brontë blew her nose. "He tried to give me a business." Her face crumpled. "So I could 'make something' of myself."

"Ouch."

"I told him I loved him, and he ignored it."

"Double ouch. Okay, I can see why the lure of his money palls a bit in the face of his emotional assholeness." She glanced down at Brontë's suitcase. "Did you want to go grab a coffee and talk this out or something?"

"I guess so." She lifted her wet eyes to Audrey. "Then I guess I have to find a hotel."

"You do know how much most hotels in this area cost?"

Brontë shook her head, her stomach sinking.

Audrey sighed. "Brontë, listen. I really like you and I would love to offer my couch, but if Logan found out, he'd have kittens. So I don't mind shepherding you somewhere as a Good Samaritan, but I can't take sides in this. You know whose side I have to take."

"I know," Brontë said miserably. "I really appreciate the help, Audrey. I didn't want to get you in trouble."

The assistant brightened. "However . . ." She snapped her fingers. "I know someone who needs a roomie. Were you planning on staying long?"

"I hadn't really decided," Brontë said. She looked around the subway station and then back at Audrey. "I wouldn't mind taking a few days off to clear my head." *Before crawling back home*, she thought.

"Well, if you volunteer to pay half of this month's rent, I imagine you can stay with her a couple of weeks. I guarantee it'll end up being cheaper than a few nights in a hotel."

"Who is this person?"

Audrey smiled brightly. "My sister, Gretchen. Want me to call her?"

Brontë thought about her savings account and the tip money she'd tucked away for a rainy day or a once-in-a-life-time opportunity. She could cover half a month's rent, she supposed, even if it was crazy-expensive compared to

Kansas City. And she could take her time, see New York, and try to forget all about the man that had stormed into her life and taken over her heart so completely.

She nodded at Audrey. "Can you find out if it's available?"

———

They took the subway to SoHo, a part of town that Audrey rolled her eyes at. "Such a cliché."

Brontë hugged her suitcase close, staring around her at the subway with wide eyes. It seemed . . . crowded. Maybe she just wasn't used to it. "I don't understand. Why is it a cliché?"

"SoHo's where all the artists used to live."

Ah. "Is your sister an artist, then?"

"She likes to imagine she is," Audrey said with a grin. "Artistic temperament, yes. Artist, no. She's a ghostwriter."

"Oh, wow. That's fascinating."

Audrey shrugged. "Some days she seems to like it. Some days she seems to hate it. I suppose it depends on who she's working with." When the subway announced their stop, she grinned and gestured at the door. "This is us."

They walked a few blocks to an older apartment building. Audrey jogged up the steps and pushed the call button.

"Who is it?"

"It's your sister. Open up. I got you a roomie."

The door buzzed, and Audrey grabbed the handle, motioning for Brontë to enter. Brontë followed Audrey up four flights, the suitcase getting heavier with each step. One of the apartment doors was open by the time they got to the top of the stairs, and a woman who looked just like Audrey was looking at both of them curiously. She was tall, her form hidden by baggy clothing. Unlike Audrey's pale orange hair, this woman's was a fiery dark red, and she had the brows and pale skin to match.

"How'd you find me a roommate?" The other woman crossed her arms over her chest, looking suspicious.

Audrey put her arm around Brontë's shoulders, tugging her close and beaming. "Brontë, this is my sister, Gretchen. Gretchen, Brontë."

Gretchen studied Brontë with one raised eyebrow. "Bronty like . . . brontosaurus?"

"Like Charlotte Brontë," she replied.

"I knew that. I was just fucking with you." Gretchen adjusted square, thick-rimmed nerd glasses on her nose. She was the epitome of a writer on a deadline: Her red hair was pulled into a disheveled bun, her face was devoid of makeup, and she wore a pair of dark yoga pants and a black long-sleeved T-shirt that seemed a size too big for her. "So you want to be my roomie? You haven't even seen the place."

"Brontë here just broke up with her boyfriend and needs a place to stay for a few weeks."

Gretchen flashed an annoyed look at her sister. "I need a permanent roommate, not a temporary one."

"Yes, but Brontë's willing to pay half of the rent this month, and she can't stay with me because the boyfriend she broke up with happens to be my boss."

Gretchen's eyes widened, and she looked at Brontë like she was crazy. "Isn't he rich?"

"Too rich," Brontë said defensively. "He's let it go to his head."

The writer blinked behind her glasses. "Huh. Well, come take a look at the place."

The apartment was small but cheerful, with plants on the windowsill and bookshelves lining the living room. A computer desk covered in paper and books sat at the far end of the apartment, and more books covered the countertops in the kitchen. Brontë immediately liked it, of course. "How many bedrooms?"

"Two," Gretchen said, brushing past and opening the door to the bedroom down the hall. "It's not very big."

That was an understatement. The room was the size of her closet back home, but there was a narrow bed against the wall and a small dresser, which was really all she needed. "Looks good to me," she said. "I probably will only be staying until the end of the month, though. I still have an apartment back in Kansas City."

Gretchen shrugged. "I won't take down my want ads, then. I do have to warn you about one thing."

"Oh?"

"I have a pet. His name is Igor."

"He's hideous," Audrey said flatly.

"He is not!" Gretchen opened her bedroom door and picked a small lump up off of the corner of the bed and held it out to Brontë. "He's just a cat."

Igor blinked enormous eyes at Brontë. Gretchen's cat was hairless, apparently. It looked like a naked rat, if she was honest with herself. The thing had long, spindly legs and wrinkly gray skin. Enormous triangle ears jutted from the tiny, pointy face, and it stared up at her with wide golden eyes and then meowed.

Brontë laughed at the sight of him.

"Well, that's a better reaction than the last potential roomie," Gretchen said. "Welcome aboard."

———

Brontë curled under the blankets of her new temporary apartment. The bed was narrow and uncomfortable, with a spring sticking into her lower back, and she was pretty sure she could hear someone talking on the other side of the wall.

She got out of bed and padded over to the small window of her room, pushing it open a crack. It eased open only about two inches, just enough to let the sounds of the street below carry into the room.

The apartment wasn't glamorous, but Gretchen seemed nice, and Brontë still had a curious fascination for New York. Being here in the apartment felt a bit like hiding from reality. Back home, she'd have to deal with the fact that she'd slept with the boss and then broken up with him. But for now? She could hide away in this tiny room with a bunch of expensive clothes that would do her no good, a jillion books, a hairless cat, and a writer who was, even at two in the morning, seated at her computer and working frantically on her manuscript. It still felt a bit like an escape.

She'd left the diamond necklace behind, too. She supposed she could have sold it for rent money, but that would have been . . . painful. And unfair. And somehow wrong. It seemed to symbolize their relationship, and she couldn't have sold it. She just couldn't have.

Brontë wondered if Logan would be looking for her. She hugged her knees close, a stab of pain in her heart. The night before she'd been curled in his arms, deliciously sated after a round of incredible, blissful sex. He'd pulled her close and hugged her against him, his fingers playing over her skin as she drifted off to sleep, and she'd thought that she'd never been held so tenderly.

Funny how a day could put things into perspective. Fresh tears burned in her eyes, and she blinked them back. He hadn't wanted her. Not really. He liked her in bed. It was just out of it that she was . . . lacking.

Oh, Logan, she thought sadly. *Why did I have to fall for you? You're going to be a hard one to get over.*

But even as she said the words to herself, she knew. There were just some men you never got over, and she suspected that Logan Hawkings might be one of them.

Brontë woke up the next morning reaching for Logan. Her heart sank when the realization struck her—he wasn't there.

Not the best way to wake up in the morning. She pushed the sadness away and got out of bed, heading to the kitchen. Maybe today she'd get out and explore the city. She needed a new focus to keep her mind off of Logan. Exploring would do the job just as well as anything else. Of course, she'd be alone, which was a little depressing, but there was nothing to do about that.

Gretchen sat eating a bowl of cereal in the tiny portion of the apartment designated as the kitchen. She was dressed in a white T-shirt and black pants. Unlike the night before, she now wore makeup and her hair was up in a ponytail. The oddly naked cat rubbed against the leg of her pants, begging for attention.

"Headed out this morning?" Brontë asked in a friendly voice.

"Yup." Gretchen picked up her bowl and went to the sink. "Off to work."

Brontë sat down at the small kitchen table. "Work? But I thought you were a ghostwriter."

"I am. I have a friend who owns a coffee shop. I barista to supplement my income and help him out."

Brontë smiled. "I wish your friend was hiring. I wouldn't mind supplementing my own income."

Gretchen snorted, dropping her spoon into the sink and placing her bowl on the floor. Igor ran over at it immediately and began to lap up the milk. "He's always hiring. I have to warn you, though, he pays me off the books. He'd probably do the same for you."

"I don't mind. I need something to do."

The other woman gave her a sympathetic look. "Trying to get your mind off your ex, huh?"

"Am I that obvious?"

"No, of course not," Gretchen said. "I'm pretty good at figuring people out. Like I figured that since your eyes were all red and puffy from crying, you probably missed him."

Brontë touched her face, blushing. "Gotcha. At any rate, if you'd like the company, I could use the money and the distraction."

"Of course. Cooper'd love to have you. Do you have a white shirt to work in?"

"I think so." It probably was Gucci or something equally expensive and ridiculous. She thought of Logan briefly. Wouldn't he just hate that she was wearing the designer clothes he'd bought for her and serving drinks? "Give me ten minutes and I'll get dressed."

———————

For a week straight, Logan had called the consultant that he'd left at the Kansas City diner. Every day, the answer was the same. Brontë hadn't come back to work. She hadn't called.

She certainly hadn't called Logan. It was driving him crazy, too.

Logan rubbed a hand over his face wearily. He hadn't slept as well without Brontë there. His empty bed just felt wrong, as if it were missing something vital. His apartment, too. He'd run across a stack of books she'd left in the library for him. Real books, not the fakes he'd had lining the shelves because he'd been too busy to bother. She'd cleared the false fronts out of one of his shelves and had begun to fill it with her favorites. He'd found a book on top of the stack with a yellow Post-it stuck to the dust jacket.

The Post-it had a smiley face on it. The book? *Plato's Collected Works*.

Seeing that had made his chest ache. She'd clearly been thinking of him when she'd gone shopping. Thinking of him with love.

And he'd been the asshole who doubted her. Even after everything they'd been through together on the island, he'd still not quite believed she liked him for him, not his money. When she'd gone, she'd left behind the necklace he'd bought her and taken only her clothes. He suspected that if she could have left those behind without going naked, she would have done that, too.

She truly didn't want his money. Just him. Except now she didn't want him at all. He felt like an ass. And he wanted her back, because he wanted to explain himself. To try to explain why he'd done something that was clearly so hurtful to her.

But she wasn't anywhere.

Logan called his private investigator again. "Any leads?"

"Nothing. No tickets purchased at the airport. If she's gone back to Kansas City, she hasn't flown. Maybe she hitched a ride with a friend."

But Brontë didn't know anyone in the city other than him and his friends. Worry made him grit his teeth. If anything happened to her, he'd go mad.

He needed her back. She was the only thing that felt right in his life anymore.

One Week Later

"I am ready for the day to be over," Brontë said with a smile at Cooper and Gretchen as she finished the whip on a soy mocha latte. "How's our tip jar looking?"

Gretchen leaned over the counter and peered at the tip jar. "Fat enough to order a pizza tonight. We could watch some total chick movies. You in the mood?"

"I am," Brontë said with a nod. "As long as it's not *Pretty Woman*. Something New Yorky."

"*Maid in Manhattan*?" Gretchen teased.

Brontë shot her a look. "Very funny."

"*Cloverfield*?" suggested Cooper. "I have it on DVD. I could bring it over."

"Not exactly a chick flick, Cooper," Gretchen said, tossing a hand towel over her shoulder. "And you're not exactly a chick."

Cooper flushed at her tease, heading back to the counter when a new customer lined up. Brontë winced at the adoring look that Cooper cast at Gretchen before smiling at the customers. After a week of working at Cooper's Cuppa, two things had become extremely obvious to her: one, that Cooper was one of the nicest guys she had ever met anywhere, and two, that he was carrying a major torch for Gretchen.

A torch that Gretchen seemed determined to ignore.

"How about *300*?" Gretchen asked, pulling out a mug and drying it with her towel. "That's practically a chick flick, considering it's filled with oiled-up beefcake. It's not New Yorky, but with all that man-meat, does it matter?"

"Works for me," Brontë said. "Want to invite Audrey?"

Gretchen shook her head. "She can't. A certain someone is keeping her busy on a secret project."

"Oh?" Brontë feigned casualness, even though her heart sped up at the thought. "What sort of project?"

The redhead said nothing, just continued to wipe mugs dry.

"Gretchen?"

"Don't get too excited. It's just business reports. Apparently her boss is skipping a lot of meetings lately, so she has to listen to recordings and recap them for him so he doesn't miss out on anything." She gave Brontë a pointed look. "Don't read too much into that."

"I won't," Brontë promised, but her mind was already racing. Why was Logan missing meetings? Was he all right? She squelched the rising worry and forced herself to focus. "So, a movie tonight?"

"Mmm-hmm," Gretchen said. "I want to stop somewhere first and pick up a donation."

"Donation?"

"Yeah. I pick up used books and take them in to a local retirement home."

"Oh, Gretchen, that's so sweet."

Gretchen waved a hand, dismissing Brontë's compliment. "Not so sweet. I started doing it when I kept getting so many author copies of my ghostwritten books. I didn't want them, so I donated them to my nana's nursing home. I didn't realize when I first went that so few of the elderly get out, so I bring them books. I can't imagine sitting around all day staring at the wall."

Brontë smiled. "Well, if it makes you feel any better, I love the idea and I want to help."

"Good, because Audrey bailed on me. She's working late, which means you and I get to go and pick up a few boxes from an estate sale. Someone told her there were two boxes to pick up and she volunteered us to go in her place."

An order popped up on the screen, and Brontë moved to the blender to prepare the drink. "Your sister's very dedicated to her job."

"Eh. She likes working for that soulless bastard."

Brontë bristled a little at Gretchen's dismissive tone. "He's not a soulless bastard."

"Says the now proud owner of a diner," Gretchen teased.

Brontë flushed, turning the blender on so she wouldn't have to hear more about it. Perhaps she shouldn't have shared so much of her story with Gretchen. The woman was fun to live with, and funny, but she had a caustic sense of humor and absolutely zero patience for anything related to Logan Hawkings. He kept Audrey hopping, apparently, and Gretchen resented it.

Brontë handed the blended drink to a customer with a smile, struggling to hide her heartache. After a few days, the pain had dulled into an ever-present ache that triggered tears at the slightest thought of Logan. Unfortunately for her, almost everything seemed to inspire thoughts of Logan. She and Gretchen had gone out for drinks the night before, and when someone at the bar had ordered a hurricane, she'd nearly burst into tears.

The girls working the evening shift came in to Cooper's Cuppa, and Brontë and Gretchen left the counter, heading to the back room to take off their aprons and count out their tips. As Brontë stuffed her apron into her locker, Gretchen pulled out her phone and checked her text messages, then sighed. "I have the address for Audrey's pickup. You ready to haul some books a few blocks? She says it's two boxes."

Brontë pretended to flex her muscles. "Ready."

"Let's go, then. The place should be empty. Audrey says the key's under the mat."

Hunter strolled through the empty, silent town house, regarding it with an eye long-used to appraising at a glance. He mentally sized up the asking price, tallying all the things that would make it a prize—the luxurious décor, the reputation of the prior owner, the fact that it was a historical building, and the number one thing that always made his interest perk: location. The Upper East Side was a great one.

This town house, he knew, would command several million on the market . . . provided he bothered to put it up for sale. It was a lovely gem of a home, and one of the Brotherhood might be interested in it. Griffin, perhaps, he thought, examining the Victorian wainscoting. An elegant town house would be something he'd be in the market for. Reese wanted it for a director friend of his, but Brotherhood came first. He'd probably offer to Griffin to see if he was interested, and if not, talk to Reese's friend.

Hunter stopped and cocked his head, listening. Someone had entered the town house.

At the sound of voices, he paused in the foyer of the

enormous home. Out of habit, he moved into a shadowy alcove, lest they catch him unawares and stop to stare at him. Even after years of being a scarred, ugly bastard, he was still bothered by the expressions people made at the sight of his face. It was easier to just blend in with the shadows until they were gone. He waited, his ears straining to determine who was there. The only people he'd expected to stop by were Logan's assistant, who'd insisted on picking up some of his books for a donation, and the movers who'd come to clean out the rest of what was left in the house.

He'd thought the place would be empty, so it would be a perfect time for him to inspect it. He hadn't realized someone else would be coming in, much less two women.

There was a shuffle of footsteps, and then the sound of a box thumping onto the ground.

"What is this place?" a soft, pleasant female voice asked. "It's lovely."

"Some dead celebrity's home or something. I don't care." The other woman's voice seemed full of laughter and amusement, but her tone was cutting. "All I care about is how we're supposed to get these damned boxes back to SoHo. What the heck was Audrey thinking?"

"Could we call a cab?"

The women approached Hunter's shadowed hiding place, and he stilled, waiting for them to pass without noticing him.

The redhead was standing not ten feet away from him, her head bent. He couldn't see her face, but she was curvy and tall, her ass a perfect heart from where he was standing, and her hair was a brilliant shade of red. The other girl—a pretty brunette with wide eyes—balanced two boxes and was waiting for instructions from the other woman.

"I don't know about a cab," the redhead said. "That'll clean us out, and I still want to order that pizza."

"So?" the dark-haired one asked.

"Brontë," the redhead said in a crisp voice, and Hunter came to attention. That was a familiar name.

But the redhead was still talking. "You have to understand something about my sister. She's not the most practical creature."

"She's not? She seems practical to me."

"Not when it comes to work. She thinks we're mules or something, as evidenced by all this. And if I need to call and gripe at her to get her in line, then, by golly, I'm going to do it." She put the phone to her ear. A few seconds later, she made a frustrated sound. "Voice mail. I can't believe her. She said there were two boxes. Not five boxes of hardbacks. Does she think we're bodybuilders?"

"It's not that bad," the brunette placated her, adjusting the boxes in her arms. "I'm sure we can manage."

"I blame Logan Hawkings," the redhead exclaimed, catching Hunter's attention. "He thinks the world just belongs to him, doesn't he?"

The look on the other woman's face was sad. "I suppose."

"Ugh. Look at that hang-dog expression. You're still in love with him, aren't you?"

The brunette turned sad eyes on her friend. " 'I hate and I love. Perhaps you ask why I do so. I do not know, but I feel it, and am in agony.' "

"Oh, quit quoting that crap at me. You're being dramatic. He's a jerk. You'll get over him."

The redhead turned, and Hunter got a good look at her face for the first time. She was unusual-looking, with round cheeks smattered in freckles. Her expressive eyes dominated her face despite being hidden behind square, scholarly glasses. Her chin ended in a small point, and she looked fascinating. Smart. Annoyed. "Save me from rich, attractive alpha males. They think they're the heroes from a fairy tale. Little do they know, they're more like the villains."

"That's not fair, Gretchen," the one called Brontë protested.

"Life's not fair," Gretchen said in a cheerfully acerbic voice. "I'd rather have a man who isn't in love with his own reflection than one who needs hair product or designer labels." She bent over, and that heart-shaped ass was thrust into his vision again, and his cock stirred with need.

"So you'd rather have a pizza guy with a weak chin and a knight-in-shining-armor complex?"

"Yes," Gretchen said emphatically, and a dimple flashed in her pointed little face. "His looks aren't half as important as his brain."

So she said. Hunter knew from experience that what women said they wanted in a man was soon forgetten if his physical appearance was unappealing. Still, he was fascinated with her. She was brash and clever, and a little sardonic, as if she were as weary of the world as he was. He watched as the two women, arguing and laughing, stepped out of the foyer of the empty home with the boxes of donations that he'd left for Logan's assistant.

Her name was Gretchen. Gretchen. He racked his brain, trying to think of anyone who knew a Gretchen. A lovely redhead with a charmingly unusual face and a cutting tongue. He wanted to know more about her . . .

Hunter touched the jagged scars running down the left side of his face and frowned. Would she find him as hideous as the rest of the world did? Probably. But she'd also said she could look past that. That she wasn't interested in a face as much as the brain behind it.

He was curious whether she'd been telling the truth.

Not that it mattered, since she'd just walked out the door and he'd likely never see her again.

A half-buried memory stirred in the back of his mind

as he stared at the now-shut door. The other woman had an unusual name. Brontë. He knew that name, and where he'd heard it before.

He dialed Logan's number, still thinking about the unusual redhead.

"What is it?" Logan said. "I'm about to head into a meeting."

"There can't be more than one 'Brontë' running around New York, can there?" Hunter asked.

The voice on the other end of the line got very still. "Brontë?" Logan asked after a moment. "You saw her? Where is she?"

Hunter stared at the door, half wishing the women would come back through it again, and half relieved they wouldn't. "She just left with a redhead named Gretchen. I want to know more about her."

"About *my* Brontë?" Logan's voice was a growl.

"No. Gretchen. The one with red hair. I want her."

"Oh." A long sigh. "Sorry, man. Haven't been myself lately. She left me, and I've been going crazy trying to find her." Logan's voice sounded strained, tense. "I can't believe she's still in New York. Where are you?"

"At the town house on the Upper East Side." Hunter had been overseeing it to ensure that nothing was out of place. Plus, he'd been bored and restless. And more than a little lonely.

He wasn't lonely anymore, though. He couldn't stop thinking about that redhead. Gretchen, with her big glasses and pert comebacks and red hair.

"Your assistant didn't come by to pick up the boxes," Hunter said after a moment. "This Gretchen did, and your Brontë was with her."

"I have to go," Logan said. "I'll call Audrey and see who she sent over."

"Send me information about this Gretchen woman," Hunter reminded him. *I want her.*

"I will. And thanks." Logan's tone had changed from dejected to triumphant. "I owe you one."

"You do," Hunter agreed. "Just get me information on her friend, and we'll call it even."

Things had suddenly gotten a bit more . . . interesting. Hunter glanced at the empty town house and smiled to himself, his mind full of the unusual woman who had been there minutes before.

ELEVEN

I have good news and bad news," Cooper said as Brontë and Gretchen came in to work.

Brontë pulled her apron out of her locker, frowning as she tied it behind her back. "Oh?"

"Hit us with the good news first, of course," Gretchen said. "No sense in bumming us out until you give us a bit of a lift."

Cooper beamed at them, his gaze resting on Gretchen adoringly. "I can now afford to put you both on the payroll."

"So what's the bad news?" Gretchen asked, glancing over at Brontë.

"There's a new boss. I have someone I'm answering to."

Gretchen frowned. "I don't understand."

A queasy feeling began to stir in Brontë's stomach. Oh, no.

"I sold the place."

"Holy cow! I didn't even know it was for sale." Gretchen blinked wide eyes at him. "Congrats, I think?"

"It wasn't up for sale officially, but someone approached me and made me an offer I can't refuse."

Oh, *no*.

Brontë stared at the door to the back room, then pushed it open, entering the main sitting area of the small coffee shop. Her stomach gave an unpleasant twist as she saw a familiar pair of shoulders in a tailored gray sport coat. Logan. He turned, and her heart skipped a beat even as her stomach dropped.

"Brontë." His eyes moved over her body, as if assessing whether it was really her.

"What are you doing here, Logan?"

His gaze seemed to cool a bit at her response. "I own the place."

Not again! This man was going to drive her mad. "Are you kidding me?"

"We need to talk." He stood and moved forward, reaching for her arm.

Brontë quickly sidestepped his grip and began to pull off her apron. If he owned another place where she worked, it was another one she'd have to abandon. God, this was getting ridiculous. "I don't want to talk to you."

"Allow me to rephrase that. I need to talk to you." His voice lowered and became husky as he moved to stand closer to her. He was so close that her body trembled with his nearness, but she forced herself to hold still. Remain strong.

"Please, Brontë."

It was that soft, low "please" that made her knees turn weak and her resolve melt away like butter. She looked up at his face, noticed the circles under his eyes, and gave a sharp nod. Brontë turned and glanced back at Cooper and Gretchen. Cooper was watching her curiously, but Gretchen's arms were crossed and she looked annoyed on Brontë's behalf.

"Can you give us a minute to talk?" Brontë asked.

"Use my office," Cooper volunteered, pulling the key out of his pocket and holding it out to Brontë.

She took it and turned toward the back office.

Gretchen stepped forward, concern in her eyes. "Are you sure this is wise, Brontë?"

"I'll be fine," she told Gretchen, and squeezed her hand in thanks. She'd only known her for a short period of time, but already Audrey's sister had been a great and supportive friend to her.

"We're right outside if you need us," Gretchen said, casting a scowl in Logan's direction.

Brontë nodded and went to the door of Cooper's office, not glancing behind her to see whether Logan was following. If he wanted to talk, well, he'd come after her. Her fingers were shaking as she tried to calmly unlock the door, and it seemed like forever before she could turn the key in the lock and get it open. Once the door was open, though, she stepped inside and flicked on the light. Logan entered close behind her, and Brontë shut the door after him so no one could listen in.

He immediately reached out and touched her cheek in a gentle caress before she could back away. His gaze moved over her, scanning her face and figure. "Is everything okay? You're doing all right? I've been worried about you."

She stepped aside and out of his grasp, even though every nerve ending in her body screamed for her to go back to his arms. "I'm fine, Logan. I can take care of myself."

"I know you can." His hand dropped, the movement seeming defeated. "I was just worried when you didn't return to Kansas City. No one knew where you were."

So he'd had his flunkies checking up on her? She wasn't surprised, especially considering how he'd used every means available to find her last time. That was one reason why she'd stayed in New York. "I decided to extend my vacation a little longer. Take a mental health break."

"I want you back." The words were quiet but laced with emotion.

Brontë crossed her arms over her chest, staring at the floor. She refused to meet his gaze. If she did, she might see the emotion there, and it would make her weaken. She wanted to be strong. *Needed* to be strong. "I'm not going back to you, Logan. You don't want me. You want a girl who isn't a waitress and who knows which salad fork to use. That's not me."

"I don't care about that. I want you. When you left, it felt like the lights went out. I don't care if you eat with the wrong fork at every meal. I don't care if you waitress for the rest of your life. I just want you at my side, Brontë." Logan reached for her again, and then dropped his hand before he could touch her, as if suddenly remembering to respect her boundaries. "I miss you. I miss your smile. I miss your hand in mine. I miss your laugh when you're nervous. I wish to God I was hearing it right now." His mouth crooked in a half smile. "That hurricane was the best thing that ever happened to me because it brought you into my life."

She was in danger of letting the nervous giggle escape, but she dug her fingernails into her palms until the feeling passed. "If I'm so great, why did you tell me you wanted me to 'make something of myself'?" Even now, the words hurt.

He sighed, and the sound made her look up at him. Logan's handsome face was drawn. He normally looked confident and supremely in control, but right now, he just looked . . . desolate.

Good, she thought with a little mental stab.

"I'm not a nice guy, Brontë. I don't have to be, most times, because of my money." His gaze met hers. "I told you once that my fiancée was only interested in me for my money. She was the only one I let get close enough before you. Usually women make their fascination with my money known right away, and then it's easy to just end things before someone gets hurt. I was afraid I was making the same mistake again, and I was losing my head over you. I wanted to test you, to see how you'd respond. Thing is . . ." He ran a hand down his face. "You passed the test, of course. Except I'd forgotten that you have feelings, too, and how you'd feel about my little test. I'm sorry. It was arrogant and stupid of me."

"It was," she agreed. "Why would you think I'm after your money?"

"Maybe because most of the time everyone is?" He shook his head. "It's not you, Brontë. It's me. I realize that now. I'm a cynical bastard, especially when it comes to women. That's why I didn't tell you who I really was when we were stranded together. And it's why I offered you the diner. It's not that there's something wrong with you. It's that there's something wrong with every other woman I've ever had in my life. They couldn't see past my wallet to me. You can. And that's why I want you."

Nice words. She felt her resolve weakened by them and by his entreating gaze. But she shook her head. "I can't trust you, Logan. I thought I could, but this just proved that you're not who I thought you were. You shouldn't have to 'test' me. You should be able to trust me, and me you."

"Give me another chance, Brontë. A chance to prove how much you mean to me."

She remained silent.

Logan moved forward. His fingertips touched her chin and tilted her head back until she met his eyes. "You told me you loved me that night in the limo."

A knot formed in her throat, and she met his gaze steadily. "I was mistaken."

Logan's eyes hardened. "You were *not*."

"I was," she told him, even though it was a lie. "It was silly of me to think I'd fallen in love with someone so fast, and time has proved me right."

"I'm not mistaken," he told her, and the fingers under her chin began to caress her jaw. "I'm still in love with you."

Her throat went dry at his husky words. "Logan, please."

"I'm not fighting fair," he told her. "I know. I don't care. I want you back. I don't give a shit about being fair or being the better man. I will be the most ruthless man in the world as long as I can have you at my side and in my bed. You're the only thing that matters. I love you."

"Love is not control, Logan. Love is partnership. Friendship. A wise man once said, 'If you want to be loved, be lovable.' "

His mouth quirked. "I'd say that's Plato, but I know it's not. I've been reading the book you left me, you know. 'The madness of love is the greatest of heaven's blessings.' "

Tears stung her eyes. He'd been reading philosophy? To try and understand her better? Hope unfurled in her breast, but she forced herself to be calm, careful.

"I don't know, Logan. We haven't exactly had the most normal relationship. I never know how to act around you. I'm about as comfortable in the hurricane as I am at one of your society parties. Both scare the pants off of me."

"Whatever you want to do, Brontë, I'll do it." He moved close, his mouth inches away from hers, and her pulse began to pound. Just an inch or two more and his lips would be on hers, coaxing hers into opening for him, his tongue thrusting into her mouth and conquering her all over again . . .

Brontë took a step backward, out of his grasp.

"Come home with me tonight, Brontë. We'll start over." Logan's gaze was caressing as it moved over her.

"No."

He stopped short. A flash of pain flickered in his eyes, quickly masked, and Brontë was both pleased to see that pain and saddened by it. Pleased because it meant he was genuinely invested, and saddened that she had to hurt him.

"Is this good-bye, then?" Logan asked.

"No," she said again quickly. Her mind was a whirlwind of thoughts. She needed more time to process how she felt about Logan. More time to pull herself together. More time to just be . . . her. An idea hit her, and she looked up at him with a bright smile. "I think we should date."

"Date?" His brows furrowed, as if the concept were foreign to him.

"Yes," she said, warming to her topic. "Date. You know, dinner and a movie. Bowling with friends. Going out for pizza and seeing the sights. Spending time together just to spend time together. A date. Several dates. I need to know that what I thought we had was real, Logan. And I need to know you want to be with me. I think we should date."

"I want you," he said, and his tone was nearly a growl of frustration. "Going to see a movie isn't going to change that. I love you, Brontë."

"But I need to date, Logan," she said firmly. "No fancy parties, no buying of restaurants. No hurricanes. You and me, on a few regular dates like normal people. We can see if we're truly compatible or if we're just caught up in the madness of it all."

She suspected that she was still head over heels in love with him, but dating meant that she'd have him all to herself and that they'd be on familiar territory. She wasn't at home at fancy society parties. But at a pizza place or a movie? She could relax and just be herself.

There was a challenging gleam in his eyes that made her pulse flutter with excitement. "If you want me to win you over with romantic dates, Brontë, I will."

"Great," she said enthusiastically, and when he leaned in to kiss her, she ducked away again. "Call me sometime."

"Let's go out. Tonight."

"Can't tonight," she said lightly. "I'm working. Call me." She stressed the last two words and turned to the door, then glanced over her shoulder at him. "I'm serious, Logan. I want to date like normal people. Not like a billionaire and the waitress he just bought."

She could practically hear his teeth grinding. "You know it's not like that, Brontë."

Then prove it, she thought. But she gave him only an enigmatic smile and opened the office door. "Then call me sometime."

Brontë forced herself to walk calmly through the store room and back out to the main café. With calm hands, she lifted the bar, stepped in behind it, and then let it slide shut behind her again, taking her place next to the others behind the counter.

She immediately approached the line of customers, smiled at Gretchen, and then took over manning the register. A few moments later, her heart flipped in her breast as she watched Logan's tall form walk past the bar and leave the café.

Had he given up on her? So quickly?

Confused, she concentrated on the complicated order a very patient woman was trying to place. Brontë had to ask her to repeat it twice, because her head wasn't in the right place. Had she messed things up with Logan? Had he decided she wasn't worth the effort?

"Seventeen ninety-one," she told the woman as she completed her order. Just then the phone in her pocket began to vibrate. Brontë jumped and pulled it out with shaking fingers and turned away from the cash register.

Logan Hawkings, the screen read, and her heart thumped wildly in her chest. "H-hello?" she answered.

"I'm calling you," Logan said in a gruff voice. "Go out with me."

That wild, nervous giggle escaped, and she clapped a hand over her mouth in embarrassment. When she recovered, she cleared her throat. "Where would you like to go?"

"Dinner. Tonight. Someplace casual."

"I told you. I'm working tonight," she said calmly, though she couldn't stop grinning.

He made a frustrated sound that was nearly swallowed up by the sounds of traffic. He must have still been out on the street. "Tomorrow night, then."

"Tomorrow night is good," she said, smiling. "Where should we meet?"

––––––––

As she prepared for her first date with the man she was in love with, Brontë was thankful that Audrey had dragged her out and made her go clothes shopping. Her own funds were still a little lean, and although working at the coffee shop was a good way to pass time, living in New York was expensive and she found she was constantly a bit strapped for cash. A date outfit would have been out of the question.

Luckily, she had the clothes she'd taken when she'd left Logan's apartment. She grabbed her favorite jeans, paired them with a silver belt, and tossed on a form-fitting black boatneck sweater and some ankle boots. She pulled her hair into a smooth ponytail and added a pair of hoop earrings, and then presented the ensemble to Gretchen.

"How do I look?"

Gretchen looked up from her laptop screen and squinted at Brontë. "Are you dating Logan?"

"I am."

"Then I don't care," Gretchen said and turned back to her computer.

"Be fair, Gretchen," Brontë said with a laugh. "We're just going to try each other out and see if we can have a good time like regular people."

"Oh, please," Gretchen said with a roll of her eyes. She continued to type, her hair pulled atop her head in a wild red bun. At the side of her computer, Igor curled up, looking like a naked, wrinkly bat. Occasionally, Gretchen would reach over to pet the cat and then return to typing.

"We both know that this is just some sadistic version of foreplay and you're still madly in love with him. You just want to make him dance to your tune for a while instead of the other way around."

Gretchen certainly knew how to get to the heart of the matter.

"So . . . does this outfit look okay for excruciatingly drawn-out foreplay?"

Gretchen peered up at her again; then her eyes settled on her chest. "Are you wearing a bra?"

"Absolutely."

"A big ugly girdle?"

"No."

"Mmm. You need a big ugly girdle. It'll ensure you won't want to get naked with him."

Brontë smoothed a hand over her sweater. "I'm going to assume that this looks fine, then."

"Fine, fine," Gretchen waved a hand, then returned it to scratching Igor's wrinkly skin. She didn't look away from her monitor. "I'm two chapters from the end of this stupid project, so I'm going to be chained to the computer until it's done. I'm totally fine with you staying out until all hours. Just in case you were wondering."

"Gotcha."

"Have fun."

"I will."

"Don't do anything I wouldn't do. That means most everything, by the way."

Brontë waved, grabbed her purse, and headed out the door.

The walk to the subway station was a short one. Even though the network of subway lines was still confusing to her, she knew a few stops and was glad that the one they'd agreed to meet near was among them. After she emerged from the subway, she headed for the restaurant they'd picked and scanned the crowd of pedestrians for a familiar set of broad shoulders in an expensive jacket.

Her gaze nearly skipped over a tall man in a form-fitting navy henley, and then she paused, gazing at him in surprise. Logan. In jeans and a regular shirt. She continued to stare as he moved to her side, looking just as at ease as ever, and his hand went to her waist to pull her into his embrace. His scent enveloped her, and she lifted her face for a kiss automatically.

But he only hugged her close, then released her.

Brontë was oddly disappointed.

"You look nice," she told him with a small smile. "I almost didn't recognize you out of a business suit."

He grinned down at her, looking boyishly handsome, and it made her pulse pound. "It's been a while. I admit that it seems like everything I have in my closet has somehow magically transformed into either workout clothing or a suit. I had Audrey pick me up a few things." He ran a hand down his front and lifted his chin as if posing. "Do I pass muster?"

"You do," she said with a small laugh.

"You look gorgeous," he told her, his gaze devouring her body in the form-fitting sweater and jeans. "I've missed getting to look at you every day."

Her breath quickened, and she gave another nervous laugh.

"I've missed that, too," Logan said, grinning.

She couldn't seem to stop smiling. When he offered her his arm, she placed her hand in the crook of it. "Where are we going?"

"I thought we'd grab something to eat and then see a movie."

"What movie?"

He looked perplexed for a minute, then grimaced. "I don't know what's playing, to be honest. I forgot to ask Audrey to check." He pulled out his phone.

She put her hand over his, stopping him. "We can just see whatever's showing. No big deal."

Logan's expression was a bit sheepish. "I seem to have thought of everything but the date itself."

"Oh?"

They began to walk and Logan guided her through the streaming crowd.

"Indeed. I cleared my schedule, had Audrey purchase date clothes, picked out the restaurant, memorized some Plato—the usual. I even rode the subway here, just like a normal New Yorker." He grimaced. "I'd prefer not to do that on a regular basis. The man next to me smelled like piss."

She laughed again, feeling an insane urge to hug him. "Well, I appreciate the effort."

They walked two blocks, chatting about ridiculous things like the weather, Gretchen's obvious dislike of him and her protectiveness of Brontë, Cooper's coffee shop, and Audrey's efficiency as an assistant. Simple, easy conversation. She loved it.

"Here we go," Logan said, and they stopped outside of a small pizza parlor with an old yellow-lit sign. "I thought we'd grab a slice here."

It . . . definitely didn't look like the regular sort of place Logan frequented. "You like their food?"

"I did when I was a teenager. This was my first job, you know."

She looked up at him, surprised. "You worked here?"

"I did." He stared up at the sign, the expression on his face half fond, half rueful. "I was going through a rebellious phase—drinking, smoking, staying out all night. The usual teenage boy stuff. My father couldn't deal with me. Of course, I never dealt well with my father, either. I ended up skipping classes for a few days and was suspended from school. My father wanted to teach me a lesson. He told me that I was too arrogant for my own good and that I needed to learn from someone who wasn't terrified of my family's money or position. So he dropped me off here." Logan gestured at the pizza parlor.

"A family friend?" she guessed, watching his face.

"A very old friend of his from school. It turned out my father had given him the loan to start the place, so he owed my dad a favor. That favor was taking me on as an employee for a week. Andy—that's the owner's name—was a real drill sergeant, too. He had me washing floors and scrubbing toilets and standing over the sink for hours at a time. I remember that was the longest week of my life. I hated every minute of it, but my father told me that if I didn't stay, he'd kick me out. So I stayed."

"Your father sounds . . ." She struggled for the right word. "Interesting."

"My father was a real asshole. But he was right about Andy. He kicked my ass and worked me harder than anyone ever had. And you know what happened at the end of that week?"

"Your father relented?"

"Nope," Logan said with a half smile. "Andy fired me. Said I was the shittiest worker he'd ever seen and that three-year-olds had more drive than I did. That woke me up. Here was someone who wasn't afraid of my father's money or position. He just wanted a kid to wash dishes, and he ended up with me, who'd never washed a dish in my life and wasn't about to start. But I was more afraid of my father than Andy, so I had to convince him to keep me on. Which meant working harder. I worked there all summer. Learned a lot about hard work and running a business. I respected the hell out of Andy, too." He stared up at the pizza sign fondly again. "Hungry?"

Brontë nodded, fascinated by the story he'd told her. It gave her a lot to think about. "You've been wealthy all your life, haven't you?"

"Always, but it wasn't easy, either." Logan stepped

inside and moved to the counter, pointing at one of the pizzas and then holding up two fingers.

She waited for him to continue.

"My father was a hard man."

"Surely not all hard. Your mother must have loved him."

He gave her a wry look as he handed a twenty to the cashier. "My mother was a showgirl who wanted my father's money. She tolerated his bad moods since he was rich, and he tolerated her since she was gorgeous and pregnant with me. She died when I was five."

"I'm so sorry." Brontë took her plate and followed Logan to one of the small, dingy tables in the back of the parlor.

"I am, too. That meant it was just me and my father." He shrugged. "He died two years ago."

And two years ago, Logan had broken off his engagement with Danica. No wonder he had trust issues. Brontë took a small bite, a mix of emotions swirling through her. "This pizza is good," she said, changing the subject to safer territory. "Thank you."

"So what was your first job?" He took a bite, waiting for her to respond.

She grimaced. "Babysitter, of course."

"Did you enjoy it?"

"It depended on the kids, really. Some were great, some were horrible. It gave me a lot of time to read when they were napping, though."

He grinned. "I can see why you took the job."

"I am very transparent, aren't I?" She smiled impishly back at him.

"And do you want kids someday?"

It was a tough question, but she'd been expecting it. Brontë chewed, thinking for a long minute. Then she dabbed her mouth with a napkin and gave him the only answer she could. "Someday, with the right person."

He nodded.

"You?"

Logan's eyes were on her again. "Someday. I've already found the right person. I'm just waiting for her to be ready."

Brontë's nervous giggle surprised neither of them.

———

The only movie that they could get tickets to was an action movie, but sitting in the dark with Logan was pleasant no matter what the flick. Though the movie theater was crowded, she still enjoyed herself, and spent half of the movie with her head on Logan's shoulder, waiting for him to make a move. After all, date movies were for making out, weren't they?

Except he didn't, and when they walked back to the subway, Brontë was a little confused. Their date had gone so well. She'd found out so much about him and been so comfortable with Logan tonight, but he was keeping it platonic. Extremely platonic. And she didn't know how to handle that. After all, they'd been intimate before.

Extremely intimate.

Since it was late, he walked her back to Gretchen's apartment building, and they stood on the stoop, gazing at each other.

"Are you going to give me a kiss good night?" Brontë asked.

Logan looked up at her with a slow, assessing gaze, and then shook his head. "Not tonight."

"Why not?" She flushed at how forward that sounded. "I just mean . . . we've already been lovers. I—"

"Brontë," Logan said in a soft voice, hushing her. He stepped closer, and his hand moved to her waist, tugging her a little closer to him. "It's not that I don't want to kiss you. It's that if I start, I don't think I can stop."

Her entire body felt suffused with heat at his words. "Logan, I—"

"No, let me finish," he said. "You need this to feel

comfortable with me again. You want to date without the money or the power. I understand that. And now that I've had some time to settle into the idea, I like it. So we're going to take things slow." He took her hand in his, and then raised it to his lips, pressing a light kiss to her knuckles. "We're not going to take things to the next level again until you're ready. But I don't want just sex from you, Brontë. When we go to bed together again, it's going to be you and me. Strings attached and all. So think long and hard about what you want. Because I know what I want. I want you."

So direct and to the point. She felt breathless, gazing up into his serious face. "I don't know if I'm ready for that yet," she told him honestly.

He pressed another kiss to her knuckles and smiled. "Then we date again. What are you doing tomorrow night?"

"I have to check my work calendar to see if I'm free," she began.

"Brontë," he said patiently. "We both know you can be free tomorrow night. Don't play games."

He had a point. She was just pushing to see if she could win, and it wasn't fair to him. "I'm free. What do you want to do, then?"

"Be with you."

At this rate, she was never going to stop blushing. He made her feel . . . a little excited, but strangely pleased. She rather liked being the center of his universe, even if at the moment his universe consisted of small, easy dates. "Do you want to go bowling? Dinner?"

"Have you been to Broadway yet?"

Excitement flared through her. "Oh! No, I haven't, but I'm dying to. I would love to see a show! Isn't it too late to find tickets to anything good, though?"

"Leave that up to me. I'll pick you up for dinner tomorrow." He reluctantly released her hand. "Think of me tonight?"

"I will. Good night, Logan."

She watched him descend the steps of her building and head back down the street to the subway. He didn't look back at her, but that was okay. Her entire body was still warm from his words.

What do you want to do, then?

Be with you . . . Think of me tonight.

Strange how admitting that she would think of him somehow felt more intimate than a dozen kisses.

Brontë went inside, heading up to the apartment. Gretchen hadn't moved from the space she'd occupied when Brontë had left hours earlier, except her bun now had several pencils stuck into it, and the cat had moved to curl around her feet. She looked up at Brontë as if surprised, then glanced at the clock. "Oh. Oh. It's late." She rubbed her eyes and stared at her computer screen. "Well, shit. I think I lost track of time. How'd it go?"

"Good," Brontë said with a dreamy sigh. "And bad. I'm still totally in love with him."

"Just don't tell him that," Gretchen said, reaching down to pet Igor. "I guess I'll stop hating him until you two break up again."

Brontë made a face. "Very funny. We're going out again tomorrow night."

"Fine with me. That'll give me a chance to fix this last chapter I wrote. It's horrible." She stared at the screen and grimaced. "Good thing this book won't have my real name on it."

Brontë snorted. "Well, I'm heading off to bed. See you in the morning."

Gretchen didn't look up from the screen. "See you."

Brontë went to bed, and just like she'd promised, her thoughts were entirely of Logan.

———

The next night, Logan took her out to a popular Broadway show, and she had an amazing time. She didn't even raise an eyebrow when he produced box seats instead of ones in the nosebleed section. Afterward, they went out for drinks and spent the evening talking and laughing together. She told him about her childhood in the Midwest, and he told her about his adventures at boarding school as a boy. When they parted that night, he had simply given her a hug and a kiss on the cheek.

The next night, he took her ice skating at Rockefeller, determined to show her a good time even if it meant hitting every tourist hot spot that New York had to offer. She didn't care, though. She loved the sheer fun of being out with him, seeing all the famous places around town. Holding hands with him as they careened around the ice. She laughed the entire time, and even Logan's serious face had a smile on it.

Of course, that night, he gave her just a caress on the cheek and a quick peck before leaving her on the stoop, her pulse throbbing with unfulfilled desire.

She knew he was doing it on purpose, of course. If she wanted to have a few dates just as a normal couple, they'd take it slow. Extremely slow. That had been her plan, after all. A week or two of just dating.

Unfortunately for her, the plan was backfiring in a major way. By the time they went on a walk through Central Park two days later, his every touch sent a ripple of desire through her body. Her nipples were hard enough at his nearness that she wore several layers of clothing to cover it up. And when he leaned in to nuzzle the nape of her neck in a quietly affectionate move, her knees went weak, her sex instantly wet.

This was not exactly how she'd planned for the week to go. She said nothing, of course, though she might have rubbed up against Logan's thigh a bit more than she should have in the carriage ride around the park, and when he held her close, she might have pushed her hips back suggestively. Her skin was heated and flushed with need, but he only gave her a light kiss on the lips.

If this is how he thinks normal people date, she thought wryly, *he is going to be very surprised when I jump his bones in the next date or two.* She had wanted to move slow with Logan to prove that the real spark was there between them. However, he had apparently interpreted "slow" as "glacial."

She couldn't really complain, though. His schedule kept him busy in the daytime, though he'd send her occasional text messages throughout the day to let her know what their plans were for that evening, or simply to tell her he was thinking about her. When she'd told him she was looking forward to their date, he'd sent back a quote that made her heart flutter with delight.

> *". . . and when one of them meets the other half, the actual half of himself, whether he be a lover of youth or a lover of another sort, the pair are lost in an amazement of love and friendship and intimacy and one will not be out of the other's sight, as I may say, even for a moment . . ."*

She'd been giddy over that single text. She hadn't even corrected him considering that was a quote from a satire of love. It was meant from the heart from Logan, and that was all that counted.

Meanwhile Gretchen, who was still on deadline and crankier than ever, complained that Brontë was too easily swayed. And maybe it was true.

But she knew it was love. At least, it was on her end. Love and desire and need and want all mixed into one giant bundle of nerves. And while she knew it was love, she also knew one other thing for certain.

She wasn't going to be the one to say it first. Not this time.

TWELVE

~~~~

Logan told Brontë to ask Cooper for the day off on Monday. She asked, with a bemused smile on her face. Cooper was confused about the situation, of course. Since Logan was in the process of buying the coffee shop, and she was dating Logan, did she really have to ask Cooper?

Yes, Brontë informed him. She did.

She got the day off, of course.

When Logan showed up with the limo, she should have been mad at him, but he had such an I-know-I've-been-bad smile on his face that she couldn't get upset. Instead, she eyed the car and then his clothing, noting that despite the expensive wheels, he was dressed down in jeans and a ribbed sweater. "What's with the limo?"

"We need a ride out to where we're going today."

She crossed her arms but couldn't keep the smile off her face. "We do, huh?"

"We do," he agreed, and produced a blindfold. "Unless you don't mind walking the streets blindfolded. This is for you."

Skeptical, Brontë took the length of fabric from him. "Blindfolded?"

"For our surprise date." He took it from her and gestured for her to turn around.

Obediently, she turned, biting back her smile. She could feel his fingers moving over the back of her head, and skitters of delight moved through her at even that simple touch. When his hand clasped her arm, she jumped in surprise, gasping.

"Did I startle you?"

"No, I-I'm okay." Her nipples were hard, though. Embarrassingly so. "How long do I have to wear this?"

"Until we get there," he told her, and then led her into the limo.

It was impossible to tell how far they were driving—she couldn't see a clock or see the streets to know where they were headed. Her entire world became the interior of the car and, more precisely, Logan's large body next to hers in the backseat, his thigh warm next to her own. Her senses were enveloped with his nearness, and just the occasional whiff of his aftershave was driving her wild with need.

When he put an arm around her shoulders and pulled her close, she tilted her head back, hoping he would kiss her. Instead, his thumb lightly traced the contours of her lips. The tender touch sent sensations cascading through her, and Brontë could barely breathe for the ache in her breast . . . and between her legs. God, she needed him. This was torture. Her breasts yearned for his touch, and her entire body felt attuned to him. Without the ability to see, all her other senses seemed to have come alive, and she was on fire with longing.

The car stopped, and Logan shifted next to her.

"Are we there?" Her voice was breathless and husky.

"Not quite," Logan said. He took her hand in his and led her out of the car. "This is as far as the limo goes, though."

Brontë tilted her head, wishing she could see his expression. She listened to the sounds around her—lots of people. Outdoors. But where? She wasn't familiar with the city. "When can I take this off?"

"Now," he said, and his hands moved to her hair.

He untied the knot, and she caught the blindfold in her hands, tugging it down off of her face, eyes open-wide to interpret what she was seeing.

People everywhere. A park with tall trees, and a large brick wall. Signs stood by the entrance, and she quickly scanned one. One gave ferry rates . . .

"The Statue of Liberty," she gasped, delighted. Brontë turned back to Logan, unable to contain her smile. "Is that where we're going?"

"It is." He looked pleased at her response. "Come on."

It was the most ridiculously touristy thing they'd done so far, but she loved every moment of it. They rode the ferry across the water to Ellis Island and the museum. Logan held her hand in his as they walked the grounds, their headsets on as they shuffled along listening to the tour. They stopped by the gift shop, and she got a Statue of Liberty T-shirt, postcards, and several pens for her friends back home. Once she'd finished her shopping, they went on to Liberty Island. The Statue was fascinating, and she stared up at it with wide eyes, delighted.

"Do you want a photo?" he asked. "I seem to recall that you wanted your picture taken in front of the Statue of Liberty."

She nodded, beaming at him. "Want to do one together?"

"Of course."

They took pictures in front of the Statue, pausing to switch off so they could both have photos on their individual phones. Brontë laughed at the sight of them in one shot. "Your eyes are closed in my picture, Logan. We have to take it again."

"Let's change up our pose, then," he said, and took the

phone from her, holding it low so the picture would be an uptilted view.

And he leaned in and very lightly kissed her mouth.

Immediate heat flushed through her body. Brontë clung to him, her hands going to his cheeks and anchoring her mouth against his. She'd wanted this for what felt like forever, and when his lips parted, she took advantage and swept her tongue into his mouth, letting him know her need. He groaned low in his throat at her kiss, and then his tongue was rubbing up against hers. An ache settled low in Brontë's hips, and she whimpered in response.

Logan slowly pulled away from her lips and grinned down at her. "Let's hope that photo turned out."

Dazed, she stared up at him, and reached out to take the phone back. The photo was tilted awkwardly, and the Statue wasn't even in the picture. "It's fine," she murmured, still flushed and tingling.

"It's not. We need to do it again," he said, and his hand went around her waist as he took the phone back from her. He angled it up once more, adjusted it, then leaned in and began to kiss her again. The kiss this time didn't start off delicate. His mouth immediately claimed hers, sending driving desire rocketing through her. Over and over, his mouth slanted over hers, tongue licking at hers in a way that made her knees weak. People were probably watching, and she didn't care.

She nearly sagged when he released her again, and glanced down at the phone. "Better?" she asked in a wobbly voice, clinging to him.

"My eyes are closed again," he said, and couldn't hide the triumphant expression on his face. "We should do it one more time."

"I'm starting to think you're doing this on purpose," Brontë protested, but her words were cut off by the heated kiss he bestowed on her mouth again. And oh, God, desire was hammering staccato notes through her body, and all her nerve endings seemed to be demanding one thing. His body, over hers. In hers. ASAP. All this dating and yearning seemed like one big cruel tease at the moment.

Endless, endless foreplay, she thought, lost in the feel of his mouth against hers. A low moan almost escaped her when he pulled away, but she bit it back. His gaze moved over her face with that same heated look that she was positive was plastered all over her own face. She licked her lips and nearly moaned again, because she could taste him on her skin.

Logan glanced down at her phone, and then handed it to her. "Perfect."

Dazed, Brontë stared down at the picture. A hot flush crept over her cheeks—in the photo, she was clinging to Logan, the two of them wrapped around each other, the Statue looming in the distance.

She loved that picture.

He leaned in and her breath caught. She stared up at him, hoping for another kiss, but his mouth moved to her ear.

"I want you," he told her. And he bit her earlobe.

She did moan then, the sound low and full of longing.

"Shall we find someplace private?" he asked her, still nibbling on her ear and making her bones turn to liquid. "Get to know each other a little better . . . all over again?"

"M-my place," she breathed. "Not yours."

"That's fine. Your roommate?"

"Working today," Brontë told him, and was suddenly wildly thankful that Gretchen had a job of some kind that got her out of the apartment. "All ours."

"Good," he told her, and the sound was full of so much satisfaction and promise that she went weak in the knees all over again.

Brontë clung to him on the ferry ride back to Battery Park. His arms were wrapped around her, and she had gone all too easily into his embrace. Waiting to get back to the apartment was a slow, delicious torture, but it gave her time to think . . . and stew in her own thoughts.

He'd taken her out to Liberty Island to see the Statue. Brontë thought of her comment on the plane ride to New York. She'd asked him about seeing the Statue and teased him about how clichéd it was and how she still wanted to do it. Such a small, offhand comment, but he'd remembered it. He'd remembered that she loved sightseeing and had wanted to see the city, and had taken her on a tour of New York City with every date. Even when Logan was deliberate, he was thoughtful.

And he'd completely stolen her heart.

Gretchen had warned her about falling too fast all over again, but this was Logan. *Her* Logan. Warm and delicious and handsome and thoughtful . . .

And totally loaded. And all wrong for a poor Midwestern waitress.

Well, she wouldn't worry about that right now. They were heading back to her apartment she shared temporarily with Gretchen, and they were going to make love. Her body thrummed and ached with need for him.

He hadn't told her he loved her, though.

She wouldn't tell him she loved him, either. This, she told herself, was just mutual using. Both parties seeking satisfaction. No emotions had to be involved, really. It was just the natural progression of a normal relationship, after all.

It sounded totally convincing in her head.

Truth was, their relationship had never been all that normal. From the moment she'd met Logan until now, it seemed they'd done everything half backward and sideways.

He wasn't the right guy for her in the long run, she told herself. No billionaire could see himself with a waitress long-term. Those sorts of things were generally pretty incompatible.

But she could enjoy him while she had him. And she would. She would think about the future some other time.

———

Logan rubbed Brontë's shoulder as she leaned against him in the car. The drive to Gretchen's apartment was fucking endless, and his entire body sang with a need to pull Brontë into his lap, tear down her panties, and drive into her.

But he had to be patient. She was calling the shots for now, because she needed to feel comfortable again. That was why they were going all the way across town to Gretchen's apartment instead of heading to his place on the Upper East Side. Brontë was in control.

At least until he got her naked and squirming under him. Then he was taking control, and he'd make sure she was screaming her pleasure before he even thought about his own.

He nearly swore with relief when the apartment building came into sight. He opened the door, got out, and then held the door for Brontë. He gave the driver a nod, signaling that he wouldn't need his services for the rest of the evening, and then wrapped his arm around Brontë's waist again.

She stared up at him with a soft, passion-dazed expression that made his cock hard. "What about your driver?"

"I dismissed him for the night." He met her gaze, almost daring her to contradict him and send him home with a peck on the cheek—like he'd been doing to her—and a raging hard-on.

He forced himself to be patient as Brontë fumbled with the keys, and then they climbed the stairs of the walk-up. By the time they got to Gretchen's floor, he was pretty sure he would kill Audrey's sister if they opened the door and found her standing there. His cock was so hard he ached, and he'd just spent four flights of stairs gazing up at Brontë's perfect ass as it flexed with every step.

To his relief, the apartment was dark. Brontë flipped on a light when they entered, and a wrinkly gray animal darted across the room, startling Logan. "What was that?"

Brontë seemed amused by his reaction, her laughter chasing away the soft desire in her face. "That's Igor. He's a hairless cat."

He glanced at the animal, which seemed to be all ears and wrinkles. It stared back at him with wide golden eyes. "Hideous."

"It does take some getting used to," she agreed with a smile.

"Can you shut him away in Gretchen's room?"

"I can," she said, and her voice had gone all breathy again. She bent low and snapped her fingers, and the cat darted over to her. Brontë scooped it up in her arms and disappeared into a side room, returning a moment later and shutting the door behind her. Her cheeks were flushed as if she'd been running . . . or was aroused. The anticipation was getting to her.

Good. Because it was driving him mad. Had been for the past week.

Brontë was gazing up at him, her eyes shining with a look that seemed half expectant, half anxious. Her expression was so full of emotion that it was driving him wild . . . and tormenting him. There was hurt in her eyes—hurt that he'd put there. And a little bit of fear that she might get hurt again.

They needed to move past that moment. And he had an idea of how to do that.

He pulled the blindfold back out of his pocket again and offered it to her. "Do you trust me, Brontë?"

Her eyes widened as she looked down at it, then up at him, realizing what was about to happen. "I . . . Logan . . ."

"You can say no," he told her. "I don't want you to feel pressured."

She nodded, swallowing, and then her entire face

seemed to flush red as she took the blindfold from his hand with trembling fingers and lifted it to her eyes. "Would you tie me?"

An innocent question, but it fired his blood. He moved behind her, taking the ends of the blindfold from her and tying them against the back of her head. She was standing there, stiff and wooden, so he leaned in and whispered huskily in her ear. "Too tight?"

She jumped, her elbow nearly slamming into his jaw. "N-no! It's fine." Her hands reached for him. "Just a little unnerving is all." She turned and grasped his jacket in her hands and then gave it a small tug. "Should we go to my room?"

"I'll lead the way," he told her, and swept her into his arms, enjoying the muffled sound of surprise she made and the way she clung to him. Desire surged through him, mixing with triumph. He'd won her back. She was in his arms, and he was going to make love to her and show her that he'd never wavered.

His arms tightened around her possessively. Brontë was his again.

Good.

He pushed open the door to the other bedroom. Brontë's room. There was a single twin bed in the corner of the room with a plain wrought iron headboard, and a small dresser that held a few mementos from their dates that week. A vase of flowers—flowers that he'd given her—sat in the windowsill. There were no pictures on the walls, and the entire room seemed barely lived in. The realization pleased him—she'd be back with him after tonight. His place felt empty and lonely without her.

Logan gently laid her on the bed and admired her, the curves of her body, the beauty of her face, the way the ends of her hair curled wildly. The way she bit her lip as she anticipated his touch. Carefully, almost reverently, he brushed his fingers down the length of one denim-clad leg and enjoyed seeing her shiver in response. He turned and shut the door to Brontë's small room, just in case her roommate did show up again, and she jumped at the sound.

"Everything all right?" he asked her.

A nervous giggle was his answer. "I'm fine. Just . . . a little on edge."

"That's part of the appeal of having you like this," Logan murmured. His hands went to one of her shoes and eased it off her foot, and he smiled at the way she wiggled her toes in response. "Watching your response as I touch you. Watching you anticipate my moves. All of it pleases me."

"And are you hard?" she asked breathlessly.

He took her hand and placed it on his cock. That quick caress had him nearly groaning aloud at her touch. His cock felt like steel and ached with the need to bury itself into her, but he would pace himself.

Her fingers lightly glided along his shaft, exploring and feeling him. She licked her lips, the unconscious move making his cock jerk in her hand. "You're so hard, Logan. So big in my hand."

And she was so delicate under his. "Beautiful Brontë," he murmured, leaning in to kiss her lips.

She made a small noise of protest when he kept the kiss brief, automatically reaching for him again and stroking her hands down his cheeks. "I want you."

"Let me play with you, Brontë. It would give me such pleasure."

She shuddered at his words and nodded.

"First, I'd like to undress you," he said in a low, seductive voice, intending to seduce her with words as well as touch. Her hands automatically moved to the waist of her jeans as if to help out, and he caught her hands in his. "Allow me."

Her hands fluttered at her waist, as if uncertain, and then she dropped them to her sides. "Okay."

Logan leaned in and pushed her sweater up, exposing

an inch of skin above the waist of her jeans. He kissed the skin, enjoying her shiver of pleasure beneath him. "I plan on taking my time exploring you, love. You're going to be begging for me to take you by the time I'm done with you."

She sucked in a breath. At her sides, her hands clenched and then flexed, as if she didn't know where to put them.

"Just relax," he told her with a small grin, knowing that she'd never be able to.

"Oh, sure," she said with a small laugh. "Easy for you to say."

"It is," he agreed, undoing the button of her jeans and then lowering the zipper with excruciating slowness. His cock throbbed at the sight of the sliver of pale blue satin exposed. His mouth lowered, and he nipped at her skin through the satin, enjoying her small jerk of response. "These are lovely."

"My panties or my hips?" she teased.

"Both," he teased back. He tugged the thick fabric of the jeans down her legs, tossing them aside and on the floor when he was done. Her socks went next, each one carefully removed with a light skimming of fingers over her flesh.

Now her sweater. There were no buttons that he could lovingly pull apart. Shame. He slid a hand under the soft fabric, caressing her belly.

She squirmed, ticklish. "Stop that."

"Stop touching you?" His fingertip dipped into her belly button.

Brontë sucked in a breath, and when his tongue followed the finger, she moaned in response. "Never mind. Keep touching me. I'm obviously delusional."

"Clearly," he murmured, swirling his tongue around the edge of her belly button as he pushed her sweater upward. Ah, damn. She'd worn a matching bra. The cups were the same ice blue satin decorated with little black bits of lace around the edges and between her breasts. He'd wanted to see her naked right away, but the sight of her curves cupped in that gorgeous lingerie made him rethink his idea. He'd leave her in it a bit longer, and then strip it off of her later.

But for now, her sweater had to go.

"Hands?" he asked her, sitting upright again.

Her forehead furrowed over the blindfold, and she lifted her hands in the air after a moment's hesitation. "Like this?"

"Exactly." He tugged her sweater over her head and arms in a deft move and tossed it aside, pleased at the sight of her beautiful body. "You're gorgeous. I could look at you all day and never get tired of it."

A soft smile touched her mouth, and she reached for him, brushing her fingers through his hair. "I could look at you all day, too."

"Ah, but this is about me pleasing you," he said, clasping her hands in his. "And you're not playing fair. No touching."

She did a mock pout that made him want to lean down and kiss her mouth. Instead, he took her hands and directed them over her head, to the wrought iron headboard's bars.

"Keep them here," he instructed her. "I want to play with you a little longer."

He was pleased to see the little shiver move over her body at the thought. She obeyed him, her breathing quickening with excitement.

Logan skimmed a hand down her leg, caressing the skin. The front of her thigh was smooth and soft, her calves dainty and her ankles elegant. He could indeed spend all day admiring her body. He ran a finger along her skin, tracing a light pattern over her from foot to thigh, noticing how she reacted when he touched her. She jumped when he moved over her thighs, and he repeated the motion, this time skimming the inside of her thigh, and was pleased to see her twitch even more.

"'Afflicted by love's madness, all are blind,'" she quoted suddenly.

"Oh?"

"I just . . . it felt appropriate at the moment."

Logan chuckled. "Very appropriate, except I am enjoying looking at you far too much to claim to be blind." His fingers played along the lace of her panties. "Plato?" he asked innocently.

Her lips quirked with amusement. "Sextus Propertius, I believe."

"Intriguing name," he commented. His fingers grasped her thighs, and he pulled them apart, eliciting a startled gasp from her. "Keep these open for me, Brontë. I want to get my fill of looking at you."

A whimper escaped her throat, but she did as he'd commanded, her knees falling open, her legs spread wide on the bed. He pushed them apart until they were flat on the mattress, the ice blue panties totally exposed. She was so wet that he could see it seeping through the fabric of her panties, and he palmed his cock in response, groaning. "I see how wet you are, love. Should I taste you?"

A shudder rippled through her, and she moaned, clutching at the iron headboard. He watched with fascination as her thighs quivered, as if desperate to lock together again. He ran a curious finger down the inside of her thigh, starting at her knee and moving toward her sex.

She seemed to shudder with every inch caressed, until her hips were rolling on the bed. "Logan," she breathed, her head turning back and forth despite the blindfold. "Touch me."

"Where shall I do it?" He brushed a knuckle over her belly button again. "Here?"

"Lower."

He went to her knee and caressed it. "Here?"

She moaned in frustration. "You're a horrible tease."

"Now, love," he chided. "If I was a horrible tease, I'd move in and touch you like so." And he stroked one finger up the damp satin between her legs.

Brontë's sucked-in breath was audible.

He pushed his finger, nudging at the clit under the layers of clothing. "But I'm not finished playing, Brontë. And if I continue to touch you here, you'll come. And I don't want that just yet. I'm enjoying teasing you far too much."

Her hips bucked against his hand, trying to create friction between his fingers and her flesh. Naughty woman. He spanked her sex lightly in reproach, enjoying her startled gasp. "Are you not having fun, love?"

"I'm not sure if this is fun or torture," she panted. Her body shifted on the bed, about as close to squirming as she could get away with. Her hips wriggled under his hand, still resting atop her sex. He let it remain there a moment, a silent tease, before he removed it.

A small protest escaped her throat.

It died when his knuckles brushed over the tip of one of her breasts. He could tell they were hard and tight through the fabric of the pretty bra. Tight and needing, and probably delectable. Logan's mouth watered just thinking about how she'd taste in his mouth, and he tugged at the cups of her bra, freeing her breasts. The underwire of the bra pushed her breasts upward, plumping them as if offering them to his lips. And who was he to refuse such an offering? Logan bent forward and took one succulent tip in his mouth.

Brontë moaned.

"Delicious," he murmured against her skin, rolling the tip of her nipple against his lips. Such a hard little nub. He flicked his tongue against it. He loved her nipples—a dusky rose, slightly tilted. Dark and pretty against all that creamy flesh. He began to tease the other with his fingertips as he tongued the first, flicking and teasing it with his mouth.

Underneath him, Brontë whimpered, her hips undulating again. Her hands clenched the iron headboard tight, as if she needed to hold on to something desperately. "Oh, Logan."

He kissed her flesh—the tips of each breast, the sweet valley between them, the gentle curves underneath them. She moaned wildly with each caress, her blindfolded head moving back and forth, as if in denial.

And so he paused.

"More," she demanded, arching her back so her breasts were thrust oh-so-beautifully into his face. "Please, Logan."

"Not yet, love," he murmured, kissing one nipple and then sitting up. His cock strained against his pants, so fucking eager that he could feel pre-come beading on the thick crown. He stood and began to remove his pants, desperate to free his cock.

She whimpered, confused. "Logan? Where are you going?"

"Nowhere, love," he told her. "Just getting undressed. My cock's so hard it's aching and my clothes are too tight."

A smile curved her lips, and she licked them, which nearly made him come in his pants. "I love your cock."

"Do you, now?" He stripped off the rest of his clothing, kicking it onto the floor before kneeling back alongside her again. His cock thrust into the air, hard, the head slick.

"Mmm-hmmm," she said with a small sigh of delight.

He wrapped a hand around his cock, stroking it while looking at her lying in the bed, legs spread for him, panties wet, her breasts thrust up. Her head was tilted slightly, as if she were listening for his movements since she couldn't see him.

Logan moved back over her, leaning in to kiss her mouth. His hand went to her breast, palming it, and he settled between her legs. She responded to his kisses eagerly, her tongue meeting his and rubbing against it with soft mews of desire. He moved down a little, settling his cock against her wet core and thrusting.

She gasped, her hips rocking against his flesh.

"Feel good?" he asked her, thrusting his cock against her sex again. The wet fabric prevented him from pushing deep inside her, a teasing barrier.

"Oh, God, yes," she moaned. "Logan, I need you so bad. I want you inside me."

He wanted to be there, too. But he wasn't done playing. He thrust again, enjoying her moans of response.

When she parted her lips and licked them again, a mental image formed in his mind that made him groan aloud. He had to get up.

She whimpered a protest, turning her head and looking for him.

"I'm here," he told her, standing by the head of the bed.

He caressed her breasts, plucking at the nipples. Then, he ran a thumb over her lower lip, unable to resist that mental image in his mind. "Do you trust me, Brontë?"

Her entire body seemed to tremble with anticipation, and then she took his thumb in her mouth and bit down lightly. "I trust you."

"Do you want me?"

"More than anything."

He grasped the headboard and leaned forward until the head of his cock pressed against her mouth. "Then taste me."

Her lips parted, and she ran her tongue over the head of his cock, licking up the salty pre-come there. He groaned when her tongue slipped down the shaft, flicking against it. Then she opened her mouth and tilted her head, taking him in deeper. The sight of her lips wrapped around his cock was almost enough to send him over the edge, and he clutched at the headboard, trying to keep control. "Brontë," he groaned. "Ah, God, your mouth."

Her tongue licked against the underside of his cock, running along the thick vein there. So trusting and loving. So incredibly erotic.

She sucked, trying to take him deeper, but he pulled out of her mouth. It was too much pleasure too fast, and it would be over with far too quickly if he let her continue.

He wanted her to come first. Logan moved a step back from the bed, eyeing her all spread out and delicious. "Are you enjoying yourself, love?"

She nodded, biting her lip. Her hips lifted a little, as if unable to stay down. "More, Logan. I need you."

"I know," he told her. "I'm going to give you more. But I need you on your hands and knees."

Her little gasp was followed by a low moan, and she obediently turned over, moving to her knees and then leaning forward to rest on her elbows. The position pushed her pretty ass high into the air.

Logan ran his hand all over her exposed skin—her thighs, her calves, the small of her back, along her spine. It was a pleasure simply to touch her. She seemed to be enjoying it as well, her little breathy sighs of pleasure almost as enticing as touching her. His fingertips snagged on the waistband of her panties, and he tugged them down her thighs, exposing her wet, gleaming flesh.

Brontë moaned again, her fingers curling into the blankets on the bed, anticipation making her entire body tense.

Well, now. He had to reward that. Logan brushed his fingertips over the slick lips of her sex, then parted them, stroking up and down.

She jerked in surprise, and then a whimper escaped her when he circled the slick opening to her core. She rolled her hips, forcing his fingers to dip in, just a little. "Logan," she breathed. "I need you so badly."

He moved down to her clitoris, rubbing it between two of his slick fingers and stimulating it. Brontë jerked again, her hips flexing, and her gasps became rapid and wild, as if she were unable to control herself. She worked her hips against his hand, and he continued to rub her clit, then pushed his thumb into her core.

She went wild, writhing against his hand and moaning his name as he continued to work her. He could feel her pussy shuddering with each shallow thrust, and he pushed the pad of his thumb forward, increasing the friction even as he continued the measured, steady rubbing of her clitoris. "Logan," she cried. "Oh, please! I—"

Her entire body clenched under him, muscles quivering, and she made a soft, keening sound. Her pussy clenched around his thumb, milking it with the force of her orgasm. He continued to rub, wanting to prolong the pleasure for her, and she continued to make that low keening noise that made his cock throb with wanting her.

The orgasm seemed to go on forever, but then Brontë gave one final shudder and sagged against the blankets, resting her cheek against them. Her legs were sprawled, her sex gleaming wet from her pleasure. "Oh," she breathed. "Oh, Logan."

He licked his fingers, tasting her pleasure on his skin. "Beautiful."

A soft, sated smile curved under the blindfold, and it made his cock jump with need. "Condoms?"

She stilled, reaching for the blindfold. "Oh . . . I don't think I have any . . . I don't—" He spanked her ass lightly, and her hand flew away from the blindfold. "Pill. I'm on the pill."

"Right. Good." He was pleased to see that her hand had slipped between her thighs and she was playing with her flesh, lightly rubbing along her clit. She bit her lip as he waited, watching her. She let her hand slide away.

"No," he told her. "Keep touching yourself. I like seeing that."

He could see the hot blush stealing over her cheeks under the blindfold, but her hand returned between her legs and began to move slowly again. He watched her, fascinated by the sight of her pleasing herself. His cock jerked with need again.

Logan moved behind her on the bed, moving between her spread legs. Her ass was so beautiful, perched in the air, that he couldn't resist running his hands over it again. "Are you still touching yourself?"

She sucked in an excited breath and nodded, as if unable to trust her voice.

He thrust into her in one swift move, hands gripping her hips. She jerked in surprise, a choked moan escaping her. He stilled immediately, worried that she'd been too surprised and he'd somehow hurt her. "Brontë?"

"Move," she moaned, her hips bucking up against him. "Oh, God, move."

He groaned in response to that, thrusting hard again. He'd wanted to be so controlled in his movements, slowly driving her back up the peak of desire, but it seemed that, sheathed deep in her warmth, he'd lost all control. His thrusts were rough and wild, his hands gripping her hips to anchor her back against him. And she was out of control, too, pushing back against him to add force to his thrusts, a low scream building in her throat.

"Keep touching yourself," he demanded, his voice ragged as he continued to pump into her.

Her only response was another muffled scream, and he felt her pussy clench all around him. Logan uttered a curse, trying to retain control, trying to keep his rhythm, to make this as good for her as possible. Make it last until she was mindless with pleasure. Show her how much he fucking loved her and her body.

She made a soft sound that was almost like a sob, and then she spasmed around his cock, sucking him tight as she began to come again, her body trembling all over with the force of her passion.

He lost control. Thrusting hard into her again, he groaned her name and went over the edge, his own orgasm exploding from his body with a fierce intensity that shocked him. It seemed to go on forever, coming hard and fierce, until it left him as breathless and wrung out as the woman beneath him.

Logan pulled out of Brontë, ignoring her small noise of protest. When he turned around, she was sitting up in bed, her hands pulling at the blindfold. He moved toward her, gently undoing the knot at the back of her head and then leaning in to kiss her when she smiled up at him.

"I love you," he told her, his voice gruff. "I mean that."

Her smile faltered a little. "Thank you."

She didn't say it back. For a moment he was surprised, and then angry. And then he chuckled at himself. So this was how she'd felt when she'd confessed and he'd ignored her. Fair enough. It was a good lesson for him to learn. "You don't trust me yet." It wasn't a question.

She bit her lip, then shook her head. "I'm sorry. I'm just really . . . I just—"

"Don't apologize. You can't help the way you feel. Just know that I do love you, and I'll prove it to you somehow." Logan sat down on the edge of the small bed and grabbed the blankets. "You'd better move over if you want to get any sleep tonight."

Brontë gave a small squeal and shifted on the bed, elbowing him by accident as they tried to make all of their limbs fit in the twin bed. "We both won't fit," she protested.

"We will," he said with determination, and pulled her hips against him until their bodies were flush. The fit was tight but pleasant, and it allowed him free rein to nibble on her ear.

She was already drifting to sleep, though, her eyes drooping with exhaustion, and so he watched her doze off, his mind whirling with thoughts. One particular quotation that he'd read in another of her books came to mind, though. To test whether she was awake, he leaned in and whispered something sure to get a response.

"*Veni, vidi, vici.*" I came, I saw, I conquered.

"I heard that," she muttered sleepily, but she smiled and patted him on the arm.

He decided to keep the other to himself. *"Every heart sings a song, incomplete, until another heart whispers back."*

It seemed that loving Brontë brought out the philosopher in him as well.

THIRTEEN

The next morning, Brontë woke up to find Logan's body curled around hers, and her arm was asleep from being in a cramped position over her head. She lay in bed for a long moment, debating getting up, since there was no way she'd be able to get out of bed without waking Logan.

Sweet, gorgeous Logan. God, she loved him. Terrified of getting hurt again, she'd chickened out on saying it the night before. But he'd seemed to understand her fear, and it hadn't bothered him. He'd just kissed her, and they'd climbed into bed together, sleeping in a tangle of limbs because they didn't want to be parted. She'd been resting on a spring all night, and her leg was trapped under his, and her arm hung off the bed.

It was the best night of sleep she'd had in a long time.

Her bladder was protesting the hour, though, and she sighed and sat up, beginning to extract herself. Logan woke up and kissed her arm before rolling out of bed, yawning and stretching to work out the kinks in his back. "Morning, love."

He'd been calling her "love" all night, she'd noticed. She liked it, too. Brontë smiled at him. "I need to run to the bathroom before Gretchen gets in there. She's a shower hog."

"Go ahead," he told her, lying back. He grabbed the pillow and tucked it under his head, as if to go back to sleep.

She grinned and shook her head at him, then raced for the bathroom.

When she returned from her shower, she was surprised to see him up and moving about her room. He'd dressed in his boxer shorts and had made the bed. Her suitcase lay atop the blankets, and he'd pulled several of her hung-up clothes out of the closet.

Brontë gave him a curious look, holding back her frown. "What's all this?"

Logan smiled over at her. "Thought I'd help you get started while I waited for the shower."

"Get started with what?" She crossed her arms over her towel and tried to look open-minded about what he was going to say.

His mouth thinned a little. "We're back together now. You're moving back in with me."

She shook her head. "Logan, no."

Frustration flashed in his gaze. "Why is that a problem, Brontë?" His voice sounded as if he were trying to be patient . . . and it were causing him pain.

"Because our relationship is all messed up, Logan. You and I were 'moved in together' before we barely even knew each other, and look at how well that worked out."

"It worked out just fine in my eyes."

She snorted. Of course he'd say that. "Nothing's changed, Logan. Last night was great, but I'm allowed to sleep with a guy and not move in with him."

His face hardened as a stark look of disbelief crossed his gaze. "Is there someone else?" His voice was deathly serious.

"What? No. Of course not."

Relief flickered in his eyes. "Good." He moved forward and pulled her into his arms. "I'm not seeing anyone else, and you're not either. This thing we have, it's just you and me."

"All right."

"And you're moving back in with me." He sounded so possessive and so utterly sure of himself.

"No, I'm not. Not until I'm ready."

Logan seemed to think about that for a moment and then accepted it. "What will it take to make you ready? I want you back in my bed."

"You have me back in *a* bed."

"In *my* bed, for good. And in my life, Brontë. I want you in my life most of all. At my side."

She tugged her towel a little tighter around her naked body. Being in his bed was no problem. It was being in his life that she was struggling with. "I'm not ready yet, Logan. Please don't pressure me."

Brontë thought he would protest again, but to her surprise, he moved in and caressed her neck, lifting strands of wet hair off of her skin. "I'm disappointed, but I understand." He leaned in and kissed her lightly on the mouth. "The offer remains, of course. Accept it when you're ready."

She trembled at the sweetness of his touch and the understanding in his voice. "Thank you, Logan."

He kissed her again. "What are you doing today?"

"I work in an hour."

"Want me to clear your schedule?"

"No," she said with a smile. "I need to work, and Cooper could use the help today." Working, mindless as it was, helped keep her mind off of things like her personal life. "Maybe tonight."

He shook his head. "Tonight I'm busy."

"Oh?" That was . . . interesting. "Busy with what?"

"Meeting," he said abruptly. "I'll be free tomorrow night."

"All right," she told him. "I'll miss you tonight."

Logan gave her a curious look, and then leaned in and kissed her fiercely, as if he'd just come to some sort of bizarre realization. "I love you."

A bit surprised, she laughed at his expression. She almost blurted "I love you, too," but stopped herself. "What brought that on?"

The look he gave her was intense, making her laughter die in her throat. "I want you to come to my meeting tonight."

"You do? To a business meeting?"

"It's more of a meeting of . . . friends."

"Are you sure that's allowed?"

"It will be," he said, his smile surprisingly grim.

———————

Brontë was lost in thought as she walked the streets of SoHo, heading to Cooper's Cuppa. Gretchen hadn't been at the apartment that morning, and Brontë suspected that she had returned home late the night before and quietly left for work that morning without disturbing Brontë or her guest. It suited Brontë just fine. While they normally walked to work together, strolling by herself allowed her to clear her head and think a little.

Her night with Logan had been . . . intense. Magical. Wonderful. If she hadn't already been in love with him, she would be by now. But it was also a little troubling. He'd wanted her to move back in with him as if nothing had happened, and she was still mentally working through some of their issues.

When all was said and done, he was still a billionaire used to getting his way in everything, and she was still a waitress. Their massive power incompatibility worried her. Men like him didn't date waitresses. Men like him bought the establishment and *slept* with the waitresses, she thought wryly. That was her situation . . . and yet it wasn't. Logan had proved he wasn't what she'd expected, just as she wasn't what he'd expected, she supposed.

But she couldn't quite bring herself to fling it all away and return to being his live-in girlfriend. To have no other role in his life than being arm candy that was fun in bed.

She didn't know what to do. Logan had said the offer stood, but what if he didn't wait forever? What if he got tired of waiting for her to be comfortable with who he was and he moved on and forgot about her? Tears pricked at her eyes, and she swiped them away, pulling open the door to the coffee shop.

Gretchen was behind the counter already, her red hair pulled up in a messy knot, her glasses sliding down her nose. She looked up at Brontë's entrance and gave her a startled look. "You're here today?"

"Of course," Brontë said stiffly, heading to the back. "Why wouldn't I be?"

Gretchen stepped out from behind the counter, following Brontë to the office. "Oh, I don't know. Could it have something to do with the tall, dark, and rich guy who was over last night?"

"Why does everyone assume that just because Logan and I sleep together that I automatically decide to shirk all my duties?"

"'Cause that's what happened last time?" Gretchen asked playfully.

The words were meant as a tease, but it was too much for Brontë. She sniffed loudly and stared at her locker, willing herself not to cry.

It didn't work.

"Oh, jeez," Gretchen said, pulling one of the spare brown aprons off of a coat hook and handing it to her. "I didn't mean to upset you."

"It's okay," Brontë said, dabbing at her eyes with the apron and collapsing into a heap on a nearby stool. "I'm just all confused on the inside."

"You want to talk? I can get us a couple of coffees, and we can steal one of the booths in the back. It's kind of slow this morning."

Brontë nodded.

Five minutes later, they were settled into the smallest back booth of the coffee shop, hot mocha cappuccinos in hand. Cooper looked at them curiously from time to time, but he didn't pry, and Brontë was grateful.

"So," Gretchen said. "You had Mr. Moneypants over last night. It went badly, and that's why you're crying."

Brontë shook her head, grabbing a handful of napkins as she felt the confused tears welling up again. "It went great. It was beautiful. He told me he loved me."

Gretchen nodded thoughtfully. "And this is bad? Admission of love pre–blow job as incentive, then?"

She giggled, the sound a little choked with tears. "Post–blow job. And no, it's not bad. I just don't know what to do. I still have an apartment back in Kansas City. A life. Well, such as it is. But this morning, I got out of the shower, and Logan was packing my bags as if sleeping with him meant that I was automatically moving back in."

"That bastard," Gretchen said ironically. "How dare he want to spend all his time with you? Do you need me to talk to him and set him straight?"

She made a face at her friend. "I'm serious. My problem with Logan is that last time we did the exact same thing—we moved in together right away, and he just kind of took over my life."

"I see." Gretchen sipped her coffee thoughtfully. "Took over like how?"

"He bought me some clothes."

"That *bastard*."

"Shut up, Gretchen. I'm trying to tell you. He bought me clothes, and we went to a party and . . ." She frowned in thought. "I bought books for his library."

"Well," Gretchen said huffily. "What a douche bag. How dare he spend his billions on you?"

Brontë glared. "You're not helping."

"Of course I am," Gretchen said, matter-of-factly. "I'm making you realize how silly you're being."

Brontë continued to glare at Gretchen.

The redhead shrugged. "Look. He's got so much money he could roll in it. You, meanwhile, count the change in your wallet for a slice of pizza. Is it weird that he wants to shower you with presents and nice things? Maybe he likes buying them for you."

"He doesn't like gold diggers, Gretchen. Everyone always uses him for his money. I don't want to be like everyone else."

"Then don't be. Don't go running off buying a truckful of Birkin bags. Though if you do, remember your bestie, Gretchen, and her sister, Audrey." When Brontë glared at her again, Gretchen sighed. "Look. It doesn't sound like the problem is his money. It sounds like the problem is you."

"What?"

"As in, Logan doesn't need you. He likes you, he finds you fun, but he doesn't need you to survive. So you don't know what to do with yourself. That's a little unhealthy, don't you think?"

"That's not the case at all!"

"No? What did you do when you moved in with him?"

Brontë opened her mouth to protest, then snapped it shut again. "I shopped with Audrey, and then I sat around in his apartment."

"Gee, exciting. I'm amazed he let you get away the first time," Gretchen said drily.

"Oh, my God," Brontë said. "All this time I've been thinking I can't be with him because I can't be who he wants me to be. What if it's because I *am* the problem?"

"Well, you are a waitress," Gretchen said. "It's not as

if you can continue waitressing if you're living with a billionaire."

She was right, Brontë realized. Oh, God. Everything she was saying was right. Brontë was blaming Logan for being . . . Logan. Logan was who he was—a little alpha, take-charge, and always thinking ahead. And she'd been punishing him for being who he was instead of loving him for it.

She'd been the problem all along.

Her stomach gave a sick little lurch. "I don't know what to do, Gretchen. If I move in with him again, I worry that I'm going to turn into one of those women he hates. Sitting around all day spending money and doing nothing."

"That won't happen. You're smart. You're constantly spouting ancient wisdom and writing little sayings on customers' cups. They love that. Do something with that big philosophizing brain of yours instead of serving coffee."

Brontë stared down at her cappuccino. "I really wanted to do something with my philosophy degree, you know. Show the world just how wise and intelligent they were in classical times. Make others love the ancients just as much as I do."

"Then maybe you should go back to school. Teach. Or write books about ancient philosophers. I know a great editor or two. Or you could set up charity foundations with all of your boyfriend's ridiculous money that he wants you to spend." Gretchen leaned over and clasped Brontë's hand. "My point is that the money's not a problem. It's not an obstacle if you don't make it one. If he wants to shower you with money, use it and really make something of yourself, Brontë. Be who you want to be, not just a Midwestern waitress with big dreams. Understand? You can always pay him back."

Strange how a friend telling her to make something of herself came across far more gently than when Logan had. Brontë smiled at Gretchen. "So if you were me, you'd move back in with him?"

"Hell, no," Gretchen said. "If I were you, I'd have killed him in a week. But you're wimpy. You're great with him."

Brontë stuck her tongue out at Gretchen.

The redhead grinned, and gave Brontë's hand another squeeze. "If he makes you happy, don't set up obstacles that don't have to be there. Love is more important than anything else in the world. Well, almost, but you've got the money thing taken care of already. I'd kill to have a man look at me the way Logan looks at you."

"Cooper looks at you that way, Gretchen," Brontë said carefully.

The look of chagrin on Gretchen's face was terrible to see. "I keep hoping he'll grow out of it," she said quietly. "I like Cooper, but he's not the right guy for me. He's so . . . normal. Bland. I need someone different." She smiled at Brontë, and her smile was sad. "I'm a bit of a hopeless romantic, you know. Holding out for a hero and all that."

Brontë nodded and squeezed Gretchen's hand back. "You'll find the right guy. I'm sure he's out there somewhere."

"He might be, or he might just be fictional. Or broke. Or both." Gretchen gave her a teasing laugh. "It'd help if he was half as rich as your boyfriend, though."

For the first time in years, Logan felt an emotion that had become foreign to him.

He was nervous.

Tonight was going to be a clusterfuck. It was one of the brotherhood meetings. They had a strict rule that no additional parties were allowed. No siblings. No buddies. No parents. No business partners. Just the original six. No one had ever thought of breaking the rules, because it would have been unfair to the others in the group.

And here Logan was, their leader, about to bring the woman he loved to a meeting and explain to her that he was part of a secret society of billionaires. The tattoo on his arm? A badge of membership. His success? Interlocked with that of his brothers.

He hoped she'd understand. He knew there couldn't be any more secrets between them, not if he wanted to keep her. And he was laying it all on the line, betting everything he had, because he needed her to realize just how much he loved and trusted her. And how different she was from everyone else.

The others would be furious. They wouldn't understand. None of them were married or even had steady girlfriends, though Reese had a steady stream of women. But Logan had to do this.

He couldn't risk losing Brontë forever. So he'd show her everything . . . and hope she wouldn't be put off by the nondisclosure agreement she'd have to sign. Danica had balked at the prenup and shown her true colors. What would Brontë do?

Was he going to lose everything just by trying to include her in his life? He hoped not.

———

Brontë studied her closet. She had no idea what to wear to this mystery meeting. Meeting implied business, but Logan said it was friends. She studied the clothes hanging in the small closet. Go casual? Or dress up in anticipation of something fussy? She couldn't decide. Tonight felt important for some reason, though she had no idea why.

Her mind was still on this morning's conversation with Gretchen. Logan had offered himself just as he was, and she had been the one with the problem. It was a bit humbling. There was nothing wrong with being a waitress, of course. She liked her job and liked working with people. But she couldn't be a waitress and be with Logan. The two were completely incompatible. Waitressing was hard work with odd hours. She didn't want to be too tired to see him—or too busy. And it didn't make sense for her to bust her butt for tips when he had money.

She had to choose.

And she was going to pick the gorgeous man she was in love with, of course. It was just a matter of admitting it to herself.

She decided on a simple black sweater and dark gray skirt with heels. Dressy enough that she could pass for formal, but it wouldn't look out of place if the evening was casual. She smoothed her hair, applied a bit of makeup, and waited for Logan to arrive, her stomach fluttering with nervousness.

She had a feeling tonight was going to change everything in their relationship.

———

The dark sedan had shown up for their date, and Brontë didn't even blink when the driver got out to open the doors. She would just have to get used to that sort of thing in the future, she told herself.

Logan got out of the car and kissed her lightly, then held the door open for her to get in. Brontë smiled at the driver as she entered, then slid over to make room for Logan. When he was seated next to her, she asked, "Is what I'm wearing all right?"

"It's fine," he told her, seemingly distracted, but he reached for her hand. With a nod to the driver, the car pulled away from the curb, and they began to head back toward midtown.

Brontë watched the buildings that passed, noting streets and trying to determine where exactly they were going. Where was this meeting being held? To her surprise, they pulled up in front of a small bar.

She gave Logan a curious look, but followed him out of the car and onto the street.

He put his hand on the small of her back and guided

her forward. Inside, the bar was quiet, only a few patrons seated at wooden tables. It looked very . . . ordinary. A hockey game was playing on a TV set in the corner, and no one was paying a bit of attention to them.

"Is this where the meeting is?"

"I'll explain everything later. I promise."

Curious, she let him lead her to one of the back doors. A dark, narrow hallway was lit by a single unadorned lightbulb, and at the far end stood a large hulking man next to a door.

Logan stepped in front of her and headed toward the man, and unease grew in her stomach. This . . . wasn't normal. Was this some kind of under-the-table business deal? Something illegal? Oh, God. Was Logan into trafficking? The drug trade? Her stomach twisted with anxiety. Surely not. She'd never expected such a thing from Logan, but what were they doing down here in this dingy hallway for a business meeting? She didn't understand.

The man eyed them with a cold expression, saying nothing, and Brontë resisted the urge to step behind Logan and let him shield her.

Logan lifted his hand and placed two fingers over his heart, then moved it up to his shoulder, and slid them down his sleeve. A very specific gesture. The man nodded as if satisfied, and his glare fixed on Brontë.

"She's with me," Logan told him.

The man's eyebrows went up, but he simply nodded and gestured at the door. "The others are inside."

This was clearly some sort of secret meeting. Her stomach clenched again. Surely Logan wasn't in the Mafia, was he?

Then again, this was New York City.

Logan pushed the door open and then gestured for Brontë to enter.

She did, stepping down a narrow line of cement stairs into . . . a basement. A very well lit basement. Cigar smoke hung in the air, and she could hear the murmur of conversation that abruptly stilled as she descended the last stair and came into the others' view.

A poker table sat in the center of the room. A drink table at the far end. Chips were scattered about, along with half-full glasses and ashtrays. Around the table sat five men, all scowling at the sight of her.

And . . . she recognized four of them. Jonathan, who'd been their helicopter rescuer—and who was as fabulously wealthy as Logan—sat on the far end of the table, a cigar held between his teeth. Cade sat in the middle, his expression more welcoming than the others, but equally perplexed. To his right she recognized Reese, whom she'd met only briefly. And Griffin. And there was one man with his back to her, only part of his face visible.

Reese threw down his cigar and cards, getting to his feet. "What the hell is this, Logan?"

Logan adjusted the cuff links of his jacket as if nothing were amiss. "This is Brontë. My girlfriend."

"You can't bring your girlfriend to—" Griffin abruptly stopped short, as if realizing what he was about to say.

Brontë's heart sank. They were all wealthy. All wealthy and conducting secret meetings together? It could only be one thing. She turned to Logan, and tears shimmered in her eyes. She didn't know whether she was hurt or terrified. "Why didn't you tell me you were with the Mafia?"

"The Mafia?"

Loud bursts of laughter rocked the table behind her, and Brontë turned, confused, then looked back at Logan. "I don't understand."

"I'm not with the Mafia, love," he said patiently. "But I do need you to understand this if we're going to make a life together. These men are my . . . friends."

"Logan," Jonathan said in a warning voice. "Don't you dare."

Logan ignored him, his gaze on Brontë. He took her

hand in his. "They've been my friends since college. We were in the same fraternity together. We made a pledge to assist each other in business and remain friends for life." He studied her face. "Do you understand what I'm saying?"

"God fucking damn it," Reese said.

"Leave him alone," another gruff voice said. It was the man Brontë didn't know. "He has to have his reasons."

Brontë's head swirled with what he was telling her. He was watching her and it seemed to be important, but she didn't understand. "You're college friends? But why the basement? Why—"

She stopped when he put his hand on his biceps, over the tattoo. Two fingers. A two-dollar bill. It had seemed so odd to her that someone like Logan would have such a bizarre tattoo. It made sense now, though. She gasped. "A secret society."

"A brotherhood," Logan agreed. "We help each other out, no matter what."

"Hey, I can write down my social security number and my PIN if we're giving her all of our information," Reese said sarcastically.

But Logan's gaze was serious as he stared down at her. "Do you understand?"

She thought for a moment, then took her clutch purse and whacked Logan on the arm with it. "You scared the shit out of me. I thought you were in the Mafia for a second."

"This is just as secret, Brontë. If word got out that we had business dealings together, people would be crawling all over us. Feds, auditors, you name it. This is a secret. Our secret." After a long, serious moment, he added, "And I'm trusting you with it. I love you."

Brontë gazed up at Logan, shocked. This . . . this was a big secret. He was trusting her with everything. Giving her everything that he was.

He wanted—needed—her in his life that badly?

She realized then that Danica had been wrong about Logan. He didn't treat everything like business. He'd come down into this basement knowing full well that his friends—and business partners, it seemed—would be utterly furious with him. He was risking everything.

For her.

"I love you, too," she told him with a catch in her throat. "But I think your friends are going to kill you."

A grin lit his face, and he pulled her close. "They'll get over it." He kissed her—long, hard, and fierce. So fiercely that her knees went weak, and she sagged against him.

Behind them, someone cleared his throat. "This is really quite moving," Griffin said in a cultured voice. "But you seem to forget the implications for the rest of us. *We're* not in love with her."

She turned to look at them, unhappy that this moment of trust was going to cost Logan so much. "You're all such close friends—I don't want this to be a problem."

"Too late," Jonathan said flatly.

Brontë looked at Logan. "Is there something I can sign that would prove it? That I can stay quiet? That you can trust me?"

"A nondisclosure agreement?" Logan asked.

"Yes, that's it," she said with a nod, glancing back at the table. "Would a nondisclosure agreement work?"

"It depends," Reese said. "Exactly how many other women are we going to be dragging in here and sharing all our secrets with?"

"Only this one," Logan said, grinning. "I'm not in love with anyone else."

A warm feeling swept through her, and she couldn't stop smiling.

"Oh, jeez," Reese said. "They're so cute together I want to puke."

"Be nice," Cade said. "I'm happy for you both, Logan

and Brontë. Come have a seat. We'll get things worked out as we play."

Logan moved to the table and pulled out his chair for Brontë, motioning for her to sit down. She did, pretending she didn't see the wary looks on the men's faces. While Logan had invited her in for the evening, it was clear that she still wasn't exactly "invited" in their eyes. "Get an extra chair," Logan said.

"There are no extra chairs," Griffin pointed out succinctly. "There's never anyone else down here but us."

"We need to get another chair for in the future, then," Logan said.

It got very quiet. Cade began to push some chips toward her, but Brontë shook her head. "I don't know how to play poker," she lied, sensing that her playing would push a few of the men past their comfort zone. "And I don't think I'll be coming back." She smiled at Logan reassuringly. "Just because we're a couple doesn't mean we have to be together every moment. This is your time with your friends."

"Marry this one," Reese proclaimed, picking up his cigar again.

"I plan on it," Logan said.

Brontë blushed, getting up from the chair so Logan could sit down. Was that just more guy talk? It was far too early to be thinking about marriage. But their banter and her backing off from the table had the desired effect. She immediately sensed a bit of the tension easing off the table and knew she'd made the right decision. These were Logan's friends, and Logan's club. He was welcome to it, and she wouldn't share the secret.

As if he could tell what she was thinking, Logan sat down in the chair and dragged her into his lap. Two drinks were set in front of them—whiskey or brandy from the looks of it.

"Drink up," Jonathan said.

They did, and Brontë coughed at the burning taste of

the drink, which made the men laugh. Her face flushed with embarrassment, but Logan only pulled her closer, settling her on his lap. "This meeting of the brotherhood is called into session," he said, grinning up at her.

———————

As the evening wore on, drinks, cards—and business advice—flew freely around the table. Brontë lost track of most of the conversation due to the drinks that the men kept sending her way—deliberately, she suspected, to distract her. That was fine. She ended up spending half the night discussing the exaggerations of the account of Atlantis in Plato's *Timaeus*. Griffin was funding an archaeological dig in Spain for a theoretical site near Cadiz, and they chatted about it while the men played cards. It seemed that while Plato thought Atlantis was an island in the ocean, recent theory was that Atlantis was on the Spanish coast, and it intrigued him to investigate it. He even offered to take her and Logan to see the site sometime, which made her brighten and Logan scowl.

"Quit flirting with my woman, Griffin."

"I'm not flirting with her, you Neanderthal. We can discuss mutual interests without it being flirting," Griffin said, but he winked at her as if sharing a joke.

Logan snorted. "I'd believe it if I thought that talking archaeology didn't give you a hard-on."

Griffin just shook his head, but Brontë noticed he didn't meet her gaze again, which told her that Logan had hit pretty close to the mark.

At some point, Logan kissed her ear and stood up, sliding her out of his lap. "I'm heading upstairs to chat with Reese and Jonathan, love. We'll be back in a moment."

"All right," she said, clutching her newly refilled glass to her breast, her head buzzing. "Don't take too long."

"I won't. We're just going to discuss . . . your nondisclosure agreement."

She nodded, her brain fuzzy, and sat back down in Logan's chair.

Cade frowned as the three men left and then stood himself. "I'd better go and see what they're up to."

He left, and Griffin followed him out. That left Brontë holding her glass and the man seated next to her, who had been quiet all night. He'd been careful not to look over at her, and she was curious about him.

Hunter. Did he not like her? Brontë frowned and took another swig of her whiskey, watching him over the rim of her snifter.

"Your friend," Hunter said after a long moment. His voice was deep and gravelly. He spoke as if the words were a chore. He was an odd man. "The redhead. Tell me about her."

"You mean Gretchen?"

"Gretchen." He repeated the name, as if tasting it. "What is her last name?"

"Why? How do you know about Gretchen?"

"I saw her with you the other day. Tell me more about Gretchen."

Brontë frowned, her thoughts slow and diffuse from alcohol. Something about giving her friend's information to a stranger seemed . . . not right, but she was having a hard time reasoning as to why. "Why should I tell you about Gretchen? So you can stalk her?"

Hunter stared down at his cards, and she realized he was carefully hiding one hand behind the other. Interesting.

"I am an admirer of hers . . . from afar."

"Like a stalker," Brontë repeated drunkenly.

"Not a stalker. I simply wish to know more about her."

"That's what a stalker would say," she pointed out, taking another sip of her drink.

He ground his teeth and glared over at her. Brontë got her first good look at his face . . . and she suddenly understood why he'd been so careful to turn away from her, and why he hid his hand. Thick white scars stood out in relief against his tanned skin. They crossed his face in an irregular, scattered pattern that indicated massive trauma. One corner of his eye was tilted down, as if the repairs had altered its shape, and the side of his mouth had a jagged white line curving from it—a seam that had been torn open and repaired. Even the hand he'd covered showed the white, gouging lines of scarring.

It was not a pretty sight. Not in the slightest. Brontë swallowed hard, her stomach churning from the alcohol.

"Your friend is quite safe from my romantic interests," Hunter gritted out. "I simply wish to learn more about her."

"Oh," Brontë said, forcing herself to turn away from the hideous webbing of scars. She stared down at her glass, which seemed a little too empty at the moment. "Petty," she said. "Her last name is Petty. She writes books."

"What kinds of books?"

"Books with other people's names on them."

His gaze seemed to pin her to Logan's chair, and she wished she had a bit more to drink. "A ghostwriter?"

Brontë nodded, then stopped because it made the room wobble. "That's right. And Cooper's in love with her."

"Cooper?" He rasped the word out harshly.

"It's okay, though. He won't make a move. He knows Gretchen isn't interested in him that way. She wants adventure or a fairy tale or something."

The scarred man snorted and lifted his own drink, and Brontë peeked over at him. Nope, the scars didn't look any better on the second glance.

"Is Logan coming back?" she asked, feeling a little faint. "I think I'm going to be sick."

Hunter smiled grimly over at her. "Depends on whether Jonathan and Reese have given him a few black eyes yet."

She stared at him in surprise, then bolted to her feet. The room shifted woozily, and she grasped at the chair. "But . . . they . . . I don't want them to hurt Logan! I said I'd sign the nondisclosure agreement."

"The agreement takes care of the future. Fists take care of right now," Hunter said. "Sit down before you hurt yourself."

Brontë flopped back to her seat, holding her stomach. Suddenly, being drunk in a dark, smoky room didn't seem like such a good idea. "I need a drink of water, I think. And Logan. I want Logan."

Hunter set a tumbler in front of her and filled it with water. When she reached for it, he laid a hand over it, blocking her. "Tell me more about Gretchen."

Brontë glared at him and brushed his hand aside. She took the glass anyhow and started sipping it. When her stomach stopped doing flips, she began, "Well, she has a cat . . ."

FOURTEEN

⌒

When Brontë woke up the next morning, her head was pounding and her mouth felt like a dirty, old sock. She groaned, rolling over in the bed and smacking into Logan's broad chest.

His arms went around her, and he pulled her close, nuzzling her ear. "Morning."

Even that small word made her head hurt insanely. She groaned and closed her eyes, pressing the heel of her palm to her forehead. "I hurt."

"Do you need aspirin?"

Just the thought of dry, medicinal-tasting aspirin sticking to the roof of her mouth made her want to vomit. "Dry toast, please?"

He kissed her cheek. "Coming right up."

The bed shifted as he climbed out of it, and Brontë spent the next five minutes trying not to throw up from the quaking that small movement had produced. There was something not quite . . . normal about where she lay. There was a roaring in her ears.

God, had she ever been so drunk in her life?

She had vague memories of a smoky room and a man with scars, and lots of poker chips being passed back and forth. That was it, really.

Logan returned, his hand smoothing the messy hair off of her brow. "You okay?"

She forced herself to sit up in bed slowly, her eyes squeezed into slits, and she reached for the glass of water he put in her hand and began to drink. After a moment, she said, "My head's so fuzzy, it feels like the ground is moving."

"Huh."

Logan's innocent syllable made her frown. Unfortunately, the bright light in the room was killing her, so she couldn't glare at him. She lay back down in the bed and reached for a pillow to pull over her head, ignoring Logan's chuckle of amusement. The bed shook again, and her stomach gurgled in response.

That shaking . . . was not her imagination.

Brontë's eyes flew open as the jet's thrusters started roaring. Pressure made her ears pop and pushed her down on the bed, and she tried to struggle to her elbows. "Are we . . . are we flying?"

"Don't get up," Logan said, pressing a hand to her shoulder. "Lie down and relax. You're hungover."

Her gaze moved to his face, and she gasped. Her handsome, contained, so-in-control billionaire boyfriend had a hell of a shiner. A dark purplish-green ring lined his eye, and it was puffy and swollen.

"Your face!"

He grinned and touched his fingers just below his eye, wincing. "Yeah. The guys and I had a little talk. When we land, the nondisclosure agreement will be waiting at my office for you to sign. The others insist."

"That's fine," Brontë said, eyeing him for other bruises. "Whatever gets them off your back."

"I'm sorry if you feel I'm pushing you into it," he told her in a guarded voice. "I know you're probably not happy about it."

She shrugged, holding the pillow close to her throbbing head. "I actually don't care," she told him, closing her eyes and trying to relax to ease her throbbing head. "It's not a big deal. I wouldn't go telling all your secrets anyhow, but if the paperwork makes them feel better . . ." When he said nothing, she opened one eye. "Why?"

Logan shook his head, staring down at her. "I just . . . I guess I expected you to be upset." A smile curved his mouth again, and he leaned down to lightly kiss her brow. "This is why I love you, Brontë."

Because she wasn't like Danica? She snorted, and that tiny move made her head hurt all over again.

"Rest, love," Logan told her, brushing a hand over her cheek and pulling the covers back up around her chest. "You have a few hours before we land."

"Where are we going?" she asked sleepily.

"It's a surprise. One I think you'll enjoy."

———

It was a surprise, all right. Hours later, after she'd taken aspirin for her hangover, Brontë stared in surprise at the small airport where they'd just landed. It looked . . . familiar. She looked up at Logan questioningly.

"Come on. We'll miss the ferry to Seaturtle Cay if we don't hurry."

"We're going back to the resort?" She wobbled behind him a few steps as he began to head down the tarmac briskly. "I don't understand. Isn't it wrecked? How can it be open for business?"

"It's not open," he told her. "But not all the rooms are destroyed, and I thought you wouldn't mind having another look at the place when a hurricane isn't bearing down on you."

Brontë was silent as they took the ferry out to Seaturtle Island, then drove out to the resort. The downed trees had been cleaned up and the power lines restored, she noticed as they drove. When they pulled up to the main resort, the sounds of drills and power saws greeted her, and she looked at the hotel in surprise. Large swaths of the entire eastern wing of the resort were covered in construction plastic. There was no broken glass littering the lobby any longer—everything had been cleaned up and repaired. Trees had been righted, or replanted, and the entire place seemed different from when she'd last seen it.

Brontë passed by the gift shop and noticed a floral beach dress, very similar to the one she'd salvaged from the place when they'd been stranded, hanging on the mannequin. The diamond necklace was still there, which made her smile ironically at the sight. To think she'd been worried about Logan taking it because he wouldn't be able to afford it. How he must have laughed at her concern. She shook her head and tucked her hand into the crook of his arm, and felt warm when he automatically placed his hand over hers.

They entered the hotel, and a curly-haired man with a swarthy tan and wearing a suit appeared, extending his hand for Logan to shake. "Mr. Hawkings. It is a pleasure to see you here."

"Mr. Douglas," Logan said. "Things look like they are proceeding well."

"Indeed they are. Repairs have continued around the clock, and once the upgrades are decided upon, we can continue with the renovations." Mr. Douglas smiled at Brontë. "This must be Miss Dawson."

Brontë extended her hand politely, smiling at the manager. "Pleasure to meet you."

"Miss Dawson is tired from our trip," Logan said in a crisp voice. "Is our room ready?"

"It is," Mr. Douglas exclaimed with a bright smile.

"Everything that you have asked for is ready and waiting."

Both men paused for a moment, and then Logan looked down at her. "Love, I need to meet with Mr. Douglas to discuss some things. Would you like to go up and check out our suite? Let me know if there's something that's not to your liking."

She nodded absently. It felt like Logan was trying to get rid of her at the moment, but the need for a shower outweighed everything else at the moment. "What floor are we on?"

"I will have someone show you the way, Miss Dawson." The manager turned and waved over a tall, willowy woman. "Luz, please escort Miss Dawson to Mr. Hawkings's personal suite."

"Right away," Luz said, smiling at Brontë. "Please follow me."

Logan kissed her temple and whispered in her ear, "I'll be up shortly."

She nodded and pulled away from him, following Luz across the lobby. Brontë paused when Luz stopped in front of an all-too-familiar elevator. "Can we take the stairs?"

Luz seemed surprised at her request. "It is twenty floors up. Are you sure you wish to take the stairs?"

Brontë grinned. "Oh, I'm sure. Very sure."

"Very well," Luz said, leading her farther down the west wing. At the end of a long hallway, they opened the door to the stairwell. It was well lit and there wasn't a single mattress in sight, which was almost disappointing. Brontë thought of the long nights she'd spent there, curled up with Logan. Funny how at the time she'd been wondering what he was thinking about her.

Funny how she was back to square one in that aspect.

Since she'd been living in Gretchen's fourth-floor walk-up for the past two weeks, the flights of stairs were not so bad, and she handled them better than poor Luz. They paused repeatedly between sets of stairs, and it took longer than anticipated to get up to the top floor. But she was in no hurry to step back into that elevator, so she didn't mind.

When they finally got to the twentieth floor, Brontë noticed the hall had been recently recarpeted, and art hung on the walls. New art? she wondered. The smell of paint was still strong, the walls crisp and fresh with color. Had they remodeled this portion of the building first, knowing that Logan would be stopping by for a visit?

And was there anywhere in the world that Logan Hawkings's every whim was not catered to? She smiled wryly at the thought.

Luz moved to the door and tapped in a code on the keypad. "There are no keys for this room, Miss Dawson. You simply need to use the access code. It is five-five-four-three." She opened the door and gestured for Brontë to enter. "Please call down and let me know if there is anything else I can do for you during your stay."

"I will," Brontë said. "Thank you, Luz."

The other woman nodded and left, and Brontë stepped into the suite with a dumbfounded look on her face. She'd been expecting the room to be posh, but once again she was surprised at the wealth and luxury that Logan enjoyed.

The room was palatial. Slow-moving fans lazily whirled overhead from the high-beamed loft ceiling. A breeze ruffled white curtains on the balcony. The room was full of sweet-smelling flowers, vases artfully perched on end tables and countertops. Those were the only splashes of color—everything else was stark, brilliant white—from the fluffy bedspread to the artful netting hanging over the bed to the thick carpet beneath her feet. There were even white couches in the "living room" area, offset by dark teakwood furniture accompanying it.

It was lovely and cool and tropical, and she immediately felt relaxed at the sight. How beautiful. Brontë moved to the small kitchen area, looking for bottled water to soothe her dry throat. She laughed when she opened the mini fridge and saw it was full of M&M's. Logan truly seemed to recall every small thing she'd ever mentioned, and the thought made her feel warm inside.

The bed was gorgeous, but Brontë wanted to wash up first. She groaned with pleasure at the sight of the shower. It was made entirely from stone instead of tile and the showerhead was a built-in waterfall, meant to mimic a tropical paradise. It was also heaven on her skin, and she took a long, exceedingly hot shower, enjoying every minute of luxury. Then she curled up in one of the fluffy white robes left for her and headed to the bed, intending to try it out only for a moment.

She woke up hours later, when Logan's heavy weight sagged on the bed next to her. She smiled as he pulled her close and turned her face up for his kiss.

His mouth lightly touched hers. "Do you like the room?"

"It's gorgeous," she said with a small sigh. "I could stay here forever."

His lips continued to move along her jawline. "How about a week? I have some business to attend to while we're here and need to stay until next Saturday."

Brontë sat up, pushing him away. "How about you ask before dragging me onto your jet?"

"I did ask," he said, his stern lips quirking with amusement. "If I recall, you told me that you loved the idea. And then you fell over and began to snore."

She scowled at him. "How about asking me when I'm *sober*? I'm supposed to work for the next week."

"Gretchen says they will be fine without you."

"You talked to Gretchen?"

"She packed a bag for you. Don't you remember?"

Brontë blinked, trying to recall. Nope, the night before was still a whiskey-filled blur. "I'm sure it'll come back to me."

"I'm sure," Logan said, kissing her neck. He sounded amused.

Her hands went to his thick hair, and she ran her nails over his scalp, sighing with pleasure when he licked at the sensitive dip in her throat. "Logan, I want to talk to you."

His teeth grazed her collarbone. "Talk, love. I'm listening."

"You're being very distracting."

"I've only started to be distracting," he told her in a husky voice. His hand slipped inside her robe and cupped her bare breast, thumb playing over her nipple.

Heat and longing shot through her body, and she moaned, her hips moving reflexively. "That's not fair," she gasped, her words rising an octave when he continued to circle her nipple with the pad of his thumb, making the sensitive peak stiff. "I'm trying to have a serious conversation with you."

"I'm very serious right now," Logan told her, tugging open the belt of her robe and exposing her breasts. His head moved down, and he kissed the other nipple. "I've wanted to touch you all day, and I'm very serious about getting to do so right now."

"Logan," she breathed, her fingers gripping his hair tightly. "I wanted to talk about you and me."

His teeth gently bit her nipple. "How good we are together?"

She moaned as he raked his teeth lightly over her nipple again, then tongued the sensitive flesh. "I've been thinking . . ."

Grinding to a screeching halt, Logan jerked up, his gaze meeting hers. Those warm, delicious eyes were now staring back at her warily, and his voice was cold. "What were you thinking?"

Oh. Brontë felt a twinge of shame at his immediate wariness. His reaction was so strong as a result of her constant running away. He was expecting her to bail on him again. She reached up and stroked his strong, tense jaw. "I was thinking that . . . I've been unfair to you."

He stared down at her, no emotion showing. Those hard eyes glittered. "You have been unfair . . . to me? Explain."

"Yes," she said, and skimmed her thumb over his lower lip. It was really unfair that he was so sensual and masculine. "Whenever things got a little frightening for me, I ran away. I should have stayed and talked to you. And . . . I'm sorry. I want this to work between us. I want you. I want to be with you."

Logan's cold expression finally cracked. He exhaled loudly, and then buried his face against her.

"Logan?" She touched his hair.

"I thought you were going to leave me again." The relief in his voice was evident, and he began to press kisses on her stomach. "You scared the shit out of me."

"Sorry," she said, the nervous giggle escaping her throat. Damn stupid giggle. "I'm . . . I won't run again. Not without talking to you first. I just . . . it's hard to know where I fit in your world when I've always had trouble even fitting into my own."

"I know where you fit," Logan said, sitting up suddenly. He pressed a fist to his heart. "Right here, Brontë."

Sudden tears pricked her eyes. "I love you, Logan."

"I love you, too," he told her, leaning down and kissing her mouth lightly. "And I want you to be comfortable with me. If something bothers you, tell me so I can fix it or change it."

"I think it's me more than you, Logan. I thought that if I came to you and did nothing but sit around your house, I'd turn into one of those women that you hate. I'd do nothing but spend your money on shoes and purses all day long, like Danica."

"It wasn't that Danica spent my money, love. If you dedicated your life to shopping, you wouldn't be able to spend all my money. It was that she valued the money more than she valued our relationship. You've never been like that. You never will be. It's not in your nature." He picked up her hand and kissed the palm of it tenderly. "That's one reason why I fell for you so hard."

"I might spend some of your money," Brontë blurted, waiting for him to react. But he didn't; he only continued to smile at her. "I've realized that I was resenting you for my being a waitress, which is stupid. It isn't your fault I picked a major that wouldn't get me anywhere except waiting tables. It wasn't that you wanted me to make something of myself. It's that I wasn't happy with who I was. That doesn't change with or without money, really. But Gretchen woke me up, and I realized that only I can make myself satisfied with my career path. All I know is I that being without you made me unhappy even when I was waiting tables again. So . . ." She breathed deep and blurted, "I want to go back to college and get a graduate degree. Or start a charity to donate books to schools and retirement homes like Gretchen does, but on a bigger scale. Or do both. Or all of it. I'm not sure. But I want to do something with myself. I'll get bored sitting around your apartment all day."

A smile curved his hard mouth. "Love, I want you to do whatever makes you happy. And if going back to school helps you—or starting a charity—then we'll do both. As long as we do it together."

"Together." She blinked rapidly, overcome. "I'm sorry I've made this so difficult. I—"

"Shhh," he told her. "You didn't. You were just frightened, and I tend to be overbearing and controlling. It's part of my nature."

"It is," she agreed with a small smile. "You're used to handling the situation. But a girl likes to be asked every now and then."

"I promise to ask more," he said, and his eyes grew serious again. He reached into the inner pocket of his jacket and produced a small box. Logan held it out to her. "Starting now."

She sucked in a breath, staring at the small, dark blue box. Her fingers trembled as she reached for it, and slowly snapped the case open.

An oval diamond the size of a pebble was set into a thick gold band. She stared at the ring in surprise, then at Logan.

"I picked the inscription for you," he said, his voice a little gruff. "Do you like it?"

"Inscription?" She pulled the ring out of the box and peered at the inside of the band, turning the ring to read the tiny lettering printed there. " 'Every heart hears a song, incomplete, until another heart whispers back.' " Her eyes filled with the tears she'd been unable to hold back. "It's beautiful. Ovid?"

"Plato, actually," he told her with a grin. A laugh escaped her, wild and free. Plato. Of course it was. How very perfect.

"You're my heart, Brontë. I know it feels like such a short time together, but I want to wake up every day with you at my side and in my life." He took the ring from her trembling fingers and held it out to her. "Will you marry me?"

"Of course I will," she said, throwing her arms around his neck. "I love you so much."

"I love you, too," Logan told her. "Waitress, philosopher, or charitable organizer, I'll love you all the same as long as you'll be mine."

Slipping the ring on her finger, she kissed him with all the love in her heart.

EPILOGUE

It didn't take long for Brontë to decide what she wanted to do with her life. Gretchen's book-donation charity had inspired her, and after signing up for continuing education classes at NYU, she worked with Logan's financial advisors to set up a charity. Philosophy Reads was soon born, complete with a fancy website and nonprofit status. Her goal? To bring her love of reading and knowledge to those who couldn't afford it or couldn't get out. Brontë selected two books—one classic and one modern—and then purchased hundreds of copies. These she had delivered to local libraries, retirement homes, and hospitals, and she set up weekly meetings for people to meet and discuss them.

She nearly danced with delight when her first meeting—at the retirement home where Gretchen had dropped off books before—had an attendance of nearly fifty people, all of them brimming with enthusiasm to discuss that month's reads, *The Iliad* and *Harry Potter and the Sorcerer's Stone*. She wanted to eventually introduce them to heavier reads, but she'd start them out slow. The discussions were a success in some venues, and in others, not as much—she had a few that were sparsely attended. But it was a work in progress, and she was determined to fine-tune her charity and turn it into a well-oiled machine that would help bring the joy of reading to those who might otherwise overlook it.

That part of her life had become incredibly satisfying—almost as much as living with Logan. As soon as she'd moved back in, she'd quietly begun to refill his library with new reads—some classics, which Logan read out a sense of obligation to her, but when she caught him quietly reading a Tom Clancy paperback, she also added men's action thrillers to his section and even read some of them herself so they could discuss the books over dinner.

Logan was proud of her charity, and never objected to the amount of money she spent. At night they twined around each other, locked in bliss.

She'd signed the nondisclosure agreement without a word of complaint and had offered to sign a prenup. Logan turned down her offer vehemently and then spent the evening kissing her back into submission. The fact that she was willing, he told her, was more than enough for him.

Life was just about perfect for Brontë, and she grew to love Logan more each day. Every morning, she woke up eager for what the day would bring and excited about how much she enjoyed being with Logan. And every day she held her engagement ring—that big, audacious diamond she would have run from a few months prior—and read the heart-melting inscription to herself again.

Every heart sings a song, incomplete, until another heart whispers back.

And Brontë's heart was complete now that Logan's was whispering back.

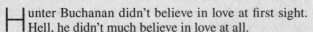

Hunter Buchanan didn't believe in love at first sight. Hell, he didn't much believe in love at all.

But the moment he'd seen the tall redhead standing in the foyer of one of his empty houses, a box of books in her arms and a skeptical look on her face, he'd felt . . . something. She'd been bold and fearless with her words, something that attracted him as a man who clung to the shadows.

And when she'd admitted to her quiet friend that most men bored her and she wanted something different in a relationship than just a pretty face?

Hunter knew she was meant for him.

She was pretty, young, and single. She had a smart mind and a sharp tongue. He liked that about her. She was unafraid and laughed easily. Days had passed since he'd glimpsed her and he still couldn't get her out of his mind. She haunted his dreams.

Hunter was smart as well, and rich, and only a few years older than her. It shouldn't have been unattainable.

Unconsciously, he touched the deeply gouged scars on his face, fingers tracing the thick line of the scar at the corner of his mouth where damaged tissue had been reconstructed.

There was one thing preventing Hunter from pursuing a woman like that. His face. His hideous, scarred face. He could hide the scars on his chest and arm with clothing. He could clench his hand and no one would notice that he was missing a finger. But he couldn't hide his face. When he chose to leave his house, people crossed the street to avoid him. Men frowned as if there were something unnerving about him. Women flinched away from the sight of it.

Just like the woman next to him currently was doing.

Brontë, Logan's big-eyed girlfriend, sat next to him at the Brotherhood's poker table. The dark basement was filled with a haze of cigar smoke and the scent of liquor. Normally the room was filled with his five best friends, but they'd gone upstairs to 'talk' to Logan about the fact that he'd brought his new girlfriend with him to a secret society meeting. Brontë had stayed behind . . . with him. It was clearly not by her choice, either. She sat at the table quietly, nursing her wineglass and trying not to look as if she'd wanted to bolt from the table once she'd gotten a good look at his face. Her gaze slid to his damaged hand, and then back to his face again.

He was used to that sort of thing. And he wondered if the redhead who was her friend would react the same way to his face.

Experience told him that she would. But he remembered the redhead's sarcastic little smile and that shake of her head. The words she'd said.

"Save me from rich, attractive alpha males. They think they're the heroes from a fairy tale. Little do they know, they're more like the villains."

And he found he had to know more.

"Your friend," he said to Brontë. "The redhead. Tell me about her."

She looked over at him again, those dark eyes wide and surprised, pupils dilated from alcohol. "You mean Gretchen?"

"Yes." He knew her first name, but he wanted to know more about her. "What is her last name?"

"Why? How do you know about Gretchen?"

"I saw her with you the other day. Tell me more about Gretchen."

She frowned at him. "Why should I tell you about Gretchen? So you can stalk her?"

Hunter glanced down at his cards and tried not to suppress the annoyance he felt at her caginess. Couldn't a man ask a simple question? "I am an admirer of hers . . . from afar."

"Like a stalker."

"Not a stalker. I simply wish to know more about her."

"That's what a stalker would say."

Hunter gritted his teeth, glancing over at her. She automatically shied back, her expression a little alarmed as she studied his scars. He ignored that. "Your friend is quite safe from my romantic interests. I simply wish to learn more about her."

After all, what woman would want to date a man with a grotesque face? Only ones that wanted his money, and he wasn't interested in those. He wanted a companion, not a whore.

"Oh," Brontë said, and studied her wineglass as if it were fascinating to her. "Petty," she said. "Her last name is Petty. She writes books."

Now they were getting somewhere. He mentally filed the information away. Gretchen Petty, author. He could see that. She had a sharp mind. "What kinds of books?"

"Books with other people's names on them."

He gave her an impatient stare, hating the way she shrank back in her chair just a bit. "A ghostwriter?"

Brontë nodded. "That's right. And Cooper's in love with her."

"Cooper? Who is Cooper?" Whoever it was, Hunter fucking hated him. Probably good looking, smug, and not nearly good enough for her. Damn it.

"Cooper's her friend. It's okay, though. He won't make a move. He knows Gretchen isn't interested in him that way. Gretchen likes guys that are different. She likes to be challenged."

He snorted. Well, she'd definitely get a challenge with him.

They chatted for a bit longer, the conversation awkward. Brontë kept turning her face to the door, no doubt anxiously awaiting Logan's return. Logan was a good-looking man, tall, strong, and unscarred. Brontë was a soft, sweet creature, but he doubted she'd ever look at someone like him with anything more than revulsion or pity.

He'd had his share of pity already, thanks.

Gretchen Petty, he repeated to himself. A ghostwriter. Someone that wrote books for others and hid behind their names. Why, he wondered. She didn't seem like the type to hide behind a moniker. She didn't seem like the type to hide behind anything. And that fascinated him. What would draw a woman like her to him? Did he even want to try? Did he want to see if she looked at him with a horror that she was trying desperately to hide for the sake of politeness, just like Logan's woman? Or would she see the person behind the scars and determine that he was just as interesting as any other man?

"I'd rather have a man not in love with his own reflection than one that needs hair product or designer labels."

A plan began to form in his mind.

It wasn't a nice plan, or a very honest one. The good thing about money, though, was that it allowed you to take control of almost any situation, and Hunter definitely planned on using what he had to his advantage.

———————

The Brotherhood played poker on into the night while his bodyguard stood at the door, keeping out anyone that would disturb them. They drank, they smoked cigars, and they played cards. It was one of their usual meetings, if one could ignore the quietly sleeping woman curled up on the couch in the corner of the room, Logan's jacket a blanket over her shoulders. Business was discussed, alcohol drank in quantity, and notes taken for analyzing in the morning. Tips were shared back and forth, investment opportunities and the like.

The Brotherhood had met like this once a week since their college days, vowing to help one another. At the time, it had seemed like an idealistic pledge—that those born with money would help the others succeed, and as a result, they would all rise to the top of the ladder of success.

It had been an easy vow to make for Hunter. When Logan had befriended him in an Economics class, he'd been oddly relieved to have a friend. After being home schooled for the majority of his education, Dartmouth seemed like a nightmare landscape to him. People were everywhere, and they stared at his hideous face and scarred arm like he was a freak. He had no roommate or companions to introduce him to others on campus, and so he'd lurked in the background of the bustling campus society, avoiding eye contact and silent.

Logan had been popular—wealthy, handsome, and outgoing, he knew what he wanted and pursued it. Women flocked to him and other guys liked him. It had surprised Hunter when Logan had struck up a conversation with him one day. No one talked to the scarred outcast. But Logan had stared at Hunter's scars for a long moment, and then gone right back to their Economics homework, discussing the syllabus and how he felt the class was missing some of the vital concepts they would need to succeed. Hunter had privately agreed, having learned quite a bit of his father's business on his own, and they'd shared ideas. After a week or two of casual conversation, Logan had taken him aside and suggested that Hunter attend a meeting he was putting together.

It was a secret meeting, the kind legendary on the older Ivy League campuses and spoke about in hushed whispers. Hunter was immediately suspicious. As a Buchanan, his father was one of the wealthiest men in the nation, a legend among business owners for the sheer amount of property he owned. Their family name was instantly recognizable, and several of their houses landmarks. His father's real estate investments had made him a billionaire, and Hunter was his only heir. He'd learned long ago to suspect others of ulterior motives.

But Logan was incredibly wealthy in his own right. He had no need for Hunter's money. And Hunter was . . . lonely, though he would never admit such things to anyone that asked. So he'd gone to the meeting, expecting it to be a scam or a joke—or worse, a shakedown.

Instead, he'd been surprised. The six men attending had come from all walks of life and had a variety of majors. Reese Duncan was attending college on a scholarship, and his clothes were worn and ill-fitting hand-me-downs. He'd been ribbed about being a charity case by the other wealthy students, and had gotten into a few fist fights. Ditto Cade Archer, though he was a favorite on campus with his easy, open demeanor and friendly attitude. His family did not come from money, and rumor had it that they were up to their necks in debt to send Cade to college. He did recognize Griffin Verdi, the only foreigner. British and titled, the Verdi family was well connected with the throne and still owned ancestral lands. And there was Jonathan Lynde, whose family had some wealth, but had lost it all in a business scandal.

It was an eclectic group to say the least, and Hunter had been immediately wary. But once Logan had begun to speak, the reality of their gathering came to light: Logan Hawkings wanted to start a secret society. A brotherhood of business-oriented men that would help each other rise to the top of their selective fields and assist one another. He believed that the ones that had power could use that power to elevate their friends, and in doing so, could expand upon their empire. And he'd selected like-minded individuals that he hoped would have the same goals as him.

Hunter had been reluctant at first, since his family had the most money of all of the attendees. The others had been equally skeptical, of course. But once they began to talk, ideas were shared and concepts and strategies born. And Hunter realized that these men might not be after his family's wealth after all, but to make some of their own.

He'd joined Logan's secret society. The Brotherhood was formed, and over the years, he'd gone from no friends to having five men that were closer to him than brothers.

And even though years had passed, they still met weekly (unless business travel prevented it) and still caught up with each other and shared leads.

Until tonight, a woman had never been invited. The others had been unhappy at Logan's invitation to Brontë, but Hunter didn't mind. He was actually inwardly pleased, though he'd shown no outward reaction.

Brontë's inclusion into their secret meant that she would be around a lot more. And Brontë was good friends with his mysterious redhead—Gretchen.

This was information that Hunter could use. And so he didn't protest when Logan had brought her in. She'd given him plenty of information, too. His Gretchen was a writer. A ghostwriter. There had to be a way to get in contact with her. Spend time with her without arousing her suspicions. He simply wanted to be around her. To have a conversation with her. To enjoy her presence.

Of course he wanted more, but a man like him knew his limits. He knew his face was unpleasant. He'd seen women clutch their mouths at the sight of him. He'd never have someone like Gretchen—smart, beautiful, funny—unless she was interested in his money. And the thought of that repulsed him.

He'd take friendship with a beautiful woman, if friendship was all he could have.

Jessica Clare also writes as Jill Myles and Jessica Sims. As Jessica Clare she writes sexy contemporary romance. You can contact her at jillmyles.com, or at twitter.com/jillmyles, facebook.com/jillmyles, or pinterest.com/jillmyles.

FROM *NEW YORK TIMES* BESTSELLING AUTHOR

JESSICA CLARE

BEAUTY
and the
BILLIONAIRE

A Billionaire Boys Club Novel

Real-estate tycoon Hunter Buchanan has a dark past that's left him scarred and living as a recluse on his family's palatial estate. Hunter is ready to give up on love—until he spots an enigmatic beauty and comes up with an elaborate scheme to meet her.

Gretchen Petty is in need of a paycheck—and a change. So when a job opportunity in an upstate New York mansion pops up, she accepts. And while she can overlook the oddities of her new job, she can't ignore her new boss's delectable body—or his barely leashed temper.

Hunter worries that his scheme might be unraveling before it's truly begun, but Gretchen is about to show him that life can be full of surprises…

Now available as an e-book!

jessica-clare.com
facebook.com/AuthorJessicaClare
facebook.com/LoveAlwaysBooks
penguin.com

M1446T0214